ROXANNE

Jane Claypool Miner

SCHOLASTIC INC.
New York Toronto London Auckland Sydney

This book is dedicated to Jennifer Kyle, who is a fine dancer and pretty enough to be a movie star. With love from Granny Jane.

ISBN 0-590-33686-X

12 11 10 9 8 7 6 5 4 3 2 1   8   5 6 7 8 9/8 0/9

Printed in the U.S.A.   06

ROXANNE

A *Sunfire* Book

SUNFIRE

Chapter One

"HOLLYWOOD?" she stared at her mother in amazement. "You're going to spend all our money on a trip to Hollywood?"

"Not a trip, Rosie. We're moving there. Don't you want to be a movie star?"

Rosie Wilson shook her head angrily and said, "Ma, if Pa could hear you now, he'd turn over in his grave."

Her mother's face took on a petulant, angry stubbornness, as it often did when Rosie mentioned her father. It seemed wrong and very sad that her mother was still so angry, even though he'd been dead over three months. Rosie sighed and said in a softer voice, "That check for three hundred dollars is all the money we have in the world, Ma. It will barely keep us till June, when I'll graduate from high school and can start looking for a job."

"Job?" Her mother looked really angry now as she asked, "This is 1938 — don't you know we're in the middle of a depression? Who's gonna give you a job? Grown men have been out of work for ten years, and you think someone's going to give a kid like you a job?"

"Henry's uncle promised I could wait tables on weekends," she answered. Even to her own ears that didn't seem like much of a job. She added, "It's a beginning. And you can keep on making those fancy aprons. People will be sure to buy them for Christmas. We might even take a trip to Tulsa and talk to the big department stores about taking some. Wouldn't you like to see your aprons sold in Halliburton's, Ma?"

"I'd rather see my daughter in the movies."

"Ma, it's a dream. Do you know how many pretty girls go to Hollywood each year? There are lots of better ways to make some money."

Mrs. Wilson pulled a folded-up magazine from her purse and said, "It says right here that they're looking for new girls every week. There's a story here about a girl who was ushering in a movie house and a producer saw her. She's making a hundred dollars a week now. Think what we could do with a hundred dollars a week, Rosie. I'd buy a big house and get a maid right off. No more standing on my tired feet all day."

"You'd get fatter," Rosie said, and laughed. "Come on, Ma. Put down the dreams and get to work on the aprons. I have to do my homework."

"Not anymore. You've dropped out of school as of today. I just told Mrs. Lester that we were leaving on tomorrow's bus."

Fear grabbed Rosie by the throat. Her mother had been talking about moving to California ever since her pa died three months ago, but she'd never really believed that she could be serious. She knew that her mother was a foolish woman. Laureen Wilson had a reputation for empty-headedness. Folks said Mr. Wilson had fallen for her golden curls and small feet, not checking to see what else he was getting.

"I changed your name at the same time. Told them to mail your grades to Roxanne Wilson, care of general delivery, Hollywood, California. Roxanne . . . that's a name for a star." Laureen's eyes were bright with hope as she hugged her daughter and said, "Just pack your best blue dress and shoes, honey. We'll buy you some new clothes when we get there."

"You can't really mean it!"

Her mother was laughing now and swinging her around the floor while she hugged her at the same time. For a moment Rosie's eyes filled with tears as she remembered that this woman was her mother. It was almost a new thought. For so many years she'd followed her father's lead and thought of Laureen as a younger child who had to be protected and coddled. A sadness welled up in her throat as she longed for the mother she'd never had . . . a sensible woman who could be depended upon.

"I'm not going," Rosie said. There was no use crying for something you couldn't have, she told herself. The important thing was to talk her mother out of this latest foolishness and get on with life. She'd have to make up some story to explain to Mrs. Lester when she appeared at school on Monday morning, but that was a small matter. "Pride is a rich man's privilege," her pa always said. She both needed and wanted that high school diploma, so she would go back to Norman High School and face Mrs. Lester.

"Roxanne, you have to go," her mother said. She faced her daughter and tucked the magazine into her purse. Her face was closed and angry again as she complained, "How can you deny your mother her one chance for a decent life? If we stay in this hick town, I'll just die of boredom. You'll marry that silly boy, Henry, and I'll be an old grandmother before I've even seen anything in life. I'm a young woman, Roxanne, and I'm entitled to some of the good things in life."

"My name is *Rosie*." She had no reply to her mother's other words. They were well-known complaints. She knew the story that her mother delighted in telling well enough to recite it by heart. According to her mother, she was well on her way to an acting career when she was swept off her feet by an older man. Rosie knew that the facts were a bit different. Her mother had been sixteen, but her father was only twenty, and according to the town gossips, the wedding was her mother's idea.

Rosie looked at the photograph of her father that sat on the kitchen table. She was fascinated as always by his youthful and happy appearance. The photograph had been taken in 1922, the year she'd been born. He'd had a good job, money in the bank, and his own house then. Then the Depression and the years of poor health had worn him away. The father she remembered was a good man and she loved him, but he bore no resemblance to the happy young man who stared out at her from the tin frame.

"You're my child and you have to do what I say," her mother repeated. "So pack your suitcase while I go say good-bye to the folks in town."

"I won't go." Her words were clipped and angry.

"What are you going to do, Rosie? Roxanne? Live with your cousin Margaret? She's so stingy, she won't give you any more than a crust of bread to eat. And she'll work you from sunup to sundown for that. Marry that boy and live with his crazy father? You've got to come."

"I won't go."

"You'll go," Laureen said. She turned to the mirror over the kitchen sink and patted her hair into place. Then she looked around the small kitchen and said, "Be glad to leave this dump. It was never home."

In her heart she agreed with her mother. The small, cramped wooden house they rented for ten dollars a month had served as refuge after they'd had to sell their own. But none of them had ever thought of it as their own. "Pa died here," she reminded her mother.

"Dying don't make it a home," Laureen retorted. She took out a lipstick and painted a bright red Cupid's bow mouth, gave her hair another pat, and walked to the door. Turning, she said, "You'd better make up your mind to it, Roxanne. We're gonna go to Hollywood and you're gonna be a movie star."

Chapter Two

"MARRY me," Henry said. He pulled her close. "Rosie, we can live with my dad and I'll get a job. You can work for Uncle Henry and we'll make out."

"What about Mother?" It wasn't really as much a question as an argument. There was no way Henry could stretch his proposal to include a home for Laureen. Though his father wasn't as bad as Laureen implied when she called him crazy, he was a very difficult man to live with. As long as she could remember, Mr. Scott had been known for his terrible depressions and drinking bouts.

"I don't know," Henry said. "Could your mother live with your cousin?"

"They can't stand each other. It won't work, Henry. We're just not old enough to get married."

"But if we love each other enough. . . ." Henry's argument was offered softly. He trailed his fingers along her shoulder and neck, nestling his hand in her soft blonde hair, looking into her bright blue eyes. Then he kissed her on the mouth softly and said, "Make her stay home, Rosie. In June we'll both graduate, and then we'll find a way."

"I can't handle her the way Pa did," Rosie admitted. "He could always get around her silliness, but she doesn't listen to me. She's changed my name. Did I tell you? She calls me Roxanne now."

"Roxanne?"

She shivered. What was it about that name that gave her a thin stab of excitement every time she heard it? "She says that's what she wanted to name me in the first place, and my pa talked her into naming me after his sister who died. She says she was playing Roxanne in the school play when she met my pa and that it's the most beautiful name in the world."

"Why doesn't your mother go to Hollywood and be an actress herself and leave you alone?"

Roxanne ignored his bitter question. "The play was called *Cyrano de Bergerac*, and I guess it was a real hit. She still remembers all her lines. She taught me some when I was a little girl. You know, I think Ma's crazy, but I do kind of agree that Roxanne is a pretty name."

"You sound like you *want* to go Hollywood," Henry accused.

"No, I just said I thought Roxanne was a pretty name, and I don't see anything else to do but go with her to Hollywood."

"Live with your cousin until June, then we'll get married."

She couldn't help but notice that his offer of immediate marriage was retracted. She smiled and said softly, "Henry, you don't even know if you *want* to marry me. You're too young."

"I'm seventeen. I love you."

"Do you?" She looked at the handsome young man sitting beside her. He was so good. There was a clear, honest look in his eyes that had always made her feel wonderful just to be with him. People thought they made a fine-looking couple, she knew, just because they were both so blond and good-looking. But while she was slender and delicate, he was strong and sturdy with large, muscled shoulders and wide, competent hands. She leaned her head against his shoulder and said, "We can write. In a few weeks or months Ma will see that we're better off back here in Oklahoma. We'll wait and marry later when things make more sense." Suddenly, she felt a hundred years old and she wondered if things would ever really make more sense than they did now.

His arms gripped her shoulders, and there was fear in his voice as he asked, "Do you want to go to Hollywood?"

"I think it's a silly idea." But at least Hollywood would be different than this constant poverty and worry.

"Do you want to leave me?"

"I don't see any other way."

"Do you love me?"

Now there was an accusation in his voice. She wondered why he thought he had a right to be angry with her because her mother was making her do something foolish. She bit her tongue to hold back sharp words and said, "Of course, but I don't see what else to do."

"Marry me." He kissed her then, holding her close and pressing her lips with his in a demanding, insistent way. It was almost as though the kiss were designed to persuade her and show her how much he loved her all at once.

She pulled away and said softly, "I'll write a lot and I'll come back as soon as I can."

But her answer didn't satisfy him, and he sounded angry as he asked, "Are you doing this for your mother or because you *want* to be a Hollywood movie star?"

She was startled at the way he put the question, and she asked, "Do you think I have a chance? To be a star, I mean?"

"Of course. You're prettier than all of them." Then he frowned again and said, "If you really love me, you won't go away."

"I'll be back." She was sad about parting from Henry, of course. She was also very angry with her mother for making her do this foolish thing. But behind those two emotions she was beginning to detect something else, something new and different, a feeling that she couldn't quite label. It tickled the back of her mind, sending small shivers of excitement through her, even in the midst of this tragic good-bye.

They kissed again, and Henry walked her back to the small, run-down wooden house she called home. As the time drew near for them to part, she had less and less to say to Henry.

He was also very quiet, and by the time they got to the rickety front porch, there was a catch in his voice as he said, "Good-bye, Rosie. I think you're making a big mistake."

She stood on her tiptoes to kiss him one more time, knowing that her love for Henry would always be important to her. They had been sweethearts for two years, and he had become a quiet, stable presence in her life, during the difficult time when her father was dying and she was trying so desperately to put things together.

She kissed him one time, then touched his lips with her fingertips and whispered, "I'll miss you so much. I do love you, Henry, I really do."

She went into the house and shut the door, letting the tears run freely down her cheeks. But the minute she closed the door, the feeling that was in the back of her mind came forward. She was an honest person, and she'd known all evening that there was something besides loss and grief in her good-bye to Henry. What had it been? As she reviewed their conversation she went back to the point where she'd asked him if he thought she had a chance to be in the movies, and he'd answered so casually, "Of course."

She knew what the feeling was now that she looked around the poor, run-down room where she lived. She let her eyes roam over the pink-flowered couch with the hole in the arm, the orange-flowered wallpaper with the faded spots and frayed edges, then down to the dark-red and green-flowered rug that was so old that they'd placed a smaller rug over the spot that was worn clear through. "When I get to be a movie star," she announced to the empty room, "I'm going to have a beautiful house full of beautiful things, and the only flowers in it will be real. Everything will match."

Then she laughed and repeated, "When I get to be a movie star." The nagging feeling she'd been trying to identify all evening had been hope.

Chapter Three

IT was a long, miserable bus ride to Kansas City, and Roxanne didn't even try to look out the window as the big bus lumbered down the highway. What was there to see, anyway? Nothing but dingy little farmhouses and dying crops. The drought that had plagued the Midwest for the last eight years was at its height now, and Oklahoma, Missouri, and Kansas were known as the dust bowl.

It was cold even though there was a heater at the front of the bus, so Roxanne was glad she'd worn her navy-blue sweater under the old tweed coat that was a hand-me-down from Cousin Margaret. Laureen had not been as sensible, and she shivered in her best blue-print dress and a short, thin blue gabardine jacket.

The two women ignored each other as the

bus jostled them, because they'd fought up until the moment they'd boarded the bus at seven in the morning. Finally Roxanne had thrown up her hands and said, "I'll go because you're my mother. Not because I think you're right."

After they'd traveled for about two hours Laureen ventured, "You'll thank me when you're a big star, Roxanne. And I'll be so proud of my little girl. Every time I see your pretty face on the screen I'll love you so much."

"Don't you love me now?"

"Of course I do, honey. I just mean that I'll be so proud of you."

"Aren't you proud of me now?"

Her mother turned toward the window, staring out at the barren landscape as she said, "When I was a girl, I had dreams, and nothing's turned out right. I wanted the best for my little girl, and all you've had is sickness and being dirt-poor. These hard times are killing people's spirit. The Depression is what killed your Pa, but it's not gonna kill you and me. You'll see, Roxanne. We're doing the right thing."

Roxanne didn't answer. There was no sense trying to talk sense to her mother now. She knew her mother wouldn't turn around until they'd at least seen California. Besides, she had to agree that at least part of what her mother was saying was true. If it hadn't been for leaving Henry behind, she might have been more eager to go to California.

Even if there wasn't a real chance that she could get in the movies, they said there were jobs there.

She couldn't help but hope that her mother's dreams of making her a movie star were at least a possibility. Everyone said she was pretty, and she could sing and dance a little bit. She didn't know exactly why she believed it, but Roxanne thought she could act, too. Her hopes rose and fell as they climbed the hills toward Kansas City. Just about the time she decided she might have a chance, she asked herself how many pretty girls were on their way to Hollywood this week with exactly the same hope.

The life of a star seemed so wonderful compared to the average girl's life. No dishes to wash and no money worries. She dreamed of pretty clothes and handsome leading men, and then she chided herself for being every bit as foolish as her mother. All her life people had talked about how sensible she was, and she knew she took after her father in most ways. Why had she let her mother push her into this foolish quest? *Because you wanted to go,* a small voice whispered inside herself.

"This country's dying," her mother said. "When President Roosevelt was elected, I thought things would be better, but it seems like they're just getting worse."

"It's the drought, Ma. You know if it doesn't rain, the crops can't grow."

"Look at that poor, pitiful land," her

mother said. "When I was a girl, everything was green and pretty. Now it's all ugly. They say that in California everyone has an orange tree in his front yard. You can just pick your food off the trees. And the sun shines all the time." Laureen shivered in her thin coat and wrapped it closer around her.

"You should have worn your wool suit," Roxanne grumbled.

"You nag me like I was the daughter," her mother said. "Good thing you're so pretty or you'd never get a husband. You sound like an old lady."

It crossed her mind to say that her mother sounded like a teenager, but she kept her thoughts to herself. It was pointless to argue, and Roxanne knew she did scold her mother a lot. She sighed and stretched her legs, wishing that this interminable journey would end. Two more hours to Kansas City and then they'd start all over again. It was just more of her mother's foolishness to insist on traveling east to catch the train in Kansas City instead of simply taking the bus all the way to California. But her mother wanted to take the Super Chief, like all the movie stars did. Roxanne shook her head as she remembered that part of the argument. Her mother had insisted that it was important to her daughter's "career" to come by train.

"Don't scowl," her mother warned. "You spoil your looks when you frown."

"Do you think there's a talent scout on this bus?"

"And don't be smart with me, missy. I'm still your mother."

Roxanne returned to her own thoughts, going over all the possibilities and alternatives. By the time they arrived in Kansas City Roxanne had her thoughts and plans in order. She would try hard to get work in the movies. If she failed, her mother would have to be satisfied to return home. They could live with Cousin Margaret, and Roxanne could work for Henry's uncle till they married. Then she and Henry could live with his father, and Laureen could stay on with Roxanne's cousin.

She knew that was far from an ideal living arrangement, but she would be happy with Henry, and it was the most practical thing that two women alone could do. She also knew that this alternative to her mother's plan was grim enough to make her want to succeed in Hollywood very much. Not that she didn't want to marry Henry eventually; she did. But it would be so nice to be able to afford a little home of their own. Besides, she was still very young to marry, and a few months in California would probably be good for both her and Henry.

Once she decided to do everything she could to stay in California and make it in the movies, she began to enjoy the trip more. Now that she knew what she could do in case of failure, she could work for success.

Whatever the future held for her, Roxanne decided that it would have to include some financial stability. She was willing to work hard, but she wanted that work to pay off by providing enough money to live well. She knew that Henry agreed with her about that; he often talked about following in his Uncle Henry's footsteps and becoming a businessman. Though no one was doing very well in these hard times, Henry's uncle had managed to hold on to his restaurant and buy several farms and houses that had been in foreclosure.

Thoughts about money drifted back into Roxanne's daydreams about being a movie star. If she should be able to get a contract at a studio, she might be earning as much as fifty dollars a week. That was more than a month's wages in most jobs. Besides, there weren't any jobs, anyway.

They were coming into Kansas City now, and Roxanne sat up straight, putting all thoughts of Henry and Oklahoma out of her mind. She had never been to such a big city, and she didn't want to miss a bit of whatever there was to see.

As she stared out at the bright lights and busy streets, Roxanne reminded herself that stars made big money and the smart ones saved it. Laureen was always talking about Mary Pickford, who had been a famous silent movie star, as being the richest woman in America. Most people thought the richest woman was Barbara Hutton, who inherited all the Woolworth five-and-dime store fortune on her eighteenth birthday. But whether it was Mary Pickford or Barbara Hutton wasn't as important as the fact that Mary Pickford had made her own fortune through hard work.

"I'm a hard worker too," Roxanne whispered to herself as the bus pulled into the Kansas City depot.

The minute they stepped off the bus, Laureen said, "We've got till midnight until our train leaves. Let's go to the movies."

"Ma!" But she was laughing as she chided her mother. She loved movies almost as much as Laureen did. It had been their one extravagance all through her childhood, so it didn't really surprise her that her mother would choose to spend the extra time in a movie theater instead of walking around Kansas City. As long as she could remember, Laureen had found the money to take her to the movies every Saturday afternoon. She'd grown up on the exciting adventures of Tom Mix, and listened to her mother act like a silly girl over romantic actors like Charles Boyer and Tyrone Power.

Her mother liked all movies, and to tell the truth, Roxanne liked everything herself but the horror films. "I'll go if it isn't *Frankenstein Runs for President*," she joked. One of the first movies she could ever remember seeing was *Frankenstein*. She'd been nine years old and terrified of Boris Karloff in his monster makeup. To this day, Roxanne disliked horror films, though she'd long ago learned that the monsters were just ordinary actors with makeup.

The only horror movie she'd ever really enjoyed was *The Bride of Frankenstein* with Elsa Lanchester playing Frankenstein's wife. It was the humor that tickled her, but her mother hadn't cared for the mixing of terror and comedy. "I like my villains mean and my movies really scary," she'd complained.

Laureen slipped her arm through Roxanne's and said, "They've got one of the fanciest movie palaces in the world right here in Kansas City. The Midland Theater is just about the most beautiful movie house in the world. Your father promised to take me to see it when it was built. That was 1927, when you were five, and we kept putting it off. Then the crash came in 1929, and there was never enough money."

"Ma, we don't have very much money now, either."

"Come on, Roxanne. Don't be a grouch. We may never be in Kansas City again. Unless your studio sends you on tour, of course. Anyway, I've always wanted to see a movie in a real fancy movie palace. Everything must look a lot better if the seats are soft and everything is just right. The Bijou was a furniture store before you were born."

"I know, Ma."

"The first movie I ever saw there was Rudolph Valentino and Agnes Ayres in *The Sheikh*. That was in 1922. I always thought after that that your father looked a lot like Rudolph Valentino."

Roxanne laughed. "Rudolph Valentino! I've seen his picture; he didn't look a thing like Pa. All that eye makeup on a man!"

"They were both very handsome," Laureen defended herself. Then she linked her arm through Roxanne's and said, "Let's take a taxi to the movies."

"Maybe Rudolph is playing," Roxanne teased.

"You modern girls don't understand his appeal," Laureen said, "but he was a real romantic star. The woman in black still visits his grave every year and leaves flowers, you know."

"I know." Roxanne knew a lot more about movies than any of her friends, just because her mother was so star-struck. She knew that some of the kids in school envied her because she'd been able to go to the movies all during the Depression, no matter how tight money was. Some of her friends had gone to the movies once or twice, as a special treat. Others were never permitted inside the Bijou because their parents thought that movies would put wrong ideas in a young girl's mind.

"Let's take a taxi to the Midland," Laureen said.

"Let's find out where it is. Maybe we can walk." Roxanne went quickly to the information table in the bus station and asked for directions to the theater.

When she came back, Laureen was buying

three more movie magazines at the news-stand. Roxanne sputtered, "At the rate you're spending money, we'll be broke before we get to Hollywood."

Her mother ignored her and asked, "Where is the taxi stand?"

"We can walk—it's only six blocks," Roxanne said. "And there's a good hamburger place across the street. Hamburgers are a nickle each and coffee is free."

"I'll bet they're small hamburgers," her mother said, but she didn't complain about walking to the theater.

The suitcases they carried hadn't seemed very heavy when they got on the bus that morning, but by the time they had walked four blocks and eaten, they were both moving very slowly. "I shouldn't have had so many hamburgers," Roxanne said.

"You only had two," Laureen said. "And they were very small."

"You had three," Roxanne teased. Ever since she could remember, her mother had been a little too plump. She was a pretty woman with a sweet, round face, trusting blue eyes, and a small pointed chin. People said Roxanne looked a lot like her mother, but her cousin Margaret said that Roxanne was much prettier than Laureen had ever been. They had the same soft, curling blonde hair and light blue eyes framed by dark, double-fringed lashes. The major difference was that Roxanne's face was a perfect oval and her nose classically shaped. There was no mistaking that they were mother and daughter, but they were not exactly the same.

They turned the corner and Laureen said, "Look, there's searchlights. I'll bet they've got something special at the Midland Theater just for us."

"They're probably just giving away free dishes," Roxanne said.

"The Midland is a high-class movie palace," her mother said. "They wouldn't give away dishes like any old place."

"Dishes or dish towels," Roxanne predicted, but she could see the theater now, and she had to admit that she was impressed, even from this distance. The theater looked as much like a real palace or castle as anything she'd ever seen. It seemed to be built all of marble, and everything glittered with gold and crystal. Roxanne stopped and stared up at the marquee, which said, in large letters, GARY MARLOWE IN PERSON. Below that, in smaller letters, it said, TALENT CONTEST TONIGHT.

Laureen's hand gripped her arm and she whispered, "This is it. This is your big break."

Before Roxanne could protest, Laureen stepped up to the box office and said, "My daughter wants to enter the talent contest."

"Too late, lady. They already picked the finalists this afternoon."

"But we just got here," Laureen said. "We weren't able to be here for the preliminaries. You must let my girl in the contest. She's a very talented girl. She sings, she dances. . . ."

The girl at the box office yawned and made a big, elaborate gesture of covering her mouth. She asked, "Do you want to see the movie?"

"I want to see the manager," Laureen demanded. "I want my girl in the contest."

"Two tickets?"

"Young lady, I demand to see the manager!"

There were people behind them in line now, and Roxanne felt her face getting warm as everyone's interested gaze rested first on her mother and then on her. Was this what it would be like in Hollywood? Would she constantly be embarrassed by her mother's pushiness?

"Let's get the tickets and go in," Roxanne said.

Her mother turned on her angrily and was almost shouting as she said, "We certainly will not just go in. You deserve a chance to compete. You're a very talented girl, and they have no right to keep you out just because we're from Oklahoma instead of Kansas City." Then she wheeled back and repeated, "I demand to see the manager."

The girl in the booth yawned again and shrugged. Then she pointed over her shoulder and said, "Try his office."

Laureen walked toward the office, stopping only long enough to turn and order Roxanne, "Now, when we get there, smile."

Roxanne picked up her own suitcase and followed her mother to the beautiful golden door with figures of cherubs holding a bronze plaque that said MANAGER on it. Laureen knocked, and the door opened just a crack.

A very handsome young man asked, "May I help you?"

"Are you the manager?"

"Not exactly. . . ."

"I want to see the manager."

The young man smiled and opened the door wider. He was wearing a black tuxedo with a black cape that was lined in white satin. He was over six feet tall and very young-looking; Roxanne was sure she'd never seen such a handsome person in her whole life. His face was perfectly chiseled, and each of his features looked as though it might serve as a Greek model for perfection. His eyes were dark and seemed to flash romance, amusement, and energy all at once. His teeth were perfectly even. To make him even more irresistible, when he smiled, Roxanne saw that there was a dimple in his cheek to go with the small cleft in his chin.

She was sure that no one who looked like he did could be living in Kansas, and decided he must surely be the Gary Marlowe whose name was on the marquee. She knew that his parents were the famous Marlowes, a romantic couple who rivaled the popularity of Douglas Fairbanks and Mary Pickford before their divorce. The big difference between that famous couple and the Marlowes was that their popularity continued year after year with no sign that their public was getting tired of them as they entered middle age.

From her mother's film magazines Roxanne knew that the Marlowes had a teenage son who was going to make his movie debut very soon. She had no doubt that this was the son, making a personal appearance because they were showing his first movie tonight. If good looks were any indication of success, she was certain his career would be wonderful. She spoke up, saying, "Mother, we mustn't bother Mr. Marlowe."

"No. It's the manager we want to see."

He smiled again, with an intense look from his dark brown eyes, obviously used to charming people. "The manager is not in. But perhaps I can speak for him."

Laureen seemed to pause for a moment and reconsider the whole situation. She looked warily at the handsome young man and asked, "Are you an employee of the theater?"

"In a manner of speaking."

"He's Gary Marlowe, Ma." Roxanne was blushing now, wishing with all her heart that she could get out of there. At the same time that she wanted to run away there was a fierce message beating from her heart all through her body, calling out to Gary Marlowe to smile at her just one more time. If she hadn't prided herself on her good sense, she would have fallen in love with him at first sight.

"Gary Marlowe," Laureen said speculatively. "You don't look much like your father. Or your mother."

The young man seemed to find that funny, and he bowed slightly in mocking acknowledgment of his parents' fame. "I'm told I resemble my Uncle Herbert the most."

"Herbert Marlowe." Laureen thought that over and then shook her head decisively. "Not really. Herbert's features are much more refined. You look more like your Aunt Evelyn."

"I see you are acquainted with my whole family."

"Everyone knows the Marlowes," Laureen said. Instead of being awed by meeting one of the members of the famous acting family, she seemed to view his appearance at the door as just one more obstacle on her daughter's path to stardom. "The point is, we want to get my daughter in the talent show. Can you do that?"

He turned toward Roxanne, and his eyes seemed to burn very brightly as he asked, "Do you have talent?"

Roxanne was determined not to let him stare her down. She lifted her chin and nodded yes in defiance of his amused gaze.

He laughed then and shook his head, "You're prettier than any of the others, and you may be more talented, but I can't let you in the contest, you know."

"Why not?" Laureen demanded.

"I'm the judge," he said. "If I let you in now, it wouldn't be fair to the others."

"Why not?" Laureen persisted.

"Because I've fallen in love with you, madam, and would no doubt be tempted to give your fair daughter the prize just to please you." He delivered the lines with a straight face and bowed from the waist, flinging his cape backward before he took Laureen's free hand and kissed it. Roxanne understood that he was ridiculing her mother, and she was furious and embarrassed at the same time. Fury won, and she said, "You may think it's funny to make fun of people, but it is really very rude."

Her mother looked confused as she took her hand back and, for once, seemed to be at a loss for words.

Gary Marlowe raised one of his dark, arched eyebrows and managed to look both supercilious and amused. Roxanne decided that no matter how incredibly handsome he was, he was one of the most unpleasant people she had ever met. "I *am* sorry, but there isn't any way I can let you in the contest. Do you believe me?"

"No." Laureen's answer was prompt and angry.

Roxanne picked her words carefully as she replied levelly, "I believe you cannot let me into the contest, but I do not believe you are sorry. Actually I think you enjoy making fun of ordinary people."

"I assure you that I do not consider you

ordinary," he answered, bowing once again. "You are really quite beautiful, you know. What's your name?"

"Rosie Wilson—" she answered. Though she'd already grown accustomed to her new name, she didn't feel like telling it to him. She wasn't sure if that was because she feared he might laugh or because she wanted him to know her as she really was.

"Roxanne," her mother interrupted. "Roxanne Wilson."

Gary Marlowe threw back his head and laughed then. The laugh seemed to start very low in his chest and rumble upward in pure delight. It occurred to Roxanne that if she had heard him laugh before she'd talked with him, she might have liked Gary Marlowe very much. But a melodic laugh could not make up for bad manners, and he had the worst manners she'd ever encountered in a young man.

"Which is it? Rosie or Roxanne?"

"Come on, Mother, we'll miss the movie." Roxanne turned her back on Gary Marlowe. Practically dragging her mother back to the box office, she bought the tickets, and then they went into the theater. She was still fuming as they walked down the aisle, and sank into one of the deep-red plush seats on the aisle. It amazed her that her mother seemed to forget all about the encounter with the handsome movie star and all her disappointment about not being able to get Roxanne in the talent contest. Laureen sank back in her seat, looked up at the golden ceiling, which was all rosy circular paintings of chubby cherubs and beautiful flowers. She sighed in appreciation of the glistening crystal chandelier and whispered, "It's the prettiest place I've ever seen."

Roxanne smiled as the lights dimmed and the organist began to play a medley of popular tunes. One thing about Laureen that always impressed her was the way she could put disappointment aside and enjoy the moment. Her mother had some wonderful qualities, she knew. But Roxanne's face still burned at the humiliating encounter with Gary Marlowe. No man who was that rude had any right to be that handsome, she told herself. Suddenly, the organist swung into one of her favorite songs, "Did You Ever See A Dream Walking?"

The radio had been playing that song the first time Henry had ever kissed her. They'd been sitting on the sofa together, holding hands quietly and talking softly, when her father had wakened from his sleep and turned the radio on. The tune drifted out of her father's bedroom and into the tiny living room as Henry turned to her and asked, "Will you be my girl?"

Now, as the melody faded out and the lights of the theater went out, Roxanne realized that she missed her father very, very much. What was even sadder, because there was no sensible reason for their parting, was that she missed Henry. What was she doing in a strange city, on her way to an even stranger place? Would they find that everyone in Hollywood was as rude and unpleasant as Gary Marlowe?

She turned to beg her mother to take her home. She could make out her mother's eager profile tilted toward the silver screen. Roxanne sighed as she acknowledged the truth. She was on her way whether she liked it or not.

Chapter Four

THE movie featured the whole Marlowe family, but Gary was the star. Far from being overshadowed by his famous relatives, Gary dominated the screen whenever he appeared. Though she was still smarting from their encounter, Roxanne admitted to herself that he had real talent.

What was even more surprising, she found herself very drawn to his image on the screen, despite what she knew about him as a person. She reasoned that if he could make her fall for him, he must have a very remarkable talent indeed. The close-ups of his dark good looks were magnificent, and she had no doubt that Gary Marlowe's career was launched successfully.

The movie was an adventure tale set in Spain in the sixteenth century, and Gary wore a white shirt trimmed in lace, tight black pants, and shiny boots. In one scene he wore the same black cape with the white lining that he'd been wearing when they met earlier in the theater. About the time that Roxanne decided that his main talent was the ability to flash his dark eyes and raise his already arched black brows in interesting ways, he did a whole scene in a mask with only his eyeballs showing. Even then he dominated the screen, using his mouth to express emotion and hypnotize his audience. Roxanne found herself fascinated by his smile, the wonderful white teeth, the creases on the sides of his mouth when he laughed, and the cleft in his chin.

He was very young, Roxanne decided, and she guessed that he might be her age or a year or two older. Though his skin was smooth and unlined, his face had strong outlines and he had the look of a man. Once, when Gary Marlowe smiled directly into the camera and then spoke softly of love to his co-star, Roxanne shivered. She suspected her reaction would be worldwide.

In many ways Gary seemed to have the very best qualities of every one of his famous relatives. He had his Aunt Evelyn's dark eyes and the ability to move an audience to tears or laughter. He had his Uncle Herbert's elegant presence, but he moved more gracefully than anyone Roxanne had ever seen on the screen. There was a youthful eagerness that was irresistible. Gary Cooper had some of it and so did Errol Flynn, though they were very different kinds of actors. A lot of the special appeal that he had seemed to be because of how he moved. There was a way he had of stepping into a scene that made the others seem to shrink.

As she watched the movie Roxanne found herself studying his face carefully. She watched the way he seemed to make every little motion mean so much. A brief smile, a sudden raising of the chin to express defiance, a narrowing of the eyes to demonstrate conviction. Gary Marlowe could act.

When he took the heroine in his arms and kissed her at the end of the movie, Roxanne heard several sighs throughout the theater. No doubt she and her mother had just met the newest Hollywood idol right here in Kansas City. The most startling part of his performance was not in the close-ups or romantic scenes, though, but in his action scenes. As the undisclosed Spanish nobleman he had to ride horseback, climb balconies, scale walls, run from soldiers, and jump off high ledges before he got to his happy ending. Though Roxanne knew that they might have used stuntmen for part of the action scenes, there were too many shots that showed his face for her to ignore his athletic ability.

She hated to admit it, but it seemed to her that Gary Marlowe had everything he needed to get ahead in the world.

People clapped when the movie was over, but when the lights went on, they did not seem as enthusiastic as Roxanne would have expected. She wondered if customers in a big city like Kansas City were harder to please than in small towns like Norman. Or had she misjudged his appeal? She asked Laureen, "Did you like it?"

Laureen nodded and said, "The Marlowes always make good movies. And she's so pretty."

"But what about Gary Marlowe? What did you think of him?"

"I thought he was all right."

"Just all right?"

Laureen shrugged and said, "He's not as handsome as his Uncle Herbert was when he was that age. And he certainly can't act as well as his father."

"You're just mad because he was rude to us."

"Maybe."

"Didn't you think he was a good actor?"

Laureen shrugged and said, "Good, but not great. I don't know what I expected, but he didn't exactly live up to it. I mean, to me he'll always be just the Marlowes' little boy."

For one brief second Roxanne felt sorry for Gary Marlowe. Even though there must be a lot of advantages to coming from an acting family, she realized that there might also be some real disadvantages. Maybe if he didn't watch it, he would turn out to be "just another Marlowe."

The houselights were on now, and Laureen

was busy looking at the paintings that decorated the walls and ceiling of the fancy theater.

The first act in the show that followed was a comedian who wasn't very funny. He seemed in a hurry to get off the stage, and introduced Gary Marlowe very briefly. Roxanne decided that Gary was uncomfortable about being in front of a live audience, because he spoke very carefully and didn't make any jokes or try to entertain the audience at all. He simply introduced the acts, one after another.

The acts were all terrible, and Gary's introductions got less enthusiastic as the performances wore on. There were two sisters who sang off-key and danced. They were followed by a girl who sang all right but drowned herself out with an accordian. There was a tap dancer who was too old and fat, and the most painful act of all was a young woman who recited poetry in a high, thin voice.

As Roxanne watched the talent she began to think that she might have a chance in Hollywood after all. Kansas City was a big town, and if this was the best they could do, it was possible that she might succeed.

At the end of each act Laureen hissed, "You're better than that." For once Roxanne agreed with her mother.

Eventually Gary Marlowe gave first prize to a young tap dancer and declared a tie for second. He obviously couldn't wait to get off stage, and Roxanne decided he'd better avoid personal appearances and stick to showing his beautiful profile on the screen.

The houselights went down, and Roxanne and her mother picked up their suitcases and started out the door. Laureen said, "We have to take a taxi to the train station or else we'll be late."

Roxanne looked at her watch and agreed with her mother. They had barely thirty minutes to catch the train. When they got to the street, there were no taxis, and Roxanne said, "I'll go to the corner and see if I can find a cab."

Leaving her suitcase with her mother, she hurried to the corner and held out her arm to signal any passing taxis. A voice behind her said, "Rosie or Roxanne? Which is it really?"

She ignored the voice and kept waving her arm, hoping that she would not have to say anything to Gary Marlowe ever again. As a taxi slowed down she was relieved and moved toward it. He stepped in front of her and said, "That's my taxi, you know."

"I need it," she answered. "I have to get to the train station." She turned, and it occurred to her that they might be going to the same place. She asked, "Are you going there?"

"No," he admitted. "Just to my hotel. I'm flying home tomorrow."

Roxanne stared. She couldn't imagine anyone being brave enough to travel by flying, but she knew it was becoming more common.

There were regular commercial runs between cities now. Sometimes more than one a day.

"Rosie or Roxanne?"

"I really need this taxi. I can't miss my train."

He smiled then and bowed. "Of course, but in return for my courtesy you must at least give me your real name."

"It used to be Rosie, but I think I'm changing it to Roxanne."

"Good idea," Gary Marlowe said. "Now, allow me to present you with my taxi."

"It wasn't really yours," Roxanne snapped. "You know, you looked so nice on the screen, but in person you're very rude."

"So you said earlier. About the rudeness, I mean. I'm glad you thought I looked nice on the screen. Did you like it?"

"Yes."

His eyes held hers for a second, and he seemed to be considering several other things to say. Finally, flashing that brilliant smile of his, he said, "Thanks. I think you're a girl who always tells the truth, so if you hate *me* but like the film, it must be good."

"It's good and I don't hate you." Roxanne was strangely touched by the fact that he really seemed to care what she thought. Then she couldn't resist adding, "But don't let the fact that you come from a theatrical family destroy you."

Now he raised his eyebrow in a mocking reaction. "I could say the same to you, my dear. Don't let the fact that you come from a theatrical family destroy *you*, either."

Roxanne flushed, feeling once again that Gary Marlowe had made fun of her and her mother. She said good-night and stepped into the taxi, giving directions to the driver to pick up Laureen, never once looking back at the handsome man who stood on the curb.

Chapter Five

I T took a long time to buy the train tickets because the ticket clerk seemed convinced that they wanted sleepers instead of just coach seats. Roxanne thought it was probably because Laureen began the transaction by telling him that her daughter was going to be a star.

Finally Roxanne interrupted, grabbed the two suitcases, and said, "Come on, Ma. We've got to run for it."

They were both puffing hard by the time they boarded the Super Chief, and sure enough, within seconds the engines on the train began to chug. Roxanne and her mother selected two seats across the aisle from each other, took blankets and pillows from the porter, and curled up to try to sleep. It was after midnight, and they had a two-day, two-night journey ahead of them.

Sleeping on a moving train turned out to be remarkably easy for Roxanne, and since there was no one sitting next to her, she was able to stretch out over the two seats. The pillow did help her head some, but when she awoke the next morning, she had a stiff neck. Roxanne stretched, rubbed her eyes, and said good morning to her mother, who was sitting straight up.

"I've got a stiff neck," Roxanne said.

"I'm stiff all over," Laureen complained. "We should have bought a sleeper like the ticket teller said."

"Money, Ma. We're not rich yet."

"Been better to have made a grand entrance," her mother grumbled. "We should have gone to Hollywood in style. This is like sneaking in the back door. About the best I can say is that we are on the Super Chief." Laureen looked around her with satisfaction, rubbing her hands over the dark-red and green velvet upholstery.

"I'll go wash and then we can go to the diner," Roxanne said. "If we eat a big breakfast, we can get by on snacks the rest of the day. That will be cheaper."

"We can afford more than one meal a day, I should hope."

"Cheer up, Ma. It will be fun to have breakfast in the diner. I'll be right back."

The ladies' room turned out to be much smaller but almost as fancy as the one in the Midland Theater. There was a mirror with a gold frame, a red velvet sofa with gilded arms, and two small velvet chairs in the same green and red velvet that was on the seats in their car. Roxanne decided that the Super Chief deserved its reputation as the fanciest train in the country, and she was glad they were riding on it.

She brushed her hair and washed her face, applied some new lipstick, and looked at her reflection very critically. One way in which she knew that she was lucky was that her blonde hair curled softly around her shoulders. It was thick and golden, and she wore it parted in the middle and pulled back with two small hair bows. Nothing wrong with her face, either, she decided. Her eyes were wide enough and her nose was straight. Her mouth was not as full as some girls might like, but she liked the way her lips were shaped into a wide bow.

She frowned when her eyes traveled down to her dress, though. The navy-blue crepe she was wearing was the only really decent one she owned, and it looked very crumpled after her night's sleep. She decided that this evening she would change into her other dress and let this one hang out. Maybe some of the wrinkles would smooth out overnight.

The dress itself was all right. It had a simple, round neckline and long sleeves with a little puff at the top. There were silver buttons down the front, and the belt had a silver buckle, so she really didn't need any fancy jewelry to look complete. The best thing about the dress was the way the skirt was cut on the bias, fitting closely over the hips and then swinging out in a wider flare toward the bottom. Bias-cut skirts hadn't been in style very long, and this was the first new dress Roxanne had had in two years, so she was glad it was up-to-date.

She smiled at her reflection and then practiced narrowing her eyes to make them look angry, as Gary had in the movie she'd seen last night. Then she spent some more time practicing different expressions to see how many kinds of emotions she could convey without words. She thought her anger looked realistic enough, but there was something so phony about the way she lowered her eyelids when she was trying to look sad that she burst out laughing.

She was still laughing to herself as she and Laureen went into the dining room of the train. Walking on the train was something of a joke, anyway, especially when it went around a curve, and a couple of times Roxanne had the feeling that if she wasn't careful, she might land in some stranger's lap. By the time they'd actually made it to the diner, Roxanne had it figured out.

"You have to walk like a duck," she instructed her mother. "Put down your feet with your toes outward and make your knees stiffer and your legs farther apart."

Laureen attempted to follow her instructions, and she looked so serious as she marched stiff-legged down the aisle in the diner that Roxanne was still laughing as they sat down. "Ma, I expected you to flap your arms and say, 'Quack, Quack.'"

Her mother frowned and said, "Try to look sensible, Roxanne. There may be talent scouts here."

Roxanne raised her eyebrow in an imitation of Gary Marlowe's expression of surprise. "Do you seriously think there are talent scouts *everywhere*? Anyway, I'm too rumpled for anyone to notice me even if there were. And there aren't."

"I know a great deal more about this business than you do, young lady. After all, I started reading about the lives of stars before you were born."

"And I'll bet less than a tenth of what you read is true. I think I'll have ham and eggs. What do you want?"

"I think that's a movie star over there. I think I've seen him before."

Roxanne turned to look at a table with several men at it. She wasn't even sure which man her mother meant, since they all looked quite ordinary. The one in the center had on a dark-blue suit and was very young, but he certainly didn't look like a movie star. He had a long face and an extraordinarily long nose.

Laureen hissed. "Don't stare. I'm not sure who it is, but it's someone important. Now try to look pretty. You never know when your big break will come."

"The only break I'm going to get on this train is an arm or a leg." Roxanne burst into laughter again. "Ma, you looked so funny walking."

"Hush, anyone would think you've never been on a train before."

"I haven't."

"That's not important." Laureen brushed her words aside with a wave of her hand. "What's important is to make a good impression. I wish I knew who that man was."

During the next two days Laureen was certain that discovery was just around the corner, but Roxanne's attention was on the wonderful sights she saw from her window. She was thrilled as they climbed into the Rockies and absolutely ecstatic when they got to the desert. Lifting her face toward the sun, she said, "I feel like I'm standing in front of our kitchen stove. Imagine all this sunshine in February!"

"Wait till you get to California," Laureen promised her. "Flowers all over the place and sunshine every day. They say the Pacific Ocean is the most beautiful one in the world, and you can pick oranges off people's trees right in their front yards."

"I hope you're right about the weather," Roxanne said. "Our clothes aren't very warm." She remembered how cold they'd been as they walked on the streets of Kansas City the night before. That reminded her of Gary Marlowe, and she wondered what he was doing this morning. Was he having breakfast in his hotel? And did he have the same sort of silver and linen on his table as they had on the train? Being a movie star must be fun, Roxanne decided.

As Roxanne was settling down to sleep on the second night, Laureen came back from one of her walks and announced triumphantly. "I was right. That man was Bob Hoke. The one in the diner this morning?"

"Who is Bob Hoke?"

"I've never actually seen him in the movies," Laureen admitted. "I don't think he's made any, but he's a big Broadway star, and the porter told me he's on his way to Hollywood to be a star, same as you are."

"There are some differences, Ma. He's got a contract. All I have is your confidence in me."

"I wish you had more confidence in yourself." Laureen sighed and sat down, took off her shoes and crossed her legs, taking one stockinged foot in her hands. "Tomorrow you'll dance for Mr. Hoke."

"Good-night, Ma." Roxanne closed her eyes, hoping that her mother would have forgotten that particular plan by morning. As she closed her eyes she saw her father's face and heard him say, "Take care of her, Roxanne. I love her."

She dreamed of her father that night, dreamed that she was a very young girl again and he was explaining to her that she would soon be a movie star, just like Shirley Temple. He was laughing and looked young and happy as he said, "You're just as pretty and you can sing and dance." Then he hugged her, and when he drew away, he looked old and tired, as old and tired as he did just before he died. He said, "We need the money, Roxanne. We need the money."

Somehow, before morning, her father had turned into Mr. Hoke and her mother was on stage, tap-dancing for Gary Marlowe. Then, the next thing she knew, Gary was giving her mother a prize and kissing her hand. All of a sudden Roxanne was her mother and Gary Marlowe was kissing her, holding her close, and his embrace felt sweet, so sweet. She awoke thinking of his touch and was surprised to see her mother standing over her.

"You sure look happy," her mother said. "Good dreams?"

Roxanne blushed and said, "Mixed-up ones, really. But you won a prize for tap-dancing."

Even Laureen had to laugh at that. She was much too heavy to fit the image of a tap dancer, even if she had been younger. "Go get freshened up, we're going to talk to Mr. Hoke."

Roxanne groaned and protested, "Ma, even if he is going to be a star, and you really don't know anything except what the porter told you, how could he help me?"

"He could be a contact," Laureen said. "You've got to start building contacts."

"I hate talking to strangers, Ma. It makes me feel foolish and . . . pushy. Gary Marlowe thought we were funny."

"How do you think people get to be stars, Roxanne?" Laureen seemed angry as she asked her daughter the question. "How do you think girls get their breaks? They take every opportunity they can, that's how. Mr. Hoke could be a contact."

"When we get to Hollywood, I'll go to the casting agencies," Roxanne said. "I'll work hard."

"Hundreds of pretty girls go to the casting agencies."

"Then I'll keep going back. I'll wear them down."

Laureen shook her head. "Now go get freshened up. Put on brighter lipstick, and powder your face. Use the lipstick as rouge for your cheeks. You look pale."

Roxanne knew it was useless to argue with her mother, and though she dreaded whatever was coming next, she did her best to make herself look presentable. Then she quietly followed her mother into the diner. They were two of the first people to sit down, and her mother whispered, "Eat slowly, we'll stay until Mr. Hoke shows up."

The easiest order Laureen had given her was to eat slowly. She picked at her food, sipping her coffee carefully and asking for a refill. They sat at the breakfast table all the way through the three-hour seating, and the young Broadway star never showed up. Laureen drank at least ten cups of coffee.

Finally the waiter told them that they

were closing the diner and they had to leave, but not before Laureen asked, "That movie star, Bob Hoke, which car is he in?"

"Don't know him, ma'am."

"But the porter told me he was famous," Laureen protested. Her mother prowled up and down the train most of the morning, looking for her elusive movie star, and once in a while she dropped by to report to Roxanne on her progress.

Her mother's absence gave Roxanne a chance to think, and her thoughts kept returning to her dream of Gary Marlowe. Why had she dreamed of him instead of Henry? The question bothered her and made her feel slightly guilty, though she knew she wasn't really responsible for her dreams.

She forced herself to look out the window and watch the desert landscape. She decided that the desert was really very different than it appeared in the movies, because the sky was so blue. That color made the sand seem to sparkle. She decided that Western movies should all be shot in the new Technicolor, just to show off the beautiful landscape. So far she'd only seen one Technicolor movie, but she believed there would probably be a lot more very soon. At least, that was what her mother's movie magazines predicted.

The desert cactus and sand gave way to foothills, and Roxanne realized that they were almost there. Laureen came back just as they were pulling into the Pasadena station, and her face was flushed with anger. Roxanne knew immediately that she'd finally found her man and that the encounter was not any more successful than her attempts to get Roxanne into the talent show the other night. She sat down and said, "His name isn't Hoke, it's Hope. And he claims he can't do anything for you."

"I'm sorry, Ma." She reached out and patted her mother's hand.

"How was I to know his name was Hope? Porter said it was Hoke. He could have helped you, anyway, I'm sure of that."

"Ma, if he's on his way to make his first movie, he probably doesn't have the ability to help anyone. Besides, why should he help me? I'm not anything special to him."

Laureen crossed her hands over her chest and stared straight ahead. "I had that all figured out," she said. "Told him you were his cousin. Claimed kin on his father's side of the family. I even said that my Uncle Charlie had exactly the same kind of nose that he did. I thought, with a nose like that he'd have to believe me. But when I said our last name was Hoke, he just started laughing."

It was all Roxanne could do to keep from laughing as well. She bit her lips together to keep from hurting her mother's feelings and said, "We're in California, Ma. Almost in Hollywood."

"We should get off in Pasadena," Laureen announced. "All the stars do that."

"Why?"

"To avoid the crowds of fans."

Roxanne couldn't hold it back any longer. The laughter came tumbling out of her as she realized exactly how foolish her mother's dreams were. Might as well laugh as cry.

Chapter Six

THE sun was shining in Los Angeles, and both Laureen and Roxanne breathed a sigh of relief when they stepped out into the patio of the train station. Roxanne looked around the courtyard at the soft white stuccoed building, the bright blue tile floors, and the wonderful red flowers in pots and said, "It's beautiful. Imagine flowers in February. What are those red ones?"

"I don't know," Laureen said. Now that they were actually in California, she seemed almost uncertain about what to do next.

Roxanne walked over to examine the red flowers more carefully, touching the sharp tips of the petals with her fingertips. Never had she seen such large petals or such a glorious color. When a red cap passed them, pushing a load of baggage, she asked, "Do you know what these flowers are called?"

"Poinsettias."

Poinsettias. The word had an exotic and foreign sound to it as Roxanne repeated it. She knew that Los Angeles had once been a Spanish town and that the name meant "the angels" in Spanish. Now, looking at the train station, she realized that it was built differently than any building she'd ever seen. The doors were arched, and the whole building was covered with brilliant white stucco. She supposed that the style of the building and the tile floors were intended to look Spanish, and she thought it looked very nice and cheerful.

Laureen didn't seem to have any good ideas about what to do next, so Roxanne said, "We might as well look for a place in Hollywood. Then we can walk to the studios." She asked the porter for directions and led Laureen to the corner to wait for a bus.

The buildings their bus passed as it traveled down the main streets of Los Angeles toward Hollywood were all one or two stories tall. Roxanne was surprised and asked her mother, "Why do you think they build such low buildings?"

A woman across from them volunteered, "Earthquakes."

"Earthquakes," Laureen and Roxanne said together. Laureen shuddered at the thought, and Roxanne asked, "What is an earthquake like?"

"Earth shakes," a man answered. He was a tall, middle-aged man with a weather-beaten face and huge hands that looked almost silly carrying the carefully tied packages that peeked out from his shopping bag. His wife was a small woman with a birdlike face whose most remarkable features were a sharp little nose and pointed chin. She was well-dressed in a short fur jacket and soft beige leather pumps with pointed toes that Roxanne recognized as being from the flapper era of the 1920s.

"Do earthquakes cause a lot of damage?" Roxanne asked.

"Depends," the woman said. "Big one in '34 just about brought the whole state down. Leveled Long Beach. They still haven't finished rebuilding all the schools."

"You mean the walls collapse?" Laureen asked. "Everywhere?"

The man next to the woman laughed and said, "Not everywhere. Just where the center of the quake is. Trouble is, you never know where that might be. Take our boardinghouse, for instance. It shook but it didn't fall down. Center of the quake was Long Beach, not Hollywood."

"They don't have earthquakes in Hollywood," Laureen said emphatically. "I never read about them in my magazines."

"They've got lots of things in Hollywood you'll never read about in your fan magazines," the woman said darkly. "Where you girls from? Kansas?"

"Oklahoma," Roxanne answered. "You folks have a boardinghouse in Hollywood?"

"Yes. And I bet you came out here to be in the movies," the woman answered. "Need a place to stay?"

"My girl's going to be a star," Laureen announced.

The woman and man smiled at each other, and then the woman said, "Town's full of pretty girls who want to get in the movies." Then she added, "We're always on the lookout for paying boarders."

"I'm sure your place is nice," Laureen said, "but we're planning on finding a little place of our own. Maybe one of those little Spanish bungalows."

"Best save your money," the woman advised. "Sometimes it takes a long time to break into the movies. Besides, could be my husband might help you. He was an actor in the twenties. Made twenty westerns."

"Name is Gus Clintlock. Ever hear of me?"

Roxanne studied the older man's face carefully, but she couldn't honestly say she'd ever seen him. Still, it was interesting to meet someone who had actually acted in a movie.

Gus explained, "I fell off too many horses and had to quit. That was the days when westerns were shot in five days in Griffith Park. Those movies made me just enough to buy the boardinghouse."

"Five dollars a week for the two of you," Mrs. Clintlock offered eagerly. "That includes an egg and toast in the morning. But no cooking in your room."

"That's because of fires," Gus Clintlock explained. "But you can keep crackers and tins if you want."

"No, you can't," his wife corrected sharply. "It brings bugs. I run a clean house."

"I just thought they might want to conserve money," he explained to his wife.

"My husband has the soft heart." Mrs. Clintlock's eyes were honest and direct as she spoke to Roxanne. "I have the business sense. So you'll have to deal with me."

Roxanne smiled, understanding that Mrs. Clintlock had deliberately chosen to speak to her instead of her mother, because she knew who was the more sensible. "I think we'd like to see your boardinghouse, Mrs. Clintlock."

"But I want a Spanish bungalow," her mother protested.

"Yes," Roxanne soothed, "but in the meantime we'll be real close to Hollywood and Vine. You'd like that, wouldn't you?"

Gus helped them carry their suitcases to the boardinghouse, and Roxanne was very pleased with its handsome exterior. It was in the Spanish style and had a red tile roof and low, rambling rooms off the main part, which was two stories tall. She liked the clean, well-scrubbed look of the parlor with its Oriental rugs and dark, polished furniture. The dining room was paneled in dark wood, and there was a huge Spanish-style table with heavy, rough-cut chairs all around it. "Ranch furniture," Mrs. Clintlock apologized. "Gus always thought we'd buy a ranch and raise horses."

"It's lovely," Roxanne said, and she meant it.

The room Mrs. Clintlock gave them was somewhat disappointing, since it was only a very small bedroom with just space enough for two twin beds and one dresser. Since the dining room and living room were so spacious, she'd expected something similar from the room they were renting. "It's rather small," Roxanne said.

"Best boardinghouse in Hollywood," Mrs. Clintlock answered. "You can look around if you like."

"We'll take it," Roxanne said. Now that the possibility of settling down was presented to her, she realized that she was very tired. What she wanted most was to take a hot bath and have a good rest in a real bed. The room was clean and close to Hollywood and Vine. Though she liked Gus a lot more than his wife, they both seemed honest enough.

Mrs. Clintlock nodded and then went to the window, pulling open the shade and saying, "When the weather gets warmer, you can sit out here." Roxanne walked to the window and discovered it was really a door to a small balcony with wrought-iron railings. Though you had to step up over a foot-high baseboard to get out there, the balcony was set up for use. There was a tiny table and two wrought-iron chairs. Best of all, there were several large geranium plants in clay pots that fit into the wrought-iron cages that were attached to the balcony wall.

"Too cold for much in February," Mrs. Clintock said. "But it will be hot soon."

Roxanne stepped out onto the tiny balcony, looking down at the view below. "It's beautiful," Roxanne said. She still hadn't become accustomed to all the gorgeous flowers in bloom, despite the fact that it was winter.

Before Mrs. Clintlock left she collected ten dollars from Laureen, saying that she always collected a week in advance.

Roxanne stepped off the balcony in time to catch her mother counting her remaining money. She asked quietly, "How much?"

"A hundred and ten dollars," Laureen said. She seemed shocked at the amount.

Roxanne sat down on the bed and said, "I've got about ten dollars from the twenty you gave me for spending money. That makes a hundred and twenty. Figure ten dollars a week. Five for board and another five for food. We've got to save back the fare to Oklahoma. Subtract thirty for the bus trip." she frowned as she figured it out. "That gives us nine weeks, Ma."

"Nine weeks," Laureen said, "Why, as pretty as you are, you won't need half that time. Anyway, we have to buy you some nice clothes before you go to the casting agencies. Tomorrow we go shopping."

"Tonight I borrow Mrs. Clintlock's iron and press and spot-clean my navy-blue dress. Tomorrow I go job-hunting."

*Chapter
Seven*

LOOKING for work in Hollywood was incredibly easy in some ways. All you had to do was report to the casting agencies and leave your name. Sometimes they asked you to fill out a form, but usually the receptionist just looked bored and said, "Don't call us, we'll call you."

Roxanne visited every casting agency the first week she was there and returned the second week to deliver her photographs. Too much of their precious money went toward having a professional photographer take a simple three-quarter portrait pose of her smiling into the camera. Though the photographer gave her the best price they'd been able to find and offered to throw in several other poses for half of that, Roxanne held firm to the belief that one photograph ought to be enough. "They can see what I look like," she said. "That's all that matters."

Her mother argued with her about the photographs, wanting to order several on credit and pay for them when "our ship comes in." But even Laureen began to admit that breaking into the movies might be a little more difficult than she had believed when she'd been dreaming back in Oklahoma. Each morning she made the rounds with Roxanne, anxiously waiting outside the casting agency until her daughter returned with the same discouraging news.

The second week they were there, Roxanne joined a long line of young starlets who were hoping for a chance to try out for the part of Scarlett O'Hara in *Gone with the Wind*. There had been a lot of publicity about the famous book for several years, and though Laureen insisted that Roxanne was too young to read it, she was perfectly willing for her to try for the part of the fiery Southern heroine.

The tryout wasn't really a tryout at all, but Roxanne did get to see George Cukor, the man who would direct the film. He and several of his assistants were sitting in the lobby of a famous Hollywood hotel, and there were news photographers taking pictures of the pretty girls who were lined up for a block or more.

Roxanne stood in line two hours for a chance to walk by Mr. Cukor. When she saw how bored he looked, she decided that the rumors were true and that the talent search was nothing more than a publicity stunt designed to keep interest in the movie alive. He actually yawned as the girl in front of her walked to his table.

When Roxanne walked up to the table, he lifted his head and looked mildly interested. He asked, "Your name?"

"Roxanne Wilson."

"Where are you from Roxanne?"

"Norman, Oklahoma."

"How old are you?"

"Fifteen."

Cukor shook his head. "Too young."

"Scarlett was very young," she spoke up, knowing she had nothing to lose.

"In the beginning," he agreed. "But the book covers ten years. Sorry."

Roxanne consoled herself because she was the only one he'd actually talked with out of the whole line, but she wished she had at least been offered a screen test. They said that several young women had tested for Scarlett and been offered other parts.

Laureen decided that Roxanne didn't get the part of Scarlett because she was from Oklahoma.

"Ma, they've interviewed thousands of girls all over the country. Why should they pick me?"

"Why shouldn't they?" Laureen answered. "I think it was because you're from the Midwest. The only accents they like in this town are foreign ones." She warned her daughter to speak faster, carefully erasing any trace of a Midwestern drawl. She even suggested that Roxanne try a British accent. "Look at the big stars," Laureen said. "They're all from somewhere else. Greta Garbo still can't speak English, and she's the most famous actress in Hollywood."

"Yes, Ma." Roxanne had adopted the habit of only half listening to her mother as she worried about practical things, such as how they were going to get back to Oklahoma when the money ran out. After two weeks in Hollywood Roxanne had a chance to assess her chances, and she knew the odds were very high. But the more reality presented itself, the more Laureen stuck to her dreams. Getting her mother to admit defeat was going to be very difficult, and she'd already warned Henry in her last letter home that Laureen would probably insist on spending every penny. She had an idea her mother would have to endure actual hunger before they left the land of sunshine.

Henry wrote right back that she could call him collect and he would send fare home. She was grateful for Henry's faithfulness, and she wrote to him every four or five days, but she found she really didn't miss him as much as she'd expected. If the truth were told, she thought more about her few minutes' encounter with Gary Marlowe than her long romance with Henry Scott. In spite of everything, she was grateful to her mother for dragging her out of Oklahoma and letting her get a taste of California.

There were so many things she loved about the area. Day after day the sun shone in a blue sky. She loved the flowers and the way the people seemed so friendly. Even the beggars on the streets seemed more hopeful than they had in Oklahoma. Roxanne had long ago decided that most of the people who were living in Hollywood were dreamers who fed on hope.

She knew that she, too, had contracted a big dose of Hollywood hopefulness herself, and she found herself spinning fantasies about how it would be when she was a star, more often than she ever would have believed possible. She did her very best to make an impression on the receptionists at the various casting agencies. By the first week she knew each of them by name and was always careful to speak politely. What worried her the most was that most of them seemed to be pretty young girls who probably came out to Hollywood to be stars, just as she had.

On the morning of the fourth week she went into Star Casting Agency and tried to speak crisply instead of with a drawl as she asked, "Charlotte, how are you?"

"Hi, Roxanne. Nothing today."

"Nothing at all?"

"They're making a lot of Westerns these days, honey. No parts for pretty cowboys at all."

"Maybe I could groom the horse," Roxanne said. On an impulse she asked, "How did you get this job?"

"Got a boyfriend who got it for me. He's a guard at MGM, and it took him almost a year."

"I guess any kind of job is tough to get in Hollywood."

"You betcha. One thing there's plenty of in Hollywood is cheap labor. You have any idea how many kids come to this town to be actors and actresses and end up waiting tables or selling vacuum cleaners?"

"I'd be happy to wait tables," Roxanne said. "That's what I was going to do in Oklahoma, and it didn't seem like much of a job. But I'd take a waitress job now."

But Charlotte didn't even seem to be listening; her eyes were on the door and the three other young women who came in. One of them was wearing a mink stole, and all three were very well dressed, with expensive haircuts and lots of jewelry. Charlotte said, "We can only use two of you."

"Come on," the tall blonde said, "be a sport and send us all. What's ten dollars mean to MGM?"

"My call was for two blondes," Charlotte said. "So Ida and Maye got the call."

"I'm blonde, too," the girl with the mink said, pouting and putting her hand on her hips.

Charlotte handed a slip of paper to one of the other girls and said, "This will admit two of you to the lot. You fight it out."

As the girls left Charlotte smiled briefly at

Roxanne and said, "The call was for blondes in evening clothes. Sorry."

Roxanne was fighting back tears as she said, "You have a right to call whoever you want."

"I might have called you if you had evening clothes," Charlotte explained. "You're a little young-looking, but you're pretty. But I've never seen you in anything but your navy dress, so I figured you don't have many clothes and you didn't put down that you had costumes on your casting card."

"I understand," Roxanne said. "Thanks, anyway."

Laureen was waiting outside when Roxanne came down the steps. Her mother's first words were, "Who were those three fancy women ahead of you? Did she give them jobs?"

"Two of them got work today," Roxanne admitted. "Charlotte picked them because they had evening clothes."

"Then we'll get you evening clothes," Laureen said. "I knew we should have bought you some new dresses."

"Ma, we don't have enough money." Yet she believed that Charlotte really should have called her for that job, and the ten dollars she might have earned would have paid another two weeks' rent.

"We have almost fifty dollars left," her mother said.

"Thirty is for bus fare home," Roxanne reminded her.

"Nonsense," Laureen said. "Something will turn up before then. Besides, Cousin Margaret may be stingy, but she'll wire us bus fare if we ask. She couldn't resist a chance to see me eat crow."

"I don't know, Ma." She knew she should be more discouraged after over a month of total failure, but knowing that she'd almost come close to work had actually given her hope. "I hate to spend money on a dress when we may be going hungry soon."

"We don't have to go hungry," Laureen pointed out. "We can go to Clifton's Restaurant whenever we want."

"Clifton may give free meals, but he doesn't pass out nickles to take the bus to Los Angeles," Roxanne reminded her.

They had learned from several boarders at the Clintlocks' that there were two Clifton restaurants in downtown Los Angeles which allowed people to eat as much as they wanted and pay little or nothing. Though they knew that some out-of-work actors made it a part of their daily routine to take the bus to Clifton's for lunch each day, Roxanne and Laureen had not tried it, reasoning that for the twenty cents it cost them to take the bus, they could buy something simple in Hollywood.

Crackers and cheese didn't cost much, and despite Mrs. Clintlock's original warning, she never objected to the tin boxes where they kept them. An apple cost a nickle on the corner of Hollywood and Vine and was so big and beautiful, it could be split in half. Their egg in the morning and generously buttered toast, plus their light lunch at home was supplemented by a bowl of soup and half a sandwich at night. Despite their light diet, Laureen didn't seem to lose weight, but Roxanne was several pounds thinner than when she'd first come to town.

"Be better in the movies," Gus Clintlock assured her. "That camera makes everyone look fatter than they are."

Roxanne had never been a vain person, and she hadn't really thought much about her looks back in Oklahoma. It was just taken for granted that she was the prettiest girl in her class, and no one seemed to make much of it. But now she was depending on her appearance to get her inside a studio, and she quickly developed the ability to judge herself without getting personally involved in the verdict.

There were a lot of pretty girls in Hollywood, but she quickly saw that most of them were older and more tired-looking than she was. Even the best-dressed ones often had on too much makeup, covering little lines or tired eyes. Sometimes she passed a young woman who seemed to be in her mid-twenties and saw clearly that her best days were over. As Roxanne made the rounds her sense of urgency increased. Not only was her money running out, but she began to understand that a girl had to make it fast while that first fresh bloom was apparent, or it was too late.

There might be opportunity in Hollywood,

but it was also clear that there was room for only a few at the top. As Gus and the other boarders gossiped about how this and that star fought her way to the top, Roxanne began to understand how it could happen. A girl had to be alert to every chance if she was going to make it. Within just a few weeks Roxanne learned to be more insistent than she'd ever thought possible.

Henry wrote often, urging her to come home, but the longer she stayed in Hollywood, the harder she tried to break into the movies. Some mornings she woke with an enthusiasm that made her feel as though success were only an hour away. She hated to give up hope, and Henry's offer began to represent failure. She knew she had changed a great deal since she started out, and yet she had to admit in her letters home that absolutely nothing had happened.

That evening she was able to write to Henry that she "almost" got a job as a blonde for MGM studios, and even as she watched the dark blue ink flow from her fountain pen onto the paper, she knew it sounded like next to nothing. "I'm having fun in a way," she concluded. "But I miss you, too."

She stared at the paper a long time after that, wondering what else she could say. There was no way she could describe the excitement she felt as she mounted the steps to the casting agencies. There was no way she could explain to Henry that she'd caught some of her mother's optimism in spite of herself. Finally she concluded her letter by saying that she would be listening to the Lux Radio Theater that night, as he probably was. Then she signed it "Love, Roxanne" and folded it, even before the ink was totally dry.

Would she still love Henry when she went home to Oklahoma? Would he still love her? And if she did love Henry, why did she spend so much time thinking about Gary Marlowe?

Roxanne had taken to daydreaming about Gary a lot, though she knew it was foolish. She had developed the habit of acting out the part of the heroine in her own mind when they listened to radio dramas in the evening. She invariably found that the dashing Gary played opposite her in this mental theater. She sometimes wondered if her fondness for the Lux Radio Theater had more to do with the dreams of being held in Gary's arms than the quality of the writing in the plays.

The night after Roxanne almost got the job, Laureen went to the movies with the Clintlocks, and when she came home, she said, "Mrs. Clintlock will sell you a silver evening dress for ten dollars."

"That's very expensive," Roxanne objected. "The jobs only pay ten dollars a day."

"And I'll rent you my fur jacket for a dollar a day," Mrs. Clintlock added.

Reluctantly Roxanne followed the two women to Mrs. Clintlock's bedroom where she plowed through closets and finally found a bulky cloth bag with a zipper. She pulled out a lot of dresses and lifted up a silver evening dress. "Gus bought this for me for my birthday the year he made *Silver Saddles*. Isn't it beautiful?"

Like all of Mrs. Clintlock's clothes, it was very dated-looking. She often wore fancy dresses that Roxanne thought of as "flapper" dresses around the house when she was cleaning. What was even worse were the pointed-toe shoes that she wore. They looked absolutely miserable to Roxanne. But after an acquaintance of a month Roxanne had learned that saving money was very important to Mrs. Clintlock, not that she blamed her in these times.

This dress had an uneven hemline and a dropped waist. Roxanne shook her head and said, "It won't do. It's too old-fashioned."

"Cut the hem off and add a piece of velvet," Mrs. Clintlock suggested. She pulled out another long dress of dark green velvet and said, "Here, I'll give you this one and you can use the skirt for the bottom piece."

Roxanne shuddered to think how horrible the silver dress would look with a wide band of dark green velvet at the bottom. But she picked up the velvet dress and held it up to her. It was a very plain princess-line dress with a V neckline and long sleeves. She asked. "Will you sell me this one for a dollar?"

"It's crushed in the rear," Mrs. Clintlock admitted.

"Maybe I can steam it out," Roxanne said. "Anyway, it probably won't show in crowd scenes. A dollar?"

"Two."

"You just said it was crushed."

"A dollar and a half."

"And you'll still rent me your jacket if I need it?"

Mrs. Clintlock seemed dismayed that her profits had diminished so greatly, but she nodded her head in agreement. Roxanne said to her mother, "Give her a dollar and a half, Ma."

Laureen opened her purse and took out a crumpled dollar bill and two quarters, then she followed Roxanne into their room. Once there she said, "You'd think that skinflint would have given you this old dress. You'll never get it to look like anything."

"I think it may do," Roxanne said. "Anyway, that silver thing was horrible."

"We could have bought you a new one," Laureen grumbled.

But Roxanne was busy slipping the dark green velvet dress over her head. The dress fit because the older woman was so much shorter. The soft fabric clung to her body and felt elegant even though she knew it was worn. "How do I look, Ma?"

Her mother's expression changed from resentment to surprise. "You look beautiful," she said honestly. "Turn around."

As Roxanne twirled Laureen said, "It is

very crushed in back, but maybe if we hang it in the bathroom for a while, it will improve."

"How do you think the other boarders will like taking a bath with a velvet dress?"

"I shouldn't think they'd mind," Laureen said. "After all, one of these days they'll be bragging that they knew you when."

Roxanne laughed and kissed her mother on the cheek. "You know what I love best about you? The way you never let the facts stand in the way of what you believe."

"You're going to be a big star, Roxanne. I know it."

"I'm glad you think so," she said.

"If only you had a little more confidence in yourself," Laureen began to nag again. "Now, when you go to the casting agency tomorrow, you tell them that you're good, really good at dancing. Tell them that Madame Belinda said you could have had a career in ballet if you wanted."

"Ma, I took one year of ballet when I was ten. What's the sense of telling lies? I can dance a little and sing on key, but I'm no Ruby Keeler."

"You're prettier than Ruby Keeler," Laureen argued. "If only you had more confidence in yourself."

Roxanne sighed and said, "I'm going to hang this dress in the bathroom with a note explaining why. Then I'm going to sleep."

"And in the morning you'll go back to Star Casting and tell that girl that from now on you expect to be sent out for all calls that require evening dress."

"Yes, Ma."

She did return to Star Casting first thing the next morning, and Charlotte looked surprised as she said, "I was just calling you on the phone."

"Do you have work?" Roxanne asked. She felt the adrenaline begin to pump and her heart start to race. Was this her first break?

"It's a long story," Charlotte said. "Last night my boyfriend and I went to the movies with this guy who my sister's been dating. The guy owns a restaurant, and sometimes we all go there for a free meal. His name is Rudy, but believe me, he's no Valentino." Charlotte paused to see if Roxanne got her joke.

"But the work?"

"The work is as a waitress in his restaurant," Charlotte admitted. "He said he needed someone reliable, and I said I knew a girl he could trust. Do you want the job?"

"Of course."

"You look like a few meals would help, and I think he'll feed you every day. That's important."

"Did he say how much it pays?"

"Ten dollars a week and meals. And he says he has movie stars for customers. Maybe you'll be discovered."

Roxanne nodded. It wasn't a big break, but it was a way to stay in town awhile longer. It would keep them from having to wire for money and from having to go back to Oklahoma. It wasn't until she was outside that she thought of Henry. He was waiting for her to return soon and marry him. What would he say about this new job?

But before she could write Henry she had to convince her mother that taking a job as a waitress was a good idea. The older woman wailed, "You're spoiling my plan."

"I'm fixing it so we stay in Hollywood longer. How much do you have in your purse, Ma?"

Her mother clutched the purse to her chest and shook her head. "Something will turn up."

"I'm just working the lunch and dinner shifts. I can go to casting offices early in the morning," Roxanne promised.

"I'll take the job," Laureen offered.

"You can't stand on your feet an hour without them hurting," Roxanne said. "You might look for some other kind of work, though. Maybe a cashier in a movie theater?"

"Do you know how many people want to work in movie theaters?" Laureen asked.

"About as many as want to be movie stars," Roxanne admitted. Then she laughed and added, "I think we'd better start thinking of this restaurant job as the big break we've been waiting for."

Chapter
Eight

THE job in the restaurant was hard work, but Roxanne managed to learn how to balance the plates and give them to the right person very quickly. After she'd been there a week Rudy said, "You're a smart girl. You got a boyfriend?"

Roxanne replied very quickly, "Oh, yes."

"Nice boy?"

"Very."

"Just as long as he doesn't hang around my restaurant," Rudy warned, suddenly scowling.

"He's in Oklahoma," Roxanne assured him.

"Oklahoma?" Rudy threw back his head and laughed. "That what you are, an Okie?"

Roxanne flushed. She hated it when California natives referred to the people who came here from the dust bowl states as

Okies, or Arkies if they were from Arkansas. "I was born in Norman, Oklahoma," she said.

"How come you don't say 'ain't' and 'cain't'?"Rudy asked. Then he laughed and patted her arm. "Never mind," he said in a mock Oklahoma accent, "you cain't hep where you wuz born."

"Not everyone from Oklahoma is a hillbilly," Roxanne replied.

"You're cute," Rudy said. "Now be here early tomorrow because I got a dentist appointment."

Roxanne nodded and got her purse and coat. She was curious about the breakfast hours, because Rudy usually claimed that was when the movie stars stopped in for coffee and doughnuts. She found herself daydreaming that Gary would stop in tomorrow morning.

It was easier to daydream as she walked home than while she was on the job. Waiting on tables was very hard work and Roxanne had to stay alert all the time, so she wouldn't mix up the orders. She seldom had time to think about much of anything, except what was on the blue-plate special or whether the customer wanted his eggs sunnyside up or scrambled. Rudy talked a lot about how many of his customers were famous stars, but Roxanne never saw any.

One young customer was as star-struck as she was, though. He came in twice with his father, and both times they had horrible arguments about what the boy was going to do with his life. He was tall and lanky and about her age or a little older, and he seemed to be in college. His father was a little man with a bald head and a round belly. He wore his tweed cap inside the restaurant and gulped his coffee as he growled at his son.

Roxanne felt sorry for the son because he seemed absolutely terrified of his father. He apparently wanted to drop out of college and go to work in the movie industry, but his father kept shaking his head and growling, "No son of mine is in the movie business."

Roxanne got so that she hated the father, because the young man seemed so sweet and scared. She would have felt really sorry for the young man, except he was obviously very wealthy. He wore an expensive camel-hair coat and a different colored sweater and necktie both days they came in. Considering the obvious difference in their economic level, it was hard for Roxanne to waste much time on the young man's problems. Whatever he did would probably turn out all right. He wasn't going to starve, no matter what.

Well, they weren't going to starve, either, Roxanne reminded herself. She entered the Clintlock boardinghouse and climbed the stairs to their little room. Her mother was sitting in the one chair, polishing her nails. There were several new movie magazines strewn on top of the bed.

Roxanne couldn't resist saying, "I wish you wouldn't buy so many of them at once. They cost fifteen cents each."

"I learn a lot," Laureen replied. "Remember that Bob Hope we met on the train? He's got a contract with Paramount for three pictures. It's a seven-year contract with options, and he's getting twenty thousand dollars a picture."

"Too bad he's not really our cousin," Roxanne said. She sat down on the edge of her bed and said, "I'm really tired tonight."

"I was hoping you'd feel like going to a movie after supper."

"No need to go out to eat," Roxanne tried to keep her voice cheerful. She opened the large purse that she carried to work each day and withdrew a wax-paper bag. "Look here, a roast beef sandwich and two halves of cheese sandwiches."

"I don't feel like eating garbage," Laureen pouted.

"Ma, it's not garbage. It's good food. And you'd pay more for it at Rudy's than in the restaurant we can afford."

The next morning she almost overslept because she was so tired, but she got to work at exactly eight. Rudy looked relieved as she walked in the door, and he said, "I knew you were a reliable girl." Then he frowned and added, "But another half a minute and I would have been worried."

Rudy didn't leave until nine o'clock, and they dished out a lot of coffee and doughnuts, but as far as Roxanne could discover, there was nothing special about any of her customers. She couldn't resist asking as he started out the door for his dentist appointment, "About what time do the movie stars come in?"

"Depends," Rudy answered. "Anytime, I guess. Gary Marlowe came about this time yesterday. Had a chocolate doughnut with coconut and a Coke. Strange eating habits."

Her knees went weak at the mention of Gary Marlowe's name. It was the strangest experience. How could she be so silly? And why should that brief encounter with him have affected her so strongly?

Roxanne wiped off the counter top and dreamed of the few words she'd exchanged with the handsome young man. If only she had a quicker wit, she might have found something to say to him that would have made him notice her, that is, really notice her, not just tell her she was pretty. Telling herself that she was acting silly, she smiled at the customer who had just come through the door.

It was the young man in the camel-hair coat who'd been arguing with his father. Roxanne would have liked to have asked him if he'd dropped out of college yet, but she simply asked him if he'd like anything else with his coffee.

He looked startled and then asked, "Would you repeat that?"

"Would you like anything else? Cream?
Pie? Water?"

"Your voice is perfect," he said.

"Thank you." He didn't seem like the sort
of young man to be a problem, but she wished
Rudy would come back. In the time she'd
worked here she'd learned that there were
too many men who were too friendly to a
pretty girl.

"It's got just the right quality. Slightly
hoarse, slightly amused. Very sexy. Turn
your head. I want to see your profile."

She turned her head, not knowing what
else to do. Sneaking another look at him from
out of the sides of her eyes, she decided he
looked quite sane, even though he did seem
very young. He had a nice face with a mouth
that turned up at the corners in a small, permanent smile, and his eyes were honest. She
relaxed. Whatever this young man had in
mind, she decided she could handle it.

"Have you ever thought of trying out for
the movies?" he asked.

"Yes."

Her answer seemed to take him back for
a moment, and then he laughed and asked,
"Well, why not? You're a pretty girl and
you're in Hollywood. Ever had a screen test?"

"I've never been able to get inside a
studio," Roxanne admitted. "But my photograph is at all the casting agencies."

"What's your name?"

"Roxanne Wilson."

He nodded. "Good name. I think I can

arrange a test for you tomorrow, Roxanne."

"Then you did take that job?"

"What?"

"The one your father didn't want you to take. You didn't go back to school?" She was asking these questions to try to keep calm and delay her reaction to his offer to get her a screen test. Could he really do that? Was he kidding?

"I'm still in school," he admitted. "This is semester break. But I can get you a screen test."

"Gee, that was nice of the studio to let you work part-time," Roxanne said. "I didn't know they ever did that. I mean, I thought script boys would have to be there all the time."

"What makes you think I am a script boy?"

"Well, I thought . . ." She hated to admit the extent of her eavesdropping. "I thought that was probably what you'd do, being so young and all."

"I'll bet I'm quite a bit older than you," he said. "By the way, my name's John Randolph."

"Pleased to meet you," Roxanne said. "Are you sure you can get me a screen test?"

"Tomorrow at seven," he promised. "Shall I send a car for you?"

If her knees had been weak before, they were like jelly now. She was in shock as she whispered, "Yes, please."

"Write your address on this napkin. I'll send someone for you at seven. And no sense putting on a lot of makeup. They'll just scrub it off." He looked at his watch, frowned, and said, "I have to go now or I'll be late for class."

"Your class?" Roxanne asked. "I thought —"

"School is out of session, but I'm taking a flying class this afternoon. Ever been up in a plane?"

"No."

"Maybe I'll take you when I get my license."

He was at the door before she thought to ask him, "What shall I wear?"

"Anything. They'll dress you, too."

"What studio?"

"There's only one studio." He seemed puzzled by her question.

"I mean, what's the name of the studio you work for?"

A slow, wonderful grin spread across his face as he answered, "I thought you knew. Randolph Studios."

"You let me think you were just some college boy," Roxanne accused. "I was actually feeling sorry for you."

"I'll take all the sympathy I can get," John said. He was still smiling as he explained, "I've had free run of the studio since I was six years old, but my father wants me to have what he calls 'a real profession.' So I'm in college but I'm planning to wear him down eventually. You're part of that plan."

"If you're in college, how can you get me a screen test?"

"Simple. My dad's out of town so I'll just set it up. You'll be acting in a scene from a play I've written. I'm hoping when he sees how well I can write and direct, he'll let me drop out of school and get to work."

When Roxanne's face showed her doubt, he said, "The main thing is to sort of slip my audition in and let him think it's really yours. I can see it now. He'll say, 'Who write that brilliant dialogue?' and I'll tell him I did."

Roxanne smiled and shook her head. "You've seen too many Hollywood movies. I just hope you don't get us both kicked into the street."

"Don't worry," John said. "I'll send a car for you in the morning."

"Will it be a real screen test?" Roxanne asked.

"One hundred percent authentic," John Randolph said, and then added, "Trust me?"

Roxanne nodded her head slowly. What did she have to lose?

Chapter Nine

Laureen and Roxanne went to bed at midnight and were up at five, but Roxanne was too excited to feel tired. In fact, she was too excited even to be worried. It was Laureen who spouted doubts and fears as she finished putting the hem in the green velvet dress that they'd shortened. "What if he's just a wolf? You know, there are men who do that. Go around and offer to help pretty girls get in the movies."

"I saw his father, Mr. Randolph."

"But do you know it really was Cyril Randolph? What if it was an imposter?"

"Ma, you're going with me."

"You bet I am. I'll be with you the whole time."

By six-thirty, Laureen was stationed at the window of the kitchen where she could see cars turn the corner. Every few minutes

84

she announced, "It's coming," then she would describe a fancy car that was moving down the street.

Roxanne, who was almost as excited as her mother, felt a rush of adrenaline at each announcement. When it got to be seven o'clock and the limousine had not arrived, Laureen announced, "It was probably all a gag."

Roxanne said, "I'm sure he was sincere, Ma. He is sort of an innocent person. I was surprised when he said he was older than I am. Maybe he wasn't able to persuade his father."

In a way, worrying about whether or not the car would actually arrive seemed easier than worrying about what she would do or say if it did. She smoothed the front of the green velvet dress, then pulled her hands away abruptly, fearful that any moisture on her palms would further crush the worn fabric.

"It's here!" Laureen jumped to her feet and grabbed Roxanne by the hand. "It's white and beautiful and a mile long!" Then she turned triumphantly to Mrs. Clintlock and said, "Didn't I tell you my daughter would be a star?"

"This is just a test," Mrs. Clintlock warned. "They test lots of pretty girls."

"My daughter has talent," Laureen said with a vengeance, and pulled Roxanne toward the door.

Looking over her shoulder, Roxanne appealed to Mr. Clintlock, "You won't forget?"

"Nope," Gus Clintlock assured her. "I'll be there at exactly eight with a real sad story about how you're pretty sick but think you can be back tomorrow."

"She'll probably be signing a contract this afternoon," Laureen said.

"I hope so," Gus agreed amiably.

"Hang on to my job for me if you can," Roxanne pleaded.

The driver didn't seem surprised when they answered his knock so promptly, but when Laureen asked, "Why did you keep my daughter waiting?" he did seem taken aback.

"I'm sorry, ma'am, there was a lot of traffic at Hollywood and Vine."

"Traffic's no excuse," Laureen said. She held her head high and didn't seem the least bit impressed by the long white car that waited at the curb.

Roxanne was impressed, though, and she told herself to remember every detail of this day. If she ended up back in Oklahoma waiting on tables and married to Henry Scott, she could entertain her children with stories about the day she had a Hollywood screen test. She tried to memorize the long sleek lines of the car and to impress the smell of the new leather upholstery permanently on her brain.

Soon they were past the familiar sections of Hollywood and whizzing westward along Wilshire Boulevard. Even the air seemed to smell different as they neared the ocean.

They slowed down and turned into a long,

impressive driveway that was lined with tall palm trees on either side. The driveway led to a six-foot-tall white stucco fence with an arched opening. In the middle of the arch stood a small kiosk with a man in uniform. He waved the limousine on, and they were inside the grounds of Randolph Studios.

Once inside, Roxanne was struck by how ordinary the main building was. It was a large Spanish two-story home, similar to the one the Clintlocks owned. On either side of it were wooden wings that seemed as though they were more like railroad cars that were tacked on and painted white than anything. The stucco building with its two wooden wings stretched across the long width of the lot and as far as she could see. There was no way to drive around the building. The space between the building and the high walls looked more like an alley than a street.

The limousine stopped in front of one of the wooden buildings, and the driver got out, opening the door for Roxanne.

The chauffeur pointed to a door and said, "Just report in there. When you've finished, they'll call me and I'll drive you home."

"Thank you." Then Roxanne held out her hand to the driver and said, "I'm Roxanne Wilson. What's your name?"

"Mike," he replied. This time he was smiling as he said, "They'll have everything ready for you. No need to worry."

"Thanks, Mike," she said, and took a deep

breath, turning and walking toward the closed door. She knew that whatever happened in the next few hours could possibly change her life.

There was another pretty girl behind a desk when she walked in, and it occurred to Roxanne once again that in this town, being pretty was nothing remarkable. She introduced herself, and the girl said, "Yes. You're to report to makeup first thing. That's out back in the long wooden building marked *A*. Just turn to your right and you'll find it."

Then she turned to Laureen and asked, "Are you her mother?"

"Yes."

"You can wait right here."

"I'll go with her."

"We don't allow any unauthorized personnel on the lot," the receptionist explained.

"I'm her mother, and I'll go with her." Then, with a voice that foretold that she would win the argument, she said, "My daughter is a minor, and I'm sure that Randolph Studios wants all its stars who are underage well-chaperoned."

The girl nodded, knowing that there was nothing she could answer to that. Ever since the 1920 scandals about the private lives of movie stars, all the studios were very careful to protect young girls. Roxanne didn't know everything that had happened during that era, but she did know one girl had been killed at a wild party, and the public outcry against that sort of scandal had almost wrecked the movie business. These days, any scandal could ruin a star's career.

The receptionist was buffing her nails with a soft chamois-and-tortoise buffer. Roxanne made a note of how shiny the girl's nails looked and decided to try it. She'd never really gotten the hang of keeping fingernail polish on, and the bright red nails that she now wore made her uncomfortable.

"Come along," Laureen said, taking charge of the situation, since the receptionist was clearly through talking with them. She led the way to the makeup room and announced Roxanne's arrival. "Here is my daughter, Roxanne Wilson."

Two men who were reading the newspaper looked up and nodded their heads, then the taller one said, "All right, Roxanne, sit right down."

Roxanne sat in a chair that looked exactly like a barber's chair. The taller man, who seemed to do all the talking, waved Laureen over to the other chair and said, "You might as well sit there, sweetie. This will take an hour or so, and you'll be tired standing."

Laureen sat down, but then she realized that the chair was positioned so that she couldn't see what they were doing. She promptly stood up and said, "I'd rather watch."

"No talking," the taller man warned. "We don't like talking while we work."

"I just want to watch," Laureen promised. She stepped in as close as she could but moved back a couple of paces when the short man frowned and made a motion with his elbow to indicate that he was feeling crowded.

The tall man wrapped an oilcloth bib around Roxanne's neck and then skimmed her hair back from her face, tying it with a net scarf that kept her hair safe from the thick cold cream that the two men were slathering on her face. Roxanne shivered because the cold cream was slick and freezing cold. The tall man said, "Just relax, sweetie. Best thing you can do is put your mind totally to sleep. For the next hour or so you're a dummy. Just like Charlie McCarthy. You're made of pure hardwood, and you don't say a word unless I pull your strings. Think you can do that?"

"I'll try."

"Where you from?"

"Oklahoma." Immediately Roxanne began worrying about her accent. Would she fail the screen test because she sounded too much like an Okie?

"Think about home," the tall man advised. "You know, the cornstalks, the wheat fields, whatever they have in Kansas."

"Oklahoma," Laureen corrected.

"No talking, Mama," the taller man warned. "You wouldn't want your beautiful daughter to come out of here with one eyebrow higher than the other, would you?"

When they had all the cold cream wiped off and began painting her face with little tubes of makeup, Roxanne was very curious, but there was no mirror in front of her chair, and most of the time she had her head tilted back at a funny angle. Once or twice the two men asked each other questions about what they were doing, but during most of the hour there was only silence.

Only once did Laureen offer any advice and that was when they had Roxanne sit up and looked critically at her face, finally agreeing that they were finished with her makeup. Then the taller one asked his partner, "Part her hair on the side?"

"She has a perfectly oval face," Laureen interrupted. "She should part her hair in the middle."

Both men glowered, and the taller one said, "You'll have to leave now."

"My girl is a minor."

"We are makeup men, not white slave traders," the taller one answered. "You can wait outside."

"I will not wait outside," Laureen said. But then she added, "But I won't say another word."

"And sit in that chair, madam. Your feet are hurting you."

"How can you tell?" Roxanne asked.

"Because of the expression on her face," the taller man said. "Feet always show in the face. Now, not another word from you." He turned to his partner and asked, "Part it on the side?"

"Wig," his partner answered. "It's a costume shot."

"Why didn't you tell me?" the taller one asked. "What period?"

The short one shrugged and said, "Just says European costumes."

The tall one shook his head in disgust. "I would have done her differently if I'd known. Never mind, we'll give her a beauty mark and the white wig. Marie Antoinette, here we come."

"Not that one." He made a face, wrinkling his nose in disgust.

"All the wigs are out for the new Marlowe picture. Remember?"

"We've got that old red wig that they used in that short they did last month."

The tall one stood back and looked quizzically at Roxanne. "No. Making her a redhead won't work. She's too pink-skinned for that. Besides, we'd have to pluck out all her eyebrows and paint them in lighter. Haven't got time."

"Marie Antoinette it is," he said, and disappeared around the corner, coming back with a wooden, egg-shaped form that had a tall white wig on it. Even to Roxanne's inexperienced eye she could see that the wig was very old and in need of a total reworking.

Neither man seemed very happy with the results of the wig, but they looked at each other, clearly signaling with their eyes not to continue worrying about it. All Roxanne's thoughts were on how to hold her head up high with the heavy, stiff wig on her head. Besides, almost the minute they put the wig on, she began to feel very warm. By the time they had dismissed her, waving her on to the next building where they said she would find costuming, she was decidedly uneasy about whether or not she would begin sweating.

Once outside, Laureen said, "They weren't very polite men. When you get to be a star, you certainly won't ask for them as your private makeup men. I wonder if they were brothers?"

"They didn't look a thing alike."

"The Westmores are brothers," Laureen said. "They're just about the most famous makeup men in Hollywood. Of course, they're not at Randolph Studios, so they couldn't be the Westmores, but they could be brothers.

"Ma, I'm scared."

"Nonsense," her mother said. "You're going to be a star, so don't let this little screen test scare you. What will you do when you have to do something really hard?"

"This is really hard," she answered. "And this wig is hot and heavy."

"Just smile a lot on camera. You have a wonderful smile."

Laureen pushed open the door of the costume building and announced, "This is my daughter, Roxanne Wilson."

"You here for a test?" one fat woman with a pencil sticking behind her ear asked. She also wore a tape measure around her neck and had about a hundred straight pins sticking in the front of her dress.

"It's a European period picture," Laureen

announced. "My daughter looks very well in blue."

"It won't be Technicolor," the human pincushion assured them. "And my order says it's to be the 1900's. That wig's all wrong You'll have to go back and get another one."

"They don't have any others," Roxanne said.

"Nonsense," the woman said. Then she looked at the clock on the wall and sighed. "No sense holding everyone up just for a test." We'll put you in an eighteenth-century dress to go with the wig."

Within a minute she was back with a bright red satin dress with a huge hoop skirt and a low neckline. She frowned at Roxanne and said, "Get out of that green thing."

Laureen helped Roxanne unbutton the dark green velvet dress and slip out of it. Then the woman said, "Petticoats first. The trick is to step into them. Then you sort of jump into the dress and we pull the whole thing up. No corsets. We don't have time, and it makes it hard to breathe, anyway. Besides, you might be too nervous for corsets."

"My daughter doesn't get nervous," Laureen announced.

Roxanne wished that her mother's interminable bragging would stop. She also wished that it were true that she didn't get nervous. Though she was trying very hard, her breathing was fast, and she could feel sweat forming under the wig.

Within seconds the woman had her laced into the bright red dress and said, "You're a pretty one. Might make it. But they laid that beauty mark on pretty thick."

"May I look in the mirror?" Roxanne asked.

"Sure," the woman said, "Take a look at Cinderella."

Roxanne stepped to a long, gold-framed mirror and gasped as she saw her reflection. The girl who stood before her looked like a total stranger. Not only were her eyebrows a high, smooth circle, but her mouth was painted into a deep red Cupid's bow. What's more, her cheeks had so much rouge on them that she thought she looked like a clown. And the beauty mark was a big, black star placed high on her cheek. She had to bite her lips to keep from bursting into tears, she was so disappointed.

"Don't you look beautiful?" Laureen asked.

"No," Roxanne answered. "I look awful."

The human pincushion patted her arm and said, "You look beautiful. You're just not used to it. Now go on and give them a big smile. Wait. Smile for me."

Roxanne smiled.

"Good. Those guys sent one poor girl through here yesterday for a test, and when she smiled into the camera, she had lipstick on her teeth."

"Where do I go now?"

"Lot M. Just out this door and down the street a bit. There's a long shed, looks like a warehouse. There's a big sign that says NO ADMITTANCE on the front, but you go right on in. They're ready for you."

"And we're ready for them," Laureen said confidently.

Roxanne was silent.

Chapter Ten

JOHN Randolph looked really happy when he saw Roxanne. He had her turn her head in several poses and repeated, "Good, good," again and again. Apparently the makeup and costume departments had accomplished exactly what he wanted.

Roxanne was surprised at how glad she was to see John. He was the only familiar person on the set, of course, but that was only part of it. He was also the only one who was anywhere close to her age. She decided that she liked his eager friendliness, and his obvious nervousness gave her courage. She managed a big smile and asked, "Will I do?"

"Nervous?"

Roxanne nodded her admission. At the same time Laureen answered for her, "Of course not."

"This is my mother, Laureen Wilson," Roxanne said.

"How do you do, Mrs. Wilson. I think you'll be very comfortable over there." John pointed to a bench against the wall of the studio.

Laureen shook her head and crossed her arms over her chest, saying, "I'll stay close so my little girl can rely on me. She's used to that."

Roxanne flushed. She wished her mother wouldn't talk as though she were twelve years old, but she knew it wouldn't do any good to try to talk to her about it. Laureen couldn't help the way she acted.

Except for being embarrassed sometimes, it did make Roxanne feel a little braver to have her close. With John and her mother both on the set, she felt that she might make it all the way through the test without stumbling, fainting, or running away. Despite the fact that she was grateful for her mother's support, she hated the possibility that John would think she was a baby.

Whatever John thought, he handled the situation very easily. He took Laureen by the arm and said, "I have an idea. Why don't you sit right here in the director's chair? That way you can see everything but you'll be outside of the lights."

Laureen allowed herself to be led to the canvas chair without protest. Then John said, "This will probably not take very long, Mrs. Wilson, but if you want, I can have someone bring you a newspaper to read."

"No, thanks, I'd rather watch."

"Some tea?"

"No, thanks." Laureen patted his arm and said, "You're a very nice young man. Your father must be proud of you."

"I hope he will be someday," John Randolph answered, and then he smiled, saying, "Especially if your daughter does justice to my little scene."

"She will." Laureen was obviously really enjoying herself now that someone was paying some attention to her. "And I'm sure your scene will be fine."

This time John's smile was tinged with sadness. "I wish I had your confidence."

He left Laureen then and came back to the center of the stage where Roxanne stood, waiting for direction. As she waited she looked around the large, empty studio and wondered what famous movies had been shot here. Which of Hollywood's leading ladies and men had walked on this stage? Had Gary Marlowe stood here?

Funny that even as nervous as she was, she was thinking about Gary. The two men who did her makeup had mentioned a Marlowe movie that was being made. Was it being shot on this lot? Was it possible that she might run into Gary today? The idea was so frightening that it almost made her forget her nervousness about the test that was coming up.

"Actually," John was explaining to her, "all you have to do in this scene is look frightened, then shocked, then hurt. Do you think you can manage to cry and look pretty at the same time?"

"I'll try." She was touched by how young and eager John looked. She promised herself to do the very best job she could, not only for herself but to help John. The idea that she was helping someone else also helped her.

"Good. Now this is the way it goes. We've got Harry Burns to read the male part for you. He'll carry you pretty well because he's got that booming voice. But let me warn you that he'll try to steal the scene from you, even though it's only a screen test. He can't help it, that's the way some actors are."

"You mean he won't help me?"

"No, I'm afraid not. I tried to get a younger actor — Gary Marlowe — but he was busy today. So I had to settle for Burns because he's a swashbuckler."

"Swashbuckler?"

"It's a Hollywood expression. Means an actor or picture that is very dramatic. You know the kind. Lots of acrobatics, swordplay, and spouting big lines. Well, Burns loves to spout the lines, but he's getting a bit old to wield a sword or jump on a horse. So he may try to upstage you. Know what that means?"

Roxanne nodded. "He'll try to get between me and the camera."

John nodded and put his arm around her, hugging her briefly. "Smart girl. I'll make sure you're in the camera lens, but watch out that he doesn't rattle you. You're working with an inexperienced director."

Roxanne said, "That makes us a perfectly matched team," Roxanne quipped, but she couldn't manage a smile. She was too nervous.

"Here he comes. Harry's been around for a long time, and he's pretty good at this sort of thing. Besides, you'll look good beside him, and I may try to ad-lib a love scene. Think you can make the camera steam?"

The idea of kissing anyone in public made her extremely nervous. She'd never kissed any man except Henry, and he was her boyfriend and only a year older than she was. Harry Burns had to be over thirty-five, and the idea of kissing him repelled her. But she knew that if she were really to be offered a movie career, she would have to play love scenes.

She thought she could get used to that, if her leading man was closer to her own age. Gary Marlowe couldn't be more than a couple of years older. Roxanne couldn't help but wonder what it would be like to play a love scene with him. She was sure it would be easier than with Harry Burns. She thought she might have looked better beside Gary also, but she was sensible enough to know that his presence would make her even more nervous.

John raised his hand and waved. "Harry, over here."

A tall, broad-shouldered man in a fawn-colored jacket and dark-blue trousers strode across the stage, holding out his hand to John long before he got there. "Johnny boy, I remember the last time I saw you. It was your tenth birthday and you got a pony."

"You saw me last week, Harry. At the Olson premiere. Got your lines memorized?"

"Yes. Dreadful play. Who wrote it?"

Roxanne laughed, then she clapped her hand over her mouth, because she knew it was rude to laugh at someone else's embarrassment. Almost as fast as she covered her laughter she jerked her hand away, fearing that she would smear the bright red Cupid's bow mouth. By then she was feeling as though she'd never be able to do anything right.

But John didn't seem embarrassed by the older actor's criticism or upset at Roxanne's laughter. He was all business as he turned to look at her, saying, "I love that laugh. Do you think you could do it for the scene?"

The request froze her laughter, and she shook her head. "I just don't think I can laugh any old time. At least not like that."

"Of course you can," Laureen's voice rang over the empty stage. "You're a professional."

"Never mind," John said. "They'll really only be looking at your face, anyway. And if you look good on camera, that's all it takes."

"Women have no idea how lucky they are," Harry Burns complained. "Do you like this new hat?" He put a tall, elegant top hat on and tilted his head, waiting for John's reaction.

Roxanne decided that no girl could have been more vain than Harry Burns was. She had never really liked him in the movies he was in, and now she decided that she didn't like him in person, either. He hadn't even acknowledged her presence, but he was clearly trying to make an impression on John. Roxanne was sure it was because John was Cyril Randolph's son.

Just as she decided that, Harry Burns asked, "Will the old man be around for this test?"

"Dad? No."

"I just thought, you being the only boy, and his royal heir, so to speak — "

"Let's get going," John said abruptly. "Roxanne, you stand over there."

The test was actually done against a clear, light gray background with no sets at all. As John had said, Harry Burns had nearly all the lines, but he seemed to have a lot of trouble remembering them. He stumbled over the beginning three times, saying, "Fairfeather friends," instead of "Fair-weather friends." The third time he made the mistake, he turned to John and said, "Can't you do something about these lines? They're dreadful."

"They're supposed to be dreadful," John said. "It's a parody."

"Oh." Harry Burns looked as though he

might not know what a parody was.

"The idea," John went on quickly to save the older man any embarrassment, "is to put in every cliché that's ever appeared in one of these costume pictures. You're supposed to represent every swashbuckler whose ever wielded a sword, and Roxanne is the epitome of the fair damsel. Okay?"

After the sixth take Harry Burns got far enough along in his lines for Roxanne to get her few words in. She asked, "Kind sir, is it true that my uncle has sent for me?"

"Yes, fair damsel, but alas, I must send thee hither and yon for anon."

This time Harry Burns stopped himself and sputtered, "But what does it mean?"

"It doesn't mean anything," Roxanne explained. "It's sort of like *Alice in Wonderland*. Clever nonsense, nothing more."

"Good girl," John said, but Harry Burns did not look pleased to have a newcomer explaining things to him.

Eventually they got through the whole scene without any mistakes, and Roxanne was relieved because she had feared that the older actor would never be able to make his way through John's lines. Unfortunately she agreed with Harry Burns that the script wasn't very good. It wasn't funny, and she feared that Burns was not the only one who would miss the point. Though he seemed to be a poor writer, she suspected John had done a very fine job of directing them both.

After the last take John said, "Thanks, Harry. I think we've got all we need from you."

Harry walked off the stage without ever saying a word to her, and Roxanne was glad she hadn't had to kiss him. John said in a low voice that only Roxanne could hear, "He was never very smart, but he used to be able to remember lines. Poor guy, the bottle's got him, I guess."

"That's too bad." Roxanne wished she could feel more charitable toward Burns, but about all she was feeling at the moment was relief that the work was over.

"Yes. A lot of actors let that ruin their careers. I've seen a lot of sad stories growing up in Hollywood."

"It must have been fun, though." Roxanne realized that they were chatting like old friends while the lights were still on, and she asked, "Am I finished?"

"I want to get some close-ups," he said. "I want you to have a fair test. That means close-ups. Let's move over here and do some light work."

He directed the cameraman and crew as they adjusted the lights and equipment. Then he got behind the camera himself and directed Roxanne's actions. First he had her walk across the stage, whip around, and look surprised. Then he brought the camera much closer, adjusting the lights so that they were below and above her face. "That's to give you interesting shadows," he explained. "You're young, and your face might look flat in ordinary light. Now smile."

She tilted her head, smiled wide, then softly. John moved the camera in closer and then slowly rolled it out. She was surprised how comfortable he seemed to be with the machine. He raised and lowered it easily, rolled it smoothly, and even turned it from side to side. The major obstacle seemed to be the way the lights were set up, rather than moving the camera. Roxanne wondered why they didn't put them on casters as well.

John gave quick, clear orders to her as well as the lighting technicians. Under his directions she licked her lips, raised her chin, raised one eyebrow, then the other. Then he began calling out one-word suggestions and filmed the expressions she chose as responses. She had to change her looks as the words tumbled out: "Sad, happy, joyous, sweet, scared, terrified, angry, pouting, amused, annoyed, haughty, troubled, pensive, yearning, loving."

The words seemed to spill from John's lips, and Roxanne moved her eyes, mouth, and face as rapidly as possible. Finally she burst out laughing and said, "I've stretched my face in a thousand different directions. And you must know every freckle and line."

"No freckles, no lines. But that dimple's great," John said. He stopped the camera. "I think I got a recording of your laughter, too.

You look great, Roxanne. I'll bet you make it."

His prediction just made her nervous again. A rush of fear ran through her, and the feeling she'd come to call "jelly knees" came back. If John should be right and she should get a contract offer, then all their money troubles would be over. She thought for a moment about how happy and proud her mother would be, but the idea seemed almost too much for her. "When will I know?" she asked.

"Soon. I'll come to your house."

"You don't have to do that. We have a telephone."

"I want to."

"Honestly, you don't have to do that. Especially if it's bad news. It will just be embarrassing."

"It won't be bad news," Laureen said. Her voice was so loud that both of them jumped, they were so startled.

"I hope not," John said directly to Laureen, "but the camera is a funny thing. It loves some faces and hates others. I've seen girls, real knockouts, who look like nothing on the screen. And others who aren't pretty at all in person who just look perfect. I can't predict how the test will work out, Mrs. Wilson."

"Maybe you can't," Laureen said, "but I can. Roxanne's always been very photogenic. She's talented, too. Honey, do a little song and dance for Mr. Randolph."

"Ma!"

"And I hope you got her profile on the left, not the right," Laureen added. "That's the good side."

"I got them both," John assured her. Then he turned to Roxanne and whispered, "Let's have you sing and dance. It will please your mother."

"But there's no music."

"Just do your Bobby Shaftoe song," Laureen ordered. "You can sing that a cappella."

Roxanne nodded her head, took a deep breath, and began to sing, "Bobby Shaftoe went to sea —"

John Randolph laughed and said, "Wait for me, I give the orders around here."

He gave the camera back to the cameraman and motioned for him to film the song and dance. Roxanne went through the motions of the simple tap dance, lifting her red satin hoop skirt to show that her feet moved.

Then John ordered the lights turned off and promised, "I'll drop by with any news. You can go home now. You're probably tired."

Roxanne was amazed at exactly how tired she was when she walked back to return the red satin dress and the white wig. "I don't just feel like Cinderella's coach after it turned into a pumpkin," Roxanne said, "but I feel like the pumpkin got run over and squashed. Squashed pumpkin, that's exactly the right description of how movie stars must feel at the end of the day."

But as usual Laureen was in no mood for Roxanne's whimsy. "You have talent," her mother answered. "That nice young man recognized it right away. And it was sweet of him to say he'd come over to the house with the good news."

"But what if the news isn't good?" Roxanne asked. "That's why I told him he could call on the telephone. It will be really embarrassing for everyone if my face turns out to look like a dishpan or something."

"Nonsense," Laureen said. "You should have more confidence in yourself."

"I don't need it," Roxanne teased. "You have enough confidence for both of us."

Later, as they were riding back to the boardinghouse in the limousine, her mother said, "He's coming because he wants to see you again," Laureen said. "He's in love with you."

Roxanne laughed.

"I mean it," Laureen said. "Anyone could tell he's in love with you just by the way his eyes followed you and the way he took so many shots of your face."

"You know what your trouble is?" Roxanne teased. "You're too romantic. I think you see too many movies."

"We'll buy you a new dress tomorrow. Something suitable for going out with a young movie tycoon."

"And he's not a movie tycoon," Roxanne corrected. "He's just a college boy. His father wants him to be a lawyer."

"Anyone can be a lawyer," Laureen pronounced. "I think a pink dress if we can find it. And some new shoes. I like those with the bows on them that I saw the receptionist wearing."

"Like Minnie Mouse," Roxanne said.

"Cinderella and Minnie Mouse," Laureen said. "When are you going to learn that making movies is serious business and talk sensibly? You're not a child, Roxanne."

"Next time anyone asks me how old I am, I think I'll say I'm adjustable. When you wanted to stay by my side during the test, you made me sound very young. Now I'm supposed to be an old lady."

"Maybe blue would be better than pink. I think the blue is more suitable, don't you?"

"Maybe I could go to work this afternoon," Roxanne answered.

"Work? But John said it would be two or three days till you heard."

"I mean at Rudy's. Maybe I could go in for a few hours and say I feel better. People do recover from illnesses very quickly, don't they?"

"You'll never have to go there again," Laureen said.

"We don't know what will happen," Roxanne said. "I'll hang on to my job until we know."

"Honestly, Roxanne. You *do* sound like an old lady, you worry so much. When are you going to let loose and enjoy life? This afternoon we'll go shopping and tonight we'll go to one of the really big movie palaces to celebrate. The Mayan, I think. I'd love to see the Mayan Palace. They say the building is a real copy of an Mayan building. And the paintings are done with pure gold."

"Ma, do you really think it will happen?" Roxanne was just beginning to understand that she'd actually gotten as far as a screen test. Would the results be favorable?

Chapter Eleven

ROXANNE spent the next five days alternating between dreaming that she would soon be a movie star and worrying about holding on to her job at Rudy's. Her boss wasn't a bit happy about the day's work she missed, and he nagged her all week.

As the week progressed and she didn't hear from John, it seemed clearer and clearer that she wouldn't be a movie star. She began to imagine what it would be like to return to Oklahoma, something she was almost sure she would have to do if she lost her job. A letter from Henry arrived three days after the screen test, and he told her once again how much he wanted her to come home. Roxanne read the letter and then closed her eyes and tried to picture her old home. But the images wouldn't come; they had sold the house she was born in, and the rented house had never been a real home.

Home meant Henry, Roxanne told herself. She folded her arms close to her body, hugging herself and trying to imagine what it would feel like to be in Henry's arms once again. Yes, she could imagine the warmth and comfort of Henry's touch, but when she tried to see his face, it was very dim. There were two other faces that kept appearing, those of John Randolph and Gary Marlowe. Roxanne sighed and admitted to herself that Henry had become very hazy in her memory if these other two young men's images were stronger.

When John didn't come by the end of the week, Roxanne's nerves were stretched tight and she was too discourgaed to keep smiling, especially under Rudy's constant razzing. It was a dull, dreadful day, and when it began to rain, she felt like the storms were especially intended to accompany her mood. To make things worse Rudy finished his work in the kitchen and sat down at the counter, calling, "Bring me a cup of coffee, Roxanne. Get the lead out of your feet. Hop to it."

Roxanne brought the coffee, and he asked, "This the way you treat the customers? Where's that big smile? Gloomy face like that drives everyone away. That why business is bad today?"

"It's raining."

"Inside and out," Rudy complained. "How about cleaning out the icebox for me?"

Usually Rudy did all the cleaning in the kitchen and she kept the tables and counters neat, but she didn't dare argue with his new request. She said, "Sure," and went into the kitchen. The icebox was a big wooden one with top and bottom compartments. The bottom held a big block of ice, and the top held a much smaller one.

Roxanne began by wiping out the bottom compartment, rolling up the sleeves of her uniform to get way back in the corners. She was surprised at how dirty the inside of the icebox was and how cold her hands and arms got during the work.

Rudy called out from the restaurant, "Hey, Roxanne, come on out here."

Roxanne stood up and started toward the door, but she drew back in dismay as she saw Gary Marlowe sitting at the counter. On either side of Gary was a beautiful girl. They had obviously been caught in the storm because they were all wet, but they seemed to be having a great time. Roxanne wanted to run back in the kitchen before Gary saw her, but Rudy called out again, "Bring cream for Mr. Marlowe."

She walked out, picked up the cream pitcher, then carried it back to the kitchen where she filled it with cream. Bringing the cream back to the counter, she managed not to look Gary directly in the eye and hoped with all her heart that she had escaped his notice. But Rudy wasn't content to leave it at that. "Know who this is?" he asked.

"Yes."

"Say hello to Mr. Marlowe. Didn't I tell you he came in here?"

"Yes."

"Mr. Marlowe, you want anything else? Pie? Anything?" Rudy asked eagerly.

But Gary stood up without even drinking his coffee. He smiled briefly at Roxanne but obviously didn't recognize her, and said to his companions, "Come on, let's get back to work."

Gary Marlowe and his friends were gone almost as fast as they'd appeared. Rudy pocketed the dollar bill he'd left and frowned at Roxanne. "Will you look in the mirror? You got dirt on your face."

Roxanne turned and fought against the tears that came to her eyes at the thought that Gary had seen her looking like that. Not that it mattered, she told herself. He hadn't recognized her, anyway. She began to prepare to leave for the night.

Rudy repeated his threat as she walked toward the door. "Be sure and get here tomorrow on time if you want to keep your job. Plenty of girls waiting in line for a good job like this one."

"Go ahead," Roxanne snapped. "Get another girl if you can. See if you can find anyone who works harder or better. I've done a good job since I got here and you know it."

Rudy seemed surprised at her fast comeback. He shook his head and held up his hand as though to ward off any further blows from her. "No sense getting all excited. I was just saying —"

"You were just saying what you've been saying all week," Roxanne said. "I'm tired of hearing it. Get someone else if you want."

"I don't want," Rudy admitted. "I just want you to know that you've got a good job here."

"Any job is a good job," Roxanne answered. "I know that. But you talk as if I've been a bad worker."

"You're a good worker," he said. "But you know what? I thought you were . . . kind of shy. You've got a lot of spirit when you're riled. Lots of spunk for a kid from Oklahoma."

"That's another thing." Roxanne was honest enough to know that her anger was really frustration about not hearing from John, and the humiliation of running into Gary again and not having him recognize her. "You tease me all the time about being from Oklahoma. There's nothing funny about that."

"Maybe not." Rudy shook his head and said, "Lots of spunk. Wouldn't have thought it. You be here on time tomorrow?"

"I was on time today."

"Sure, but tomorrow?"

Roxanne realized that he thought she was quitting. She wanted to laugh at her easy victory. She'd always heard that bullies backed down when you confronted them; now she'd learned it firsthand. "I'll be here, Rudy. I need the job."

He sent half a pie home with her that night, saying it was too old to serve to customers. Roxanne was almost cheerful as she showed the pie to Laureen and told her all about standing up to Rudy. She skipped the part about Gary Marlowe, though.

"I don't care about that man Rudy," Laureen said. "Or that old job. What I want to know is why that nice young Mr. Randolph hasn't been here. I can't understand it. He was in love with you and everything."

"Maybe it was just puppy love," Roxanne teased. She didn't know why she kept trying to make jokes with her mother, who never saw the point. When Laureen failed to smile in response, Roxanne felt her spirits sinking again. The tears she'd fought against earlier in the day crowded behind her eyes again, and she wished she had a friend to talk with. If only she knew someone who was her own age, life would be so much more pleasant. How she would love to gossip with the girls in high school again. Suddenly she was very homesick, and she asked herself how she'd managed to get so far from home. And what was the point of it all?

But rather than express her doubts and fears, she tried once again to explain. "Ma, don't you know that all John Randolph really cared about was showing his script to his father? He probably showed it and they turned it down, and that was the end of that."

"He promised he'd come," Laureen complained. She seemed more depressed than she'd been since they came to California. The look on her face reminded Roxanne of the way she'd looked when her father died. Even though she was dreadfully depressed herself, she tried to cheer up her mother.

"It's the rain," she said. "Makes everything seem so gloomy. Then she hugged her mother and smoothed the older woman's hair as she said, "Ma, everything will be all right. We've got a little money, and we can always go back to Oklahoma. Henry says there are more jobs now than before. Didn't President Roosevelt promise that things were on the upswing? Remember that last fireside chat on the radio? Well, I hear the customers talking, and they all say the Depression's almost over."

"The Depression may be over in Washington, D.C., but it's not over in Oklahoma. I'm never going back there."

Roxanne sighed. There was no sense trying to talk sense to her mother when she was in this frame of mind. "I tell you what, let's go to the movies. Clark Gable's at the Del Mar."

"I'm not leaving this house until we hear from John Randolph."

"Ma, he said two or three days. It's been a week and he hasn't called. Are you going to stay in this room forever?"

"No. Tomorrow I'm going to call him."

"Ma!"

"It isn't fair to trifle with a young girl's affections that way."

"Ma, if you call that studio tomorrow, I'll

never forgive you —" Roxanne's response was broken by a knock on the door of their room. She wondered if it was Mrs. Clintlock complaining that they were talking too loudly.

But when she opened the door, Mrs. Clintlock was smiling. "A young man downstairs to see you," she said. Then she added, "He's got flowers."

"Did he ask for me?" Roxanne was startled that she had to ask. Then she decided it must be Henry who'd come all the way from Oklahoma to persuade her to marry him. Her heart began to race at the thought of seeing Henry again, and she asked, "Is he tall and blond? Good-looking?"

Mrs. Clintlock shook her head. "Brown hair but nice-looking."

For some reason Gary Marlowe's face flashed through Roxanne's mind, and she shook her head quickly, knowing that was impossible. It had to be John Randolph, and he'd brought the flowers to soften bad news. Sort of like a funeral, Roxanne decided, and she smiled wryly at her thought.

"Change into your new blue dress," Laureen said. "I'll go down first."

"No." Roxanne was determined that she would take the news bravely and simply. She didn't even bother to look in the mirror before going downstairs. John would have to take her as she was, wearing the same old navy blue dress she'd brought from Oklahoma. No sense dressing up to be let down.

John was standing in the middle of the

parlor when she got there, and he was holding a dozen roses in his hands. When she entered the room, he held them out and said, "Congratulations."

It took Roxanne a minute to understand that he was giving her good news. She took a deep breath, trying to keep her voice calm as she asked, "The test turned out well?"

"You looked great," John said. "It took awhile to get my dad to look at it, but when he did. . . . I'm here to offer you a contract with Randolph Studios. One year with a five-year option. One hundred a week."

Roxanne grabbed hold of a chair, thinking she might faint with joy. John reached out toward her, then seemed to reconsider his action and simply handed her the flowers. She took them and walked toward the small table in the center of the parlor, which held an empty vase.

As she fussed with the flowers she tried to understand what had happened to her. One hundred dollars a week was a fortune — ten times what she earned at Rudy's including the tips. In three weeks she could recoup every bit of the money that she and her mother had spent on this Hollywood adventure. She would soon be rich. Maybe not as rich as Barbara Hutton or Mary Pickford but richer than anyone she knew back in Oklahoma. She was sure that even the mayor of Norman didn't earn one hundred dollars a week.

Chapter Twelve

THOUGH it took Roxanne several minutes to adjust to the news, Laureen didn't seem the least bit startled. Her first question was, "Will they give her star billing?"

Roxanne laughed and hugged her mother. "Ma, you don't even sound surprised."

"I always told you that you had talent." Laureen turned back to John and repeated her question.

"No," John said. "This is the usual deal they offer starlets. They'll give her the glamour treatment, try her in a few parts, maybe have the publicity department do a few stories." Then he turned to Roxanne and said, "There's no way of telling whether you'll ever even get a real chance to act at all. Some girls just decorate the lot for a few months and disappear."

"My Roxanne will be a star." Laureen

frowned and asked, "Do you think they'll pay more if we turn this offer down?"

"Ma!"

"Frankly I doubt it," John said. "I have the one offer and no other instructions. I think he assumed that you'd be pleased to have the chance. I did tell my father that you were waiting on tables."

"That doesn't have anything to do with it," Laureen said. "Some Hollywood stars got their start in unusual ways. What about that new sweater girl, Lana Turner? Wasn't she discovered at a soda fountain in a drugstore?"

"I just meant that he knew that the offer he's making represents a large increase in salary." John sounded disappointed as he said to Laureen, "I thought you'd be thrilled."

"We are thrilled," Roxanne said. "I'll take it."

"Wait a minute," Laureen said. "I believe I'm the one who makes the business decisions around here. After all, you are only fifteen years old."

"I wouldn't push that point too hard," John advised. "That was his major objection. He said you were a little young for grown-up roles but too old for kid parts. Shirley Temple's studio is already worried about what to do with her when she gets to be a teenager."

"We could go elsewhere," Laureen threatened.

"Ma, we could also go back to Oklahoma,"

Roxanne said. "But I think the best thing to do is take the offer."

When Laureen offered no more objections, Roxanne remembered her manners and asked, "How did he like your script?"

John made a terrible face and then laughed. "Know what? I hated it when I saw it on the screen. The only nice part was looking at you. And Bertram, that's my dad's right-hand man, said I did a fine job directing the camera shots of you. Of course, when my dad said I had no talent at all, he backed down. I'll be back in school next week."

"I'm sorry."

"Not as sorry as I am," John said.

"When does she get paid?" Laureen interrupted. "We'll need to find a new house, buy a car, get clothes. Can we get an advance on her wages?"

John shook his head. "People are paid weekly, and the studio has a policy of not advancing any money to employees. Of course, after Roxanne's been there six months, she can join the credit union."

"That doesn't seem sensible to me," Laureen complained. "How's a girl to put her best foot forward unless the studio is willing to foot the expenses? There's a Depression on, you know."

"I can understand your concern," John said, "but I'd honestly advise you to take this offer the way it's written. I can advance you some cash, if you like."

"How much?"

"Ma! Stop this. Please."

John took out his billfold and removed four bills. "Two hundred?"

"All right." Laureen took the money as though she saw fifty-dollar bills every day.

John turned to Roxanne and asked, "Would you like to go for a drive?"

"Yes, we would," Laureen answered promptly. "We'd like to look for houses to rent."

"Ma, it's dark. We'll go tomorrow."

"The rain's stopped and there are street-lights," Laureen said, as though she were speaking to a very young child.

Within five minutes they were in John's little yellow car with the rumble seat, and driving up and down the Hollywood streets looking for for-rent signs. It was so dark, they couldn't see very well, but they did find one little bungalow on a side street not too far from Randolph Studios.

"I could walk to work," Roxanne said.

"The studio should send a limousine for you," Laureen grumbled, but she agreed that the house was cute.

"It's pink," John warned them. "I drive by it every day on my way to school. Very bright pink with a tile roof."

"Let's see how much it is," Roxanne urged.

Her mother grumbled about the house being so small, but she didn't protest too loudly as John jumped out of the car to get the telephone number written on the sign. By the time they got to the drugstore and telephoned the owner, Laureen had taken over negotiations. She came back, saying, "I told them we'd take it for three months. The price was right because I promised that her daughter would get a screen test at Randolph Studios."

John and Roxanne exchanged looks of dismay, and John said very gently, "Don't put that in writing, Mrs. Wilson."

"You can arrange it yourself," Laureen answered, "when you come over in the morning to help us move."

As they drove back to the boardinghouse no one had much to say except Laureen, who chattered all the way about what a big star Roxanne was going to be. As they pulled up to the door she said, "I'll be glad to be out of this dump."

"It seems very nice to me," John said.

"It is," Roxanne assured him. Laureen got out of the car then and said to Roxanne, "Don't be too long." Then she seemed to remember her manners and turned to John to say, "I want you to know I appreciate your help, Mr. Randolph."

"I know you do."

"I suppose some people think I'm too ambitious for Roxanne," Laureen offered. "It's just that I want the best for her. And I'm sure she has a great talent."

"I understand," John assured her.

Roxanne started to get out of the car, but her mother said, "You stay and talk with Mr.

Randolph a few minutes. Young folks should enjoy each other's company."

Roxanne was very embarrassed by the way her mother had behaved that evening, and she searched for the right words to explain her mother to John. She said, "My mother really loves me a lot. That's why she's so determined."

"Yes," John said. "You're lucky."

There was something in John's voice that told her he was thinking about his own parents and feeling sad. Did he think his father didn't love him? "What about your mother?" she asked.

"My mother was killed with my younger brother when I was five," John said. Then he changed the subject. "You said your landlord used to be an actor?"

"Gus Clintlock? He did Westerns."

John shook his head. "I don't remember the name, but I probably saw every one of them. When I was a kid, my biggest dream was to be a cowboy star and ride a white horse like Tom Mix."

"Why didn't you?"

John shook his head. "People think that if your father owns the studio, you can do anything you want. But my dad doesn't really own the whole studio. He has stockholders. Besides, it takes a lot more than connections. I haven't got that kind of looks, and I can't ride a horse very well. Then, when I got a little older, I started visiting the sets and found out that acting is the most boring job in the world. Writing and directing are the best jobs. That's where the excitement is."

"So you're going to be a famous director," Roxanne said.

"Not if my father has anything to say about it," John admitted. "About the only progress I've made is a promise that if I pass the bar exam, I can have Randolph Studios as a client."

Roxanne felt that John was an interesting person and that she would like to be friends. In some ways he was very sophisticated, but there were other ways in which he seemed very young. It wasn't just his obvious need to please his father, it was the way he expressed himself, as though he were always trying to convince people to like him. "You were very kind to Ma tonight," she said. "Thank you."

"I think your mother is . . . charming."

Roxanne laughed because she believed John really meant it. "She wasn't very gracious tonight, but sometimes she gets carried away. She's never been very practical."

"She seems pretty practical about money," John said.

"I'll pay you back as fast as I can." Roxanne's face was burning in the dark.

His voice cracked with concern as he said, "Don't worry. I've known a lot of backstage mothers in my life. You'd be surprised how many of the best actresses have an ambitious mother pushing them all the way."

"Really?"

"Jean Harlow, for one."

They were both silent then because it was common Hollywood gossip that the beautiful blonde actress's mother was to blame for her death. People whispered that her mother caused her daughter to die by keeping the doctors out and insisting on being the only person to visit the actress while she was sick.

When the silence got too long, John said, "I envy the fact that your mother has so much confidence in your talent."

"She's always believed in me."

"I don't think my father has ever believed in me," John said. Then he laughed and said, "That may be because I've changed directions so many times. First I wanted to be an actor, than an airplane pilot. Now I'm after him to give me a chance as a director."

"Maybe he'll give you a chance this summer."

"No," John said brusquely, and Roxanne understood that they'd had a terrible fight about his career. Then he changed the subject. "Your mother is ambitious for you and that's fine. But maybe you should warn her not to be too bossy on the set. The crew can make or break a star, and if they get it in for you, you're dead. Remember, there will be ten or twenty other pretty girls at Randolph in exactly the same position you're in. Competition's keen."

"I know that," Roxanne said. "And I'll try and talk to Ma, but if it weren't for her, I'd still be in Oklahoma."

John pretended to shudder and said, "That sounds like a fate worse than death."

"Not really," Roxanne said. "But I'd rather be working at Randolph Studios." Then she surprised herself by kissing him on the cheek and saying, "No matter what happens, I thank you."

He responded to her touch by turning to catch her in a full embrace, slipping his arms around her shoulders and drawing her close to him. He kissed her on the lips, holding her until she attempted to move away from him. Then he dropped his arms abruptly and said, "Roxanne, I don't want you to think . . . I really like you Roxanne, but you don't have to be nice to me because I'm the son of Cyril Randolph."

Roxanne was stunned by his actions and words. Her emotions moved quickly from surprise to anger to amusement. She managed to laugh as she asked, "Poor John. Do all the girls chase you all the time? I'll be careful not to do that. But my kiss was just an expression of friendship. You're the one who turned it into something else."

"I know that," John's words tumbled out as he tried to explain. "I liked you right from the beginning, and I've wanted to kiss you since I came in the door tonight. You looked so happy when you heard the news. My first instinct was to. . . . But I know your mother is ambitious. . . ."

"My mother isn't that ambitious," Roxanne said coldly. "Neither am I."

"You don't know what it's like having the head of a big studio as a father. If you knew how many starlets have tried to be 'extra friendly' to me."

"I can promise you that this starlet won't be extra friendly. I have a boyfriend in Oklahoma and a career to think about," she told him firmly. But she didn't add what she was thinking — that John was just too young and impulsive for her.

John took her hand and said, "I'm sorry I messed everything up. The truth is, I guess I wanted to . . . I wanted to kiss you. I guess I'd like to be in love with you."

"Well, I wouldn't like to be in love with you," Roxanne said. "For one thing, there's Henry. For another, I've seen your father, and I have a feeling I'm not ready to tangle with him. He'd be furious if you fell in love with an actress, wouldn't he?"

"Im not afraid of my father," John said, but there was no conviction in his voice, and he added, "but it would be a good idea if he didn't know we were friends for a while. We are friends, aren't we?"

"Of course."

Then he asked, "But only friends?"

John's voice was so plaintive that Roxanne laughed aloud. "John, are you one of those spoiled brats who only wants what he can't have?"

"And I can't have you?" John's voice rose with the challenge.

"We just agreed to be friends," Roxanne answered.

Chapter Thirteen

JOHN did become her friend very quickly, and Roxanne was grateful for his advice, which smoothed her entry into Hollywood life. John helped them shop for the second-hand furniture they needed to fill their small pink house. He also found a Mexican maid to keep it up while Roxanne and her mother were at the studio each day.

When Roxanne protested that it would be better to save the money, John backed up Laureen's contention that she had to keep up appearances. Roxanne wasn't sure if John agreed with Laureen simply because he wanted to please the older woman or because he couldn't imagine how anyone managed without servants. Despite her misgivings, Roxanne let Laureen hire the woman, and she wore the beautiful new clothes that Laureen selected for her.

Trying on new clothes was fun and just about the only excitement in her life during her first month at the studio. Though she got there at seven each morning as her contract required, no one seemed to have any idea what to do with her. Sometimes she posed for photographs and sometimes she read or wandered throughout the large lot, looking at the old sets and watching busier actors work.

There weren't any other teenagers under contract at Randolph Studios, and John was her only real friend those first weeks. He assured them that someone would pay attention to Roxanne eventually. She worried a lot about the long empty days at the studio, but her paychecks continued to delight her. She was able to pay John back in a month, and accomplishing that made her feel rich. The new clothes that she and her mother wore also made her feel very prosperous, even though they weren't paid for. John took them to two smart specialty shops where they could buy on credit. Laureen selected four bright silk print dresses for herself and a dozen beautiful dresses for Roxanne.

Though she worried about the bills, Roxanne loved the white silk and linen suit with the pink angora sweater that she wore the first day she reported to the studio. Never in all her dreams had she thought she would wear anything as silky and soft as the dark-blue chiffon dress with the full skirt that was hanging in her closet. She hadn't actually worn it, but John promised to take her to Earl Carrol's nightclub just as soon as his midterm exams were over.

John was obviously having a hard time in school, and Roxanne felt sorry for him because he wanted so desperately to have a career in the movies. She encouraged him to study hard because she knew he wanted to please his father so much. Sometimes John dropped by in the early evenings to visit and hear the studio gossip. They didn't actually go anywhere much because Roxanne needed to go to bed early so she would look fresh at the studio at seven the next morning. John's first class was later, so he spent his evenings studying.

On Sundays John took Roxanne and her mother out to lunch and for a drive. He always chose a destination that would distract Laureen enough so that he could really talk to Roxanne. Most of their conversation was about what was or was not going on at the studio. John gave her tips about how to get along with the crew members, and many other bits of advice.

A month after she'd signed the contract he drove them to Santa Monica for lunch. They made the trip by way of Sunset Boulevard, with several side trips so Laureen could see the houses of the famous stars. Roxanne wished John had chosen a different route because her mother had already decided that their pink bungalow was much too small. Compared to the lovely homes they passed in

Beverly Hills, even Roxanne felt that her new house was modest.

"I suppose you live in a house as big as this one," Laureen said to John as they slowed down in front of a mammoth stucco mansion with turreted roofs and brown wood trim that was supposed to represent English Tudor styling.

"Our house is about this size," John admitted.

"How many bedrooms?" Laureen demanded.

"I'm not sure . . . maybe six or seven."

"Plus the servants' quarters?"

"Yes."

"I'd like to see it sometime."

"You will, Mrs. Wilson. I want to introduce you and Roxanne to my father just as soon as possible. But we need to be sure that Roxanne is well established in her career."

"Your father won't think my girl is good enough for his son?"

"It's nothing personal. He wouldn't care whether it was Mae West or Roxanne Wilson. Any actress spells danger."

Roxanne laughed at the idea of John dating Mae West, who was supposed to be the sexiest actress in Hollywood. One of her recent pictures was banned just because of the way she said, "Come up and see me sometime."

"I should hope your father would know that my Roxanne is nothing like Mae West," Laureen sniffed.

"It was just a manner of speaking, Ma. Let's go down to the ocean now. I'm dying for some of that wonderful clam chowder we had last time. They don't have clam chowder in Oklahoma."

"I thought the studio told you to stop talking about Oklahoma?"

"I don't have to try to fool John." Roxanne laughed. "He's the one who discovered me." She said, "The publicity department hasn't decided whether they want me to be an orphan from England or a rich girl from a wealthy New York City family."

"It doesn't really matter," John said cynically. "As far as the publicity department is concerned, the important thing is not to tell the truth."

"Well, the truth is that I'm from Oklahoma where there are no lobsters, no clams, no abalone, and no sea bass. And I came to California because I love them all. Let's go, driver."

"Yes, my lady."

They went to Jack's At the Beach, which was at the end of the Santa Monica pier. They'd come there the first time John took them to lunch, and Roxanne had insisted that they come back again twice. She loved the seafood, and she loved looking at the Pacific Ocean as she ate.

After lunch Laureen said she'd just as soon sit on a bench and read her magazine while John and Roxanne strolled down the boardwalk. As soon as they were out of hearing distance, John asked, "When do you think your mother will trust me enough to let me take you out alone?"

"She trusts you. But she thinks I'm too young to date."

"You told me you almost married that guy in Oklahoma."

Roxanne laughed and said, "There's a lot of difference between Hollywood and Oklahoma."

"What's the difference?"

"Norman was a little town. Everyone knew everyone. And I didn't exactly date Henry. There wasn't really anyplace to go except school and church. The only movie was on Saturday afternoon, and I always went with Ma."

"You really went to the movies every Saturday?"

"From the time I was six."

"Maybe that's why you're such a good actress."

"I don't know if I'm any kind of actress at all," Roxanne said. "But maybe I did learn something. At least, I hope so."

"Let's not get off the subject. Why won't your mother let you go out alone with me?"

"For one thing, she really likes you. I think she looks forward to seeing you on Sundays more than I do."

"Thank you, Miss Wilson."

Roxanne ignored his sarcasm and went on. "You're the only industry person who really seems to treat her politely." She'd been in

Hollywood long enough to speak of "the industry." Industry people were anyone who had anything to do with making movies.

"I like your mother."

"You always listen to her," Roxanne went on. "It makes her feel important."

"How did you get to be so much more grown-up than your mother, Roxanne?"

John's voice told her that it was an honest question, so she tried to answer thoughtfully. "I'm like my father in a lot of ways. He always took care of Ma and he loved her a lot. She depended on him. I think she misses him a lot more than she'd ever admit."

"She doesn't seem very happy about your being at Randolph Studios. I thought the contract was her dream come true."

"It is," Roxanne assured him. "Mine, too. I'm earning ten times as much as I did when I was a waitress and for a lot less work. Know what I did yesterday?"

"Something dull?"

"Duller than dishwater, as they say. I stood on the sidelines of a movie set for five hours. I was all dressed up, and I even had a line to say, but they never got to me."

"They will. You've got to be patient, Roxanne."

"Remember what you told me that first day when you brought the contract around? You said acting was dull and that there would be ten or twenty girls who were in exactly the same position I was. Well, you were right about the dull part, but you sure can't count. There must be at least fifty beautiful girls wandering around Randolph Studios with nothing to do."

"You'll get a chance," John promised her. "Maybe they'll get to your line tomorrow."

"If they do, I'll be ready." She frowned, put her hands on her hips, and said, "The stagecoach is coming." Then she waved her arms in the air and shouted, "The stagecoach is coming!" After that she turned to him and asked, "The stagecoach is coming?"

"Good girl," he teased. "Just keep working on it. You'll get it right. One of these days you'll see your name up in lights."

"As long as I see it on those lovely paychecks I'm happy," Roxanne said, but she knew that wasn't really true. She wanted more than money; she wanted a chance to prove what she could do.

In the weeks that followed she tried to remind herself to be grateful for the fact that she was making more money than she'd ever imagined. When she learned that her one line in her first movie was cut and she wouldn't appear at all, she held up her chin and said, "It doesn't really matter. I'll get another chance."

But the other chances didn't come quickly, and she began to doubt that they ever really would. She reported to work on time each day, stood patiently for the fittings, sat quietly for the makeup and hair sessions. She was assigned to another movie and then another but never got a chance to deliver even one line.

As she grew more discouraged her mother grew more aggressive and began trying to buttonhole anyone who would listen, begging them to give her girl a chance. About three months after she arrived at the studio Roxanne overheard a conversation between two other starlets about her mother's pushiness.

"They say her mother even goes out on dates with her," the first starlet said.

"I don't doubt it," the other girl said. "She doesn't seem bright enough to make conversation by herself."

"Ever notice how when you ask her a question, her mother answers?"

"I have, but I'm not sure she has."

"It's a good thing she's pretty. She hasn't got much else."

Roxanne stepped out from behind the set and said, "Too bad I don't have a terrible tongue like you two do."

Both girls looked embarrassed to be caught gossiping. One of them said, "I'm sorry, I guess. But you know something, you'd do better at Randolph if you left your mother at home."

"When I need advice, I'll ask for it." Roxanne turned her back on the two starlets.

The incident worried her a lot, and she honestly wondered how much truth there was in what the girls had said. She knew that Laureen annoyed some people with her pushiness, but she hated the idea of forcing her mother to stay home every day. What would Laureen do to amuse herself? Besides that, Roxanne wasn't sure there was anything she could say to persuade her mother that her presence wasn't necessary on the set.

When John dropped over that evening, she asked him to take a walk with her. Once outside she said, "The evenings are so much longer now than when we got here. Can you believe it's been almost six months? I've been at Randolph four months now."

Then she told him about what she'd overheard the starlets saying that day and asked, "What do you think? Is Ma ruining my chances?"

John stopped, took both her hands in his, and said softly, "Roxanne, a lot of it is luck, you know."

"Luck?"

"Yes, luck. I walked into that restaurant and saw you. You got a chance. Someone else will see you and you'll get another chance. Or maybe you won't. I've seen girls with no talent make it. Others seem to have it all and they fail."

"What about hard work?"

"Everyone in the movie business works hard. You think my dad got to be head of Randolph Studios just because he was a hard worker? He had two partners who worked as hard as he did. One died and the other went broke."

"Your father has a great talent," Roxanne

said. "He's made some of the finest movies ever made. He made *Wagon Wheels* and *Stardust*. He's won three Academy Awards for best picture. It wasn't all luck, John."

"My father had the good fortune to run into some talented actors and directors. And he came to Hollywood just as talkies were taking off. Luck and timing, those are my father's major skills."

"There had to be more to it than that. Your father didn't just make one good picture, he's made dozens."

"It was more luck than you want to believe," John insisted.

"People make their own luck."

"Roxanne, you're living in the middle of the most terrible Depression this country has ever known. Ten million people are out of work and they're not lazy. A lot of them are just down on their luck."

Roxanne didn't have an answer for John's logic, but she knew in her heart that he was wrong. There had to be something wrong with the idea that what happened to you depended on chance. She repeated, "People make their own luck, John. And I'm going to make my luck good."

Chapter Fourteen

"IT'S a Marlowe movie," the girl in front of her said.

Roxanne felt a familiar tremor of excitement at the sound of the name Marlowe. Was she was standing in line to try out for a part in a movie with Gary Marlowe? The idea was alternately thrilling and frightening. Of course, any real part would be wonderful after four months of standing around waiting. But being in a Gary Marlowe movie would be. . . . She wasn't sure how she felt about the possibility.

But she was determined to do her best to get any part at all. Her conversation with John last night had really disturbed her. She just couldn't accept John's belief that much of her fate depended on luck. Being a good worker and having talent had to have something to do with success! It was just too discouraging to believe that someone could work hard, have everything it took to be a star, and then not make it.

Even if her chances were only one in a thousand, Roxanne preferred to believe that something more than luck was involved. That morning, when she'd received the call for a costume picture, she reported promptly, picking the prettiest dress on the rack. She also did her best to be nice to the makeup people so they would do their best for her. If professional behavior could influence anything, she was determined that her actions would help, not hinder, her.

Now, after three hours of makeup and costuming, she was standing in line with about thirty other pretty starlets. Being in competition with so many girls did make her feel like just one flower in the garden, so she had to admit that John's theory that luck played a part might be partly true. It was a long lineup of beautiful women, and all of them were wearing powdered white wigs, low-cut satin dresses, and brilliant smiles. How would they be chosen?

Roxanne had been around long enough to know that they probably wouldn't ask her to do any acting. Most of these costume calls were for the background people, and they assumed that anyone under contract would be able to deliver a few lines. The only hope she had was to attract favorable attention because of her looks, her smile, and her posture. She knew that her blonde hair was one thing that made her stand out from the others, but in a white wig, that attribute was lost. She could only hope that her smile was as beautiful and arresting as everyone said.

All the girls were standing very straight because they were laced tight into their corsets, and Roxanne was trying to stand the straightest and look the prettiest of them all. Every time anyone walked by the lineup, all the girls smiled, and so did Roxanne. She wasn't sure whether the call was for just one girl or would involve a whole group, and she didn't have any idea who would do the choosing, so she didn't want to miss any bets.

Her mother was sitting on her canvas chair, pretending to be reading, but she could feel Laureen's anxious eyes on her. She had begged her mother not to interfere, and she could only hope that Laureen would resist the impulse. Roxanne had a vision of Laureen at Cyril Randolph's knees, imploring him to give her little girl a chance. She shuddered and then fought the impulse to laugh. It was a familiar form of nervousness, this need to laugh at her most anxious moments.

"I'm hungry," the girl beside her complained. "What time is it?"

Roxanne looked at the clock on the wall at the opposite end of the studio. It wasn't very far away. "Eleven-fifteen."

"Thanks. Blind as a bat, you know."

Roxanne thanked her lucky stars that she could see well. No girl who wanted to be in the movies could afford to be seen with glasses

145

on, even if she was in danger of breaking her neck. "We'll have to eat in these, I guess," another girl complained.

Roxanne nodded. She had a lot of trouble conversing with the other starlets, because most of their talk was just a string of complaints they delivered with happy smiles. It made Roxanne almost dizzy as she tried to put the downcast words together with the sunny appearance of the girls.

"I won't be able to eat a thing," the girl complained. "This corset is so tight, I can barely breathe. Imagine what it will be like sitting down."

"We can eat standing up," Roxanne offered. It was a common sight in the studio commisary; actors and actresses in costume ate standing; some even ate leaning over to avoid spilling food on the expensive costumes. The worst thing an actor could do was hold up production because an accident forced a costume change. Careers had been ruined over too many bowls of spilled soup.

"I'm on a diet, anyway," the girl complained. "They say it's Gary Marlowe in this one. Just back from a big production on the desert. I'll bet he spent the whole winter in Palm Springs. Must be nice to be rich and famous."

"He's back?" Again that tremor of excitement. Since she'd come to work at Randolph Studios, Gary had been on location or on tour. She'd seen his famous older relatives from afar but never him. Would he remember her?

146

She told herself not to be foolish, that of course he wouldn't. He hadn't recognized her in Rudy's, had he? Why should he remember her four months later, and in costume?

"Okay, girls. This is it. Now, all you have to do is walk slowly and smile. Look pretty and smile into the camera. Got it?" A man with a megaphone shouted directions at the long line of starlets, then motioned for the first one in line to start walking.

Roxanne was too far away to see who was sitting on the set, but she could see three men in chairs plus a cameraman. When the line started moving and she got closer, her heart began to thump with excitement. Gary Marlowe was there!

He was sitting in a canvas-backed chair, looking very relaxed. He was wearing English riding boots, and since one leg was crossed over the other, the gleam of the expensive leather was so shiny that it flashed like a mirror. His pants were English jodhpurs, and he wore a tweed riding jacket with leather patches on the elbows. His shirt was a soft white flannel and open at the neck.

Roxanne decided that he was the handsomest man she had ever seen. His elegance and grace were apparent even from such a distance, and she hoped with all her heart that she could get through this test without making a fool of herself. Just seeing Gary and reacting to his style and ease made her feel awkward and inexperienced. Though she'd been through several tests like this one, she felt as though it were her first day on a set again.

"All you have to do is walk slowly and smile," she muttered under her breath.

"What did you say?" the girl behind her asked in a high-pitched, strained voice.

At least I'm not the only one who's nervous, Roxanne thought, but that wasn't much comfort.

She was close enough now to see Marlowe's dark eyes and handsome face. He seemed to be trying to keep his expression halfway between looking interested and not showing too much emotion. By now Roxanne could see that each girl was stepping onto a small stage, walking across a runway, and then, when she got to the other side, going to the right or left.

There was no way of knowing which group of girls was being selected and which was being rejected. She could see that some of the girls who had already walked across the runway were having a hard time keeping their smiles bright and cheerful. One girl looked as though she were about to burst into tears, even though she still had no idea of whether she was being chosen or not.

Now it was Roxanne's turn to walk the runway, and she took a deep breath, consciously willing herself to keep calm. By now she was aware that Gary Marlowe was the one who was actually doing the choosing. She had isolated a small movement of his left hand, waving either to the left or right.

Turning her head slightly to smile at Gary Marlowe, she tried to keep her expression friendly and to indicate with her eyes that they had met before. Making Gary notice her was her best chance of being selected, so she willed him to respond to her energetic smile.

Roxanne thought of the furniture auction that John took her to when they'd first came to town. In a way the motion that Gary was making was similar to the small, hidden signals that the professional dealers made at the auction. The idea of Gary as a dealer doing the bidding and herself as a piece of furniture that was for sale did not please her. She caught herself before the uphappy thought forced a frown. One of the most important qualities an actress could develop was the ability to look pleasant no matter how unhappy she was. Instead of frowning she widened her smile.

"Do I know you?" Gary's voice boomed out across the distance. It was a rich, full baritone, surprisingly low for someone as young as he was.

Roxanne answered, "We met once."

"Here?" Gary's eyebrow went up in amusement. He was obviously thinking that she was one of the many girls he'd dated. Since she'd come to Randolph Studios she'd learned that he had a reputation for liking pretty girls, even the ones who were older than he was.

"In Kansas City."

Gary Marlowe burst out laughing. "Rosie? You're the girl with the mother?"

"Yes." She was sorry she'd said anything now. Her cheeks were burning brightly. Why hadn't she remembered how rude he was? Why had she fallen for his handsome face once again?

"But it's not Rosie," he said. "What was it?"

"Roxanne Wilson."

"Ah, yes. The fair Roxanne. But you're wrong about meeting once. I saw you after that. And it seems congratulations are in order. You've come up in the world, haven't you?"

She didn't answer because she didn't trust herself to say anything pleasant. Why would he deliberately make fun of her in front of all these people?

He raised one eyebrow in an amused expression and asked softly, "Don't you remember? It was raining."

"I remember." She was still smiling, but it was getting increasingly difficult. If he'd recognized her that day, she wondered why he hadn't spoken. He'd rushed out of the restaurant, leaving his coffee behind. And those two girls, who were they? At that moment she felt so humiliated, she wished that she'd never met Gary Marlowe.

Roxanne saw Gary's wrist move slightly, and she knew her time was over. Of course, she had no idea whether she'd been chosen or not. For that matter she wasn't absolutely sure she wanted to work on a movie in which

Gary Marlowe was the star. She didn't look back as she stepped off the stage and into the group of girls on the left side.

It was three days before she learned that she'd been chosen as a bit player in the movie. By that time she was over her discomfort about meeting Gary again. She had a long talk with herself and decided that whatever Gary was like personally, he was a fine actor and she was a professional actress. She was prepared to work with him and get along as well as she possibly could.

When they gave her the synopsis of the movie and the script pages that included her scenes, she took them eagerly and spent the rest of the day going over the whole thing. By the next morning she had her lines memorized, as well as most of the ones the other actors would speak in her scenes. She reported to costuming early but was disappointed to discover that they would be filming the movie out of sequence. They were doing the parts that were supposedly set in America first. By that time, Roxanne realized ruefully, she was to have been long dead and lying cold and headless in a French grave.

Called *Starlight Majesty*, the movie was a love story set at the time of the French Revolution. Gary played a young nobleman who eventually escaped the guillotine and went to America, where he married his childhood sweetheart. Roxanne played a young aristo-

cratic friend who was carried to her death in
a wooden cart as the French mob shouted
curses at her.

She was pleased with her part because she
would be able to display a range of emotions.
Her first scene was a lighthearted ball, and
the last one was pure frenzy and terror. It
was a small part with only a few lines, but
Roxanne was happy with it because it was
the first time she'd had a chance to show anyone that she could act. Since she appeared in
two important scenes, there was a chance
that she would actually be noticed by other
directors and producers and get other parts.

Her mother was pleased, too, and bragged,
"You're the only one who got a speaking
part. The only one in that line of girls. See, I
told you they'd soon discover your talent."

"Yes, Ma." As usual she found it easier to
agree with her mother than to argue, but in
her heart, she knew she'd been given the
speaking part because Gary had stopped to
talk to her. She doubted that he'd been directly responsible, but his attention had
served to set her apart. The casting director
probably picked her just because he remembered her name. In a way, getting the speaking part was luck, just as John said.

She still wasn't sure that she considered
knowing Gary Marlowe exactly lucky, but
she did have to acknowledge that fate seemed
to play a part in their meeting a second and
third time. Maybe Gary was lucky for her

professionally, even if he wasn't lucky for her personally, Roxanne decided.

The Sunday after she found out she had a part in *Starlight Majesty*, she apologized to John. "I'm afraid you were right. Luck had a lot to do with my getting this. In fact, it was blind luck that I'd met Gary in Kansas City. So I'm beginning to be superstitious, just like everyone else in Hollywood."

She didn't add that she was beginning to wonder if Gary was her lucky star, her good omen in her professional life. Though she knew that most Hollywood people were great believers in astrology, fortune-telling, and other things that people in Oklahoma thought were silly, she didn't want anyone to know how foolish her own daydreams were.

"Don't underestimate yourself," John said. "You're one of the prettiest girls I've ever seen, and you can act. That day I did your screen test, your face responded to every emotion so intelligently. I'm sure you have the ability to make it big in this business."

Roxanne laughed. "You're the one who kept telling me it was all written in the stars. Now it's a business."

"That was before I was sure you'd get a break," John admitted. "You've got what it takes, Roxanne. I'm sure of it."

"You sound like Ma."

"I'll bet your mother is pleased."

"Yes. She went over to the Clintlocks' tonight just especially to brag about me. Of course, she started complaining immediately that I didn't get star billing."

"Who'd she complain to?"

"Just me."

"That's good," John said. "Any chance you can get her to stay away from the set while you're filming this one?"

"I doubt it. I tried to tell her what those girls said, but she just brushed me off."

"You've got to learn to stand up for yourself."

"Like you do to your father?" Roxanne asked. She was sensitive about her relationship with her mother because she had hated it when Gary called her "the girl with the mother." Why didn't anyone understand how much she owed Laureen? If it hadn't been for her mother, she wouldn't be in pictures at all.

"My father is a tough man to deal with," John said in a defensive voice. "You've seen him at the studio."

"I'm sorry, John. I shouldn't criticize the way you handle your father. You're always nice to Ma." She was grateful for John's courtesy toward her mother, but she feared it was founded on too great a need to please. And thinking about the times she'd seen him with his father made her sad. No doubt about it, Cyril Randolph was a real tyrant. There were a lot of stories about the famous people he fired for almost no reason. She'd once heard a well-known star refer to him at Ruthless Randolph. The next day the star was gone from the set.

"Besides, there's no real reason why my father should give me a chance to direct just because I'm his son."

"Seems like he'd encourage your talent," Roxanne said. She couldn't resist asking, "Did the Marlowes encourage Gary?"

"All the way," John said. "They started him out in children's parts when he was only two."

"So he grew up on the set. That's probably why he seems so relaxed."

"He's never had any real problems with his folks," John added wistfully.

"He's probably very spoiled," Roxanne said. "And all those starlets he dates must mean he's insecure or something."

"Maybe," John said. "He was shy when he was younger, but he got over that when he went to military school. My dad never let me go to school till I was ready for college."

"Poor little rich boys," Roxanne teased. "Are you and Gary the same age?"

"Yes. He was eighteen two months after I was." Then he asked, "How old is Henry?"

"Eighteen," Roxanne answered. She couldn't help being amused at how jealous John was of Henry. He was always asking what Henry said in his letters, and sometimes Roxanne told him. Though he still wrote weekly, Henry seemed more real to John than to her these days. Of course, that was because she usually put John's romantic advances off by reminding him of her Oklahoma boyfriend. She supposed that wasn't entirely honest, but it seemed kinder than anything else she could say.

"Did Gary's folks want him to be an actor?" Roxanne asked. She wished she could stop asking questions about him, but his dark brown eyes kept coming to her mind, teasing her and making her curious.

"I think so. At least his mother did. She's got the brains and ambition in the family, and she dotes on him."

"So Gary has a bossy mother, too." Roxanne smiled at the news.

"She's nice. And his father is a good person, too. He reads most of the time he's not working, but they were both good to me after my mother died. They're nice people. I think they're the exception for Hollywood parents, though. Most kids seem to have trouble with their parents in this town."

"Most teenagers have trouble with their parents in every town," Roxanne assured him.

"Being in the movies makes it a lot harder," John said. "Back in Oklahoma you'd still be a high school kid, but out here you're an adult."

"A sort-of adult." Roxanne laughed. "Ma thinks of my age as adjustable, depending on what the issue is."

"At least she's started letting you go out on dates with me."

"Is this a date?" Roxanne teased. "Then why don't you buy me an ice-cream soda?"

"I'd rather kiss you," John said, and leaned toward her.

Roxanne laughed and ducked away. "None of that mushy stuff or I'll have to tell my mother. I'll take strawberry."

They went to Schwaab's drugstore, because it was famous for the Hollywood writers and actors who hung out there, and they both enjoyed catching glimpses of celebrities. As they entered the small stucco building Roxanne whispered, "Looks like we're the most famous people here tonight."

They were the only customers, except for an older woman who was thumbing through the magazines. The old woman had dyed blonde hair and a dress that was much more old-fashioned than the ones Mrs. Clintlock wore. Roxanne thought this dress looked like it was in style in the early twenties.

The woman closed the magazine and shuffled out of the drugstore. "Poor old gal," John said. "You didn't recognize her?"

"No. Should I?"

"I suppose not. She was washed up before you were born. But Marion Murdock was one of the most famous actresses in Hollywood once. She came out here with Biograph Pictures, when they moved here from New Jersey, and she was almost as popular as Mary Pickford for a while."

"What happened?"

"I don't know. Her type went out of style. She spent more than she earned. Now she's a broken old woman. I'd like to write a story about someone like her someday. I'm working on a script right now that is sort of in the new realism vein."

"Why write about her? It doesn't sound like she was very successful."

"That's the point," John said. "Hollywood stories aren't all happy endings. A lot of people have a little success and then end up on the garbage heap. Some don't know when to give up, and that was Marion Murdock's problem. She hung on and tried to get parts long after anyone wanted her. Eventually she lost everything."

Roxanne shivered.

"Cold?"

She shook her head. "It's just the strawberries," she said. "And crushed ice makes me shiver." But it wasn't just the ice-cream soda that made Roxanne cold, it was fear for her own future. What if she was one of those people who got a chance in Hollywood and then got thrown away? Would she end up on the garbage heap?

Chapter Fifteen

SINCE her days were long at the studio, she began watching *Starlight Majesty* from the very beginning of the filming. Roxanne believed it would help her acting abilities to observe more experienced people, and she also found the takes and retakes of scenes sort of hypnotic.

She hated to admit to herself that some of her interest in the filming was connected to Gary Marlowe, but she couldn't deny that her eyes were often drawn to his handsome face and wonderful acting. The American part of the movie was mostly close-ups as he spoke in favor of liberty and justice for the common man. The other portion dealt with the love story, and she tried to ignore her persistent wish that she were the woman in Gary's arms.

The heroine of the movie didn't have a

very big part, but she was beautiful and Gary obviously enjoyed working with her. They looked well together, because she had light-red hair and fair skin and made a nice contrast to his dark good looks. However, she was so short that she had to play the love scenes standing on a small stool. Roxanne couldn't help but think if she were his leading lady they would be perfectly matched in size. She was five feet seven inches tall and Gary was just six feet.

They worked on the American scenes for two weeks, and during that time Roxanne spent all of her spare time on the set. She stood at the sidelines, almost hiding in the dim light as she studied every movement and every line of the stars. Gary ignored her, and she wasn't sure he even knew she was there.

Sometimes, when she was tired of standing, she sat beside her mother on a small canvas stool. The stool was a permanent fixture inside Laureen's knitting bag, along with two or three movie magazines, a deck of cards for playing solitaire, and something she was knitting, usually a sweater for her daughter.

Laureen tended to be very critical of all the other actresses at Randolph Studios, and she was especially critical of Gary's leading lady. About a week after the filming began Cyril Randolph and several other important look-ing men came to the set where *Starlight Majesty* was being filmed. As they left, Lau-reen followed them, pretending to be going to the ladies' room. She said in a loud voice,

"That girl playing opposite Marlowe can't remember her lines. I wonder why they didn't give the part to Roxanne Wilson. She's very talented."

If Cyril Randolph heard Laureen, he ignored her, but Roxanne heard her loud and clear and was afraid that several other people did as well. She was too embarrassed to show her face on the set the rest of the afternoon and spent most of her time hiding in the costume room. But as she walked up and down the rows of colorful clothing, she decided that she absolutely had to do something about her mother's behavior on the set. Much as she hated to upset her, she couldn't let Laureen go on making a fool of them both.

That evening she said to her mother, "Ma, if you get me the reputation of being hard to work with, I'll never get anywhere. Can't you understand that?"

"You've got to have more confidence in yourself. You could do that part better than that redhead."

"Ma, you're making me look like a fool on the set. You're not helping me, you're hurting. Please try to see that."

Laureen's eyes clouded with tears, and she shook her head. "I can't believe you're acting like this after I've done so much for you. Don't you think I've been right so far? Didn't I get you this contract? Well, I know best, and I'm going to make you a star if it's the last thing I do. I'm not going to let them ignore my little girl."

Roxanne put her hands on her hips and tried to sound as firm as she could. "Listen to me, Ma. If you say one more word on the set, I'm going to make you stay home. Hear me?"

"You can't make me stay home," her mother answered. "You're a minor and I'm your mother. So where you go, I go. Besides, if I weren't right there to push you, you'd never get anywhere in this business."

"You're not helping as much as you think, Ma. And comments like that one today hurt a lot." Roxanne was trembling as she tried to convince her mother that what she said was true. After years of trying to protect her mother and "handle" her as her father had, it was very difficult to actually confront her.

She wasn't sure whether she'd had any real influence on Laureen or not, because the older woman went into her room, closing the door with a loud bang behind her.

Roxanne felt terrible as she realized that her mother wasn't going to come out for supper. She was lonely without her mother's cheerful gossip, and she was so upset that she had a hard time eating. She just picked at the cold chicken and salad that Lupita left in the refrigerator. Once she went to Laureen's door and asked her if she wanted a chicken sandwich, but her mother didn't even reply. Roxanne listened carefully, but the only sounds she could hear were the strains of the Lucky Strike Hit Parade on the radio.

After dinner Roxanne washed the dish and

glass she'd used, even though Laureen insisted that now that she was a star she shouldn't put her beautiful hands in dishwater. Then she sat down and wrote a long letter to Henry. She told him a lot about the business of moviemaking but almost nothing about her real concerns, the trouble with her mother, or her feelings about Gary. As she reread the letter she sighed and thought that she and Henry were growing farther and farther apart each day. She had never realized the full extent of her loneliness until this quarrel with her mother. Now she was almost totally friendless.

She reminded herself that she did have one good friend in Hollywood. John was the one person she could share all of her dreams with. But John was busy studying for his exams this week, trying to make passing grades on his midterms so he wouldn't disgrace his father.

Thinking about John led to thoughts of her father and how unhappy he would have been to see the quarrel between his wife and daughter. But she knew it was foolish to worry about the past. Her father was dead, and she and her mother were in Hollywood, so things could never again be the way they had been; everything had changed.

She awoke the next morning worrying about her mother. Would Laureen still be angry with her? And what could she do to make it up to her? She hated to think that she'd made Laureen feel bad, but she couldn't honestly think that what she'd said was wrong. Despite her hope that her mother wouldn't be permanently wounded, she also hoped that her mother would take the message to heart.

Her mother didn't speak to her for two days, and Roxanne was miserable about that. However, the quarrel did seem to have some effect on her mother's behavior, and Roxanne was honest enough to admit that it would all be worth it if the change was permanent. Laureen was extremely quiet on the set and stopped making remarks about the leading lady or anyone else. She sat on her canvas chair and knitted with fierce motions, pretending not to watch anything that was going on at all.

John finished his midterm exams and had a week off for spring vacation. He asked if he could visit Roxanne on the set, and she laughed at the idea that he had to ask permission. "It will be fun to have you there," she said, "but what about your father?"

"He'll think I'm visiting Gary. After all, we're old friends."

That worried her a bit. How would she manage when they spoke together? Would she feel like an outsider? And what would happen if John's father should see through his game and discover that he and Roxanne were very good friends? Ruthless Randolph had been known to fire people because he didn't like the way they said hello. He would think nothing of dropping her contract if she angered him.

John seemed to enjoy his first day on the set, and he whispered a lot of information to her during the breaks. Of course, during the actual filming, no one could even breathe loudly, but Bertram, the director of this movie, didn't like anyone to talk between takes, either. Since Bertram was one of the most important people on the lot, everyone obeyed his wishes.

Having to whisper didn't slow John down a bit, and he managed to tell Roxanne more about moviemaking in one week than she'd learned in four and a half months of watching on her own. She learned that a scene was always filmed at least three times so that the person who edited would have plenty of options when he put the movie together. "They do it as a straight scene first, usually at a medium distance. Then they'll reshoot the scene with close-ups of the principal actors and actresses. If there's background, they may shoot a lot of background business to fill in."

"That's what I'll be," Roxanne whispered. "Background business."

John nodded. "Take that scene where you are carried to the guillotine. He'll film that at least three ways. He'll do close-ups of you and of Gary. Then he'll do a lot of mob background. It's up to the film cutter what stays in."

"Here's hoping it will be me."

John squeezed her hand and smiled down at her. As he did so Gary Marlowe's voice sounded behind them. "Hi, John. You on vacation?"

"Hi, Gary. You know Roxanne, don't you?"

"Miss Wilson, I believe." Gary raised his eyebrow as he said, "You seem to have a talent for meeting people."

"Roxanne is an old friend," John said smoothly. "How's *The Scarlet Plume* doing?" He was asking about Gary's last picture.

"They say I'm a star." Gary smiled, and it occurred to her that he sounded slightly ashamed of his success.

"I saw it," John said. "In fact, I took Roxanne, and we both liked it."

Gary's eyes were searching as he asked Roxanne directly, "Did you?"

"Yes."

"You still think I have talent?" He turned to John and explained, "I met Miss Wilson in Kansas City. She said I had talent."

"I also said you were rude. I haven't changed my mind about either quality."

Gary threw back his head and laughed. John joined in, and Roxanne's mood changed from annoyance to amusement. She also laughed, and their combined three voices drew the attention of Bertram, who was on the other side of the set. He yelled one word, "Quiet!"

They stopped laughing but their merriment remained, and Roxanne realized she was having a very good time. When Gary asked John, "Have lunch with me?" and then added, "Both of you?" she was inclined to say yes. But what would she do about Laureen? Somehow she didn't think she could enjoy a lunch that included Gary Marlowe and her mother. She was also reluctant to upset her mother again. The breach had barely begun to heal.

"We'd like that," John said quickly.

As Gary nodded and walked away John said, "Never turn down lunch with the star, Roxanne. That's important."

"I'd rather have lunch with you," Roxanne said. Then she added a teasing, "You're important, too, you know."

"I hope I'm important to you," John said, taking her hand again. "But Gary can be important to your career. I'm just a lowly student. Remember?"

"What about Ma?"

John frowned and then he asked, "She'll understand, won't she?"

Roxanne shook her head. "Her feelings will be hurt. I eat with her every day, you know."

"How about if I take her out somewhere and you go with Gary? She'd probably jump at the chance to go to the Brown Derby again."

Laureen was absolutely crazy about the Brown Derby restaurant, mostly because famous movie stars went there. She'd insisted that John take Roxanne's photograph in front of the restaurant, which was shaped like a man's hat. Then she sent a copy to the Norman newspaper. They ran it on the front page with a story about how Roxanne was a big star now.

When Henry saw that paper, he'd written a long letter begging Roxanne to come home where things were normal. His concluding lines were, "How can you be happy in a place where people pay a lot of money to eat inside a hat?"

Thinking about Henry always made her feel vaguely guilty, and she shook her head quickly, saying, "I don't want to have lunch alone with him. I don't like him."

"Gary's all right," John said. "Didn't you see how much he cared what you thought about his acting?"

"You always make Gary Marlowe sound very different from the person I know."

"It's because he's so handsome," John said. "A lot of people expect handsome men or pretty women to be stuck-up. You should know that as well as anyone. Come on. You'll like him, you'll see."

"I doubt that," Roxanne said sincerely, "but you're right that it will be good for my career. But you have to come with me. Ma will just have to understand."

"I'll explain it to her," John volunteered.

"You really are a wonderful friend," Roxanne said, then she took his hand and squeezed it to show how much his friendship meant to her.

"I hope I'm more than that," John answered. "Now you go powder your nose and I'll go charm the Mama Tiger."

Chapter
Sixteen

DURING the week John was on the set Roxanne got to know Gary a little bit better, and she decided he probably wasn't as bad as she'd originally believed. He was very courteous to her and seemed to think that John Randolph was a great guy. With his old friend he was young, carefree, and completely natural.

The three had lunch together twice, and both times Roxanne actually enjoyed herself. In fact, she began to hope that she could be friends with Gary, much as she had become friends with John. The second time they had lunch she said something about that possibility. "I had fun. It's good to be with people my own age. Everyone else around here is so much older."

"That's right. Us Hollywood brats have to stick together," John said.

"I'm not a Hollywood brat," Roxanne protested. "I was born in Oklahoma."

"You're not supposed to tell that," John teased. The official studio biography on Roxanne claimed that she was an English orphan.

"I can trust you two," Roxanne laughed.

"Don't be too sure," John said. "This is a tough town."

"Then I'll be tougher," Roxanne bragged, but John had turned away to greet some people he knew.

Gary responded to her statement, though. He said softly, "You'll manage."

The way he said it made Roxanne flush, and she flared. "You sound like you think I'm a hardened criminal or something."

"Just ambitious," Gary answered.

"What's wrong with that?"

"Nothing, as long as my friends aren't hurt."

Roxanne flushed again, realizing that Gary meant she was taking advantage of John's friendship. She said, "I happen to like John very much."

"And he's in love with you," Gary retorted. "Poor guy, he practically falls all over you."

"You really think I'm a terrible person, don't you?" Roxanne's voice was thick as she realized that she cared much too much what Gary thought about her.

"As I said, I think you're ambitious," Gary repeated. "And I don't want John hurt."

"What about all those girls *you* date once

and never call again?" Roxanne asked. "Don't they get hurt?"

"Jealous?" Gary asked. His eyes were not really amused. In fact, he looked very angry, but the minute John rejoined them, his face smoothed over and the party resumed its happy tone.

That one incident showed Roxanne what Gary really believed about her, and she gave up all thoughts of ever trying to be his friend. When John went back to college, she and Gary dropped any pretense of friendship. They spoke on the set and that was all.

Only once in the remaining three weeks of filming did she exchange more than a few words with Gary. That was the day his leading lady was out sick and the director asked her to stand in. Bertram said, "I'll see you get the stand-in's wages as well as your salary, Roxanne."

Her job was to stand next to Gary as he went over some line changes. The camera wasn't turning, and nothing was required of her except to be there. She tried to keep as still as she could, ignoring the fact that it made her nervous to be so close to Gary.

But as she stood next to him she could smell the scent of his makeup, and his warm breath touched her neck. She was so close, she could see a tiny mole on the side of his face. The mole surprised her because she thought she knew everything there was to know about Gary's face. She had seen *The*

Scarlet Plume several times now, telling herself that she wanted to study his actions on camera.

Standing so close to Gary made her feel a little dizzy, and she began to breathe more deeply, knowing that long, slow breaths would calm her down. Gary didn't seem to notice her at all as he repeated the lines, trying to get them right. Finally Bertram said, "I think you've got it. Try it one more time."

"This comes just before I kiss her? Right?" Gary asked.

"Right."

Somehow Roxanne knew what was coming next. Gary delivered his lines perfectly and then took her in his arms, holding her close and kissing her passionately. She was angry at him, but she was even more angry at herself for the reaction she felt. Her pulse started racing, and she responded to his kiss, willing it to never stop.

When Gary pulled away from her, his eyes were quizzical and confused, as though he wanted to ask her something. Obviously the joke was on him, and Roxanne realized he had expected her to fight or be flustered. Without planning she had done the one thing that was designed to throw him off-balance. Her response was so passionate that he was clearly confused.

"You're quite a little actress, aren't you?" he asked.

Roxanne shrugged. She was determined

that he would never know that her response had been genuine. "I'm ambitious, isn't that what you said?"

"Thanks, Roxanne," Bertram said, and the moment was over. She went back to the wings. No one paid any attention to her the rest of that day, and Gary left the set with two new starlets, a beautiful redhead and a short, cute blonde.

They filmed her scenes the next week, and Roxanne thought it was the most exciting week of her life. On Monday and Tuesday she was dressed in a gorgeous satin gown and a tall white wig. The wig was so beautifully powdered and curled that she began to laugh when she saw it.

"Is something wrong?" the hairdresser asked her.

"I did my screen test in a wig like this," Roxanne explained. "Only all the good ones were out for a Marlowe movie and I got the moth-eaten reject. Now I'm in a Marlowe movie myself."

When the hairdresser still looked confused, she explained, "This wig shows me that I've come up in the world."

"The people who wore the real ones used to carry fancy sticks to scratch underneath," the hairdresser said. "They all had lice in those days."

Roxanne shuddered and said, "If you told me that to depress me, it won't work. This is my first real movie part, and I'm going to enjoy every minute of it. Besides, they chop my head off on Wednesday, so I might as well have fun at the ball."

She danced all day, laughing into the camera, swinging around and around on the wooden stage with the other background actors. The brightly lit chandelier sparkled overhead, and the painted set in the background looked like a real ballroom.

All she had to do was dance with the hero's best friend and look pleased as Gary signed her dance card. Most of the time the camera was following the other dancers, and Roxanne noticed anxiously that Bertram was using a lot of overhead shots of the whole scene.

Overhead shots were a fairly new idea in the movies. They'd been developed primarily for the fancy musicals of the early thirties, and now lots of directors of dramas were using them as well. They put the camera on a moving platform and suspended it from the air, roving back and forth over the scene, filming the tops of heads in crowd scenes. Since Roxanne knew it was perfectly possible that many of the close-ups of her could be replaced by overhead shots, she watched anxiously as Bertram continued to order them.

She was exhausted at the end of the second day but looked forward to tomorrow when she would get her only real chance to act in the movie. As she and Laureen started walking home that evening her mother said, "I noticed that the cameraman photographed your left side. That's because I spoke to him."

"Ma, you promised!"

"But your left side is best."

Roxanne was too tired to argue, but she felt really discouraged about the way Laureen was gradually resuming her bossy ways. The worst thing that could happen to a Hollywood actress was to have the crew members get down on her. They could destroy a career faster than a wink of the eye.

"I've also got plans for starting the Roxanne Wilson Fan Club. Wrote to Cousin Margaret today and asked her to be president."

"Ma, Cousin Margaret doesn't even like movies."

"She likes you, doesn't she?"

"I'm not sure about that, either." Roxanne was so happy to be approaching her home that she was ready to make jokes. She took out her key, opened the door of the little pink bungalow, and said, "I love this house."

"It's too small," Laureen said. "Now that you're a real star, I've started looking for a bigger one."

"How much money do we have in the bank, Ma?"

"A few hundred dollars," Laureen said evasively.

"How many is a few?"

"I'm managing our finances very well."

"Ma, I may not make it. We may need that money." Roxanne sat down and took off her shoes. She lifted her legs and stretched her feet forward, pointing her toes.

"If you had more confidence. . . ." Laureen began.

"Not tonight, Ma," Roxanne begged, but her mother went right on with her standard pep talk about Roxanne's lack of confidence. By the time she'd heard a few minutes of it Roxanne was certain that if she didn't get right to sleep, she'd never make it to the set in the morning. She stood up, interrupting her mother in the middle of a sentence, and said, "I'm going to take a long bath and go to bed."

"It's only seven o'clock," her mother protested. "What about supper?"

"I'll eat a big breakfast," Roxanne promised, and left the room before her mother could answer.

She was nervous the next morning as she reported to the makeup room, but she managed to calm herself by the time they'd smudged her face and disheveled her real hair. She was breathing normally and felt fine as she slipped into the dirty, torn dress that she was to wear in the last scene. She walked onto the set as though she'd had speaking parts in a thousand movies.

As was often the case in the making of movies, she spent the whole day waiting to begin. The next morning the makeup and costuming was repeated, and she was too bored to be nervous at all. Roxanne sat in her wooden cage on a small stool for three hours before they actually got around to filming her. Then she got a chance to shout her lines, "I don't want to die! I'm too young to die!" three times before they broke for lunch.

Walking into the commissary in costume and makeup was fun because most actresses and actors were always trying to look handsome or pretty. There was a reverse pleasure in looking like a mess, and Roxanne enjoyed her lunch as much as any she'd ever eaten in Hollywood. Her mother hated the way she looked, though, and fussed all during the meal about the fact that they'd made her so ugly.

"I'm not ugly," Roxanne assured her. "Imagine what the real girl would have looked like. She'd probably be starving and have a few teeth knocked out. Be glad they didn't blacken my teeth, Ma."

Her mother shuddered in revulsion and ignored Roxanne during the rest of the meal. Roxanne wished there were some way she could get her mother to stop showing her displeasure by these angry silences. But more and more often her mother wasn't speaking to her for one reason or another. By the time lunch was over Roxanne was truly depressed, and it was easier to put her heart in making terrible faces, rattling her cage, and shouting her lines.

Friday was a repeat of Thursday, although Roxanne noticed with alarm that there were more overhead shots than before. She began to understand why John said he wanted to be a writer and director rather than an actor. It was true that actors were absolutely at the mercy of the director's decisions. Roxanne could only hope that her performance would be good enough to sway Bertram's decision about what approach to use to the scene.

At five o'clock Bertram called, "It's a wrap," and Roxanne began to climb out of her wooden cage. A small, dapper man in an ivory gabardine suit and pointed white shoes with brown tips came up to her and handed her a card. "Benny Foyle," he introduced himself. "Artistic representative." Then he added, "I'm an agent."

"How do you do?"

"I do fine. I watched you work. Think I'd like to represent you. Think you can act. You under contract here?"

"Yes."

"Too bad. I think Warner Brothers would be a better studio. Maybe we could break your contract."

Roxanne laughed. "I don't want to break my contract. I worked hard to get it."

Benny nodded his head as though he understood. "Randolph isn't the best one to work for. If you ever need an agent, let me know."

"I will." It pleased Roxanne a great deal that an agent had thought enough of her work to offer to represent her, and she was happy to tell Laureen and John about it that evening. The three of them were dining at the Coconut Grove at the Ambassador Hotel to celebrate her first real role.

"I don't know whether an agent's a good idea," John said. "My dad hates them."

"You don't need an agent," Laureen said. "I'm doing a fine job of managing your career." She stabbed her steak and cut with sharp, angry motions.

Roxanne wanted to avoid anything that would make their wonderful celebration unpleasant, so she said quickly, "Of course you are, Ma. You and John have both been a great help."

Before either of them could respond to her expression of gratitude, a familiar voice came up behind her. She heard the words, "Celebrating your first big success?" and she knew immediately that it was Gary Marlowe.

Keeping a smile on her face as she turned to face him was easy enough. She was an actress, and she knew how to mask her emotions. But when she saw Gary with his arm around two beautiful girls, she knew her cheerful expression slipped for a minute. She answered, "Yes. And you're celebrating as well?"

"Sure, I'm celebrating. Why not?" Gary's voice was defensive.

Of course, John was genuinely delighted to see Gary and insisted that the three of them join their table. Gary pulled up three chairs from adjoining tables with all the ease in the world. Roxanne thought that for a boy who'd grown up as the son of one of the most famous families in Hollywood, the Coconut Grove was probably no more intimidating than the local drugstore.

As John and Gary chatted, the four women

sat silently studying each other. Roxanne hated herself for doing it, but she compared her own youth and beauty to the two girls across the table from her. Then she decided that it really didn't matter which of them was the most attractive. She'd never seen Gary with the same girl two times in a row.

She finished her dinner while the girls sipped drinks and Gary and John talked. Then she heard John say, "That's fine." He stood up and asked the small brunette to dance with him. Gary immediately asked Laureen.

Laureen seemed surprised, but she got to her feet and followed Gary out to the dance floor. Roxanne watched with a bemused expression as the handsome movie idol and her mother danced around the floor. It seemed as though they'd come a long way from that evening in Kansas City, when her mother had almost knocked Gary down to get him to let her in the talent contest.

When the music ended, Gary escorted Laureen to her chair and held out his hand to Roxanne. She stood up, following him out to the center of the floor and willing herself not to be nervous or upset by his presence. As always with Gary, she was on her guard, wondering what he would say next. But his first comment sounded sincere. "I watched you yesterday. You can act."

"Thank you."

"I really mean it. You have talent."

"So do you."

Gary laughed and pulled her closer, then twirled her around and dipped her over in a modified tango step. He whispered in her ear, "Maybe that's what we have in common — talent."

"I hope so," Roxanne said. She wished he wouldn't put his mouth so close to her ear. It was hard to keep her balance with Gary so close.

Abruptly he stopped dancing and led her back to the table. On the way he said, "I really meant it about the talent."

"So did I." There were tears in Roxanne's eyes as she tried to figure out why Gary behaved toward her in the way he did. Then she told herself it didn't matter. All that really mattered was her career, and that was going just fine.

Chapter
Seventeen

THE week after they finished filming *Starlight Majesty*, Roxanne got a call to be in a short feature that Randolph Studios was making. It was really an advertisement for the studio, and it featured Harry Burns with a bevy of bathing beauties. Since the publicity department was in charge of the whole idea, she picked up her script from Marsha Walters, the woman who'd dreamed up her official biography.

After reading the script Roxanne asked, "How can you expect me to play an All-American bathing beauty? I thought I was supposed to be from England?"

"We need one girl who can talk. You've a good figure and blonde hair."

"But what about the publicity stories you wrote about me for *Starlight Majesty*? Won't they be releasing this feature at the same time? How can I appear in this thing and the movie at the same time? It doesn't make sense."

Marsha Walters shrugged and put her cigarette out in the saucer under her coffee cup. "When you've been around as long as I have, you won't expect things to make sense. Bertram said to use you when I asked for a blonde beauty."

Roxanne's stomach churned, and she got a sinking feeling that she knew was pure fear. She nodded slowly, taking the script, and said, "I'll have to think about it. I'm not really sure wearing a bathing suit and smiling sweetly is the best thing for my career."

"There's nothing to think about," Marsha said with a cold voice. "You're under contract, so you're going to do what we say."

Roxanne resisted the impulse to argue with Marsha. She took the script and said to Laureen, "I guess she's right. I guess I have to do it."

"You're a minor. They can't make you wear a bathing suit if I say no."

"Ma, that's not the point. The point is, if I'm in *Starlight Majesty*, it doesn't make sense."

"You can't do it."

"I may have to do it."

"I'll talk to Bertram myself," Laureen said. She rose from her canvas chair and started toward the main building of Randolph Studios.

Roxanne followed her, not sure whether

it was better to let her mother handle this or try to reason with Bertram herself. But she was a little frightened about talking to the second most important man in the studio, and so she followed the line of least resistance. Laureen was never frightened by anyone.

They had to wait thirty minutes before the receptionist ushered them into Bertram's office. Roxanne was impressed by the dark wood paneling, the two golden Oscars on the bookshelf, and the autographed photographs of some of Hollywood's greatest stars. She was very glad when Laureen began talking, even though she wouldn't have approached him in that way.

"My daughter is too young to appear in a bathing suit," Laureen said. "And it won't be good for her career, anyway. I mean, she's going to be a star, so why should she play some little nobody who's in a contest?"

Bertram frowned and twirled a gold fountain pen. He cleared his throat and then said nothing.

"I think the main point is that my publicity for *Starlight Majesty* says I'm an English orphan. Now, if the public sees me in this short feature, it will destroy the other efforts. You do see that, don't you?" Roxanne hoped that her logic would work if her mother's argument didn't. The more she thought about it, the more certain she was that this short film would hurt, not help, her career.

"My dear," Bertram began.

Roxanne's heart sank. His voice was soft and sad, as though he were going to tell her that her best friend had died. "Am I going to be in *Starlight Majesty*?" she asked.

"No," he answered.

"No?" Laureen began shouting. "My daughter is a wonderful actress. How dare you destroy her career!"

"Your scene was fine," Bertram said directly to Roxanne. "But we made an artistic decision. That's why I asked Marsha to use you in the short. I was trying to make it up to you."

"An artistic decision?" Laureen was almost screaming. "What could be more artistic than my daughter's performance? She was good!"

"Madam, your daughter was competent. No one said she wasn't." Bertram's voice was as cold as ice. "But there are many competent young women under contract here. The point of a contract is that actors and actresses are supposed to do what they're told."

"She won't march around in a silly bathing suit," Laureen said. "What will the people in Oklahoma think? I've told everyone that she's a star, and now she'll just look foolish."

"She doesn't have to wear a bathing suit, of course." Bertram's eyes were cold, and his voice was like steel. "Since, as you are always so quick to point out, she's a minor, that's your choice. However, we don't have to renew her contract, either."

"Is that a threat?" Laureen was furious

now, and Roxanne had no idea what she would say next.

Roxanne stood up, and holding her hand out to Bertram, she shook his and said, "Thank you for giving me the other part. I'm grateful." Then she literally dragged Laureen out of the director's room.

Laureen fumed all the way down the hall, and when they got out onto the open lot, she stopped still and began shouting at Roxanne. "You shouldn't have given in to him. He's a bully, and you should never give in to bullies. You know that!"

"Ma, people are listening."

"I don't care. Let them listen. I'm going to go to Mr. Randolph himself. I'll tell him you're a friend of his son's and that they can't do this to us."

"Ma, please. Let's just wait till we get home to discuss this." Several people were walking by very slowly, obviously interested in the scene before them. Roxanne recognized one of the girls who had been at the Coconut Grove the other night. She was sure that the whole story would be all over the studio within an hour. When she thought of Gary's reaction, Roxanne wished desperately that the earth would open up and swallow her. Where were all those California earthquakes she'd heard about?

"I'll take you to MGM," Laureen said, but her voice was a little lower. "I still think you'd be perfect for Scarlett. You didn't get a fair chance."

"Ma, we'll talk about it at home. Please."

It took her and John three hours that evening to convince Laureen that Roxanne had to appear in the bathing beauty short if she was to continue at Randolph Studios. Finally Laureen agreed, but not before she said, "I still think you could tell your father to be nice to Roxanne."

"Ma! If you say that one more time, I'm going back to Oklahoma on the next bus. And I mean it."

"I was just trying to help." Laureen retreated to her room after that, and Roxanne breathed a sigh of relief.

"Thanks, John. I'm sorry about Ma. It's just that she wants so much for me."

"I can't help you with Dad," John said. "I can't really help myself. If he knew I was in love with you, he'd probably fire you, not give you better parts."

"I understand that, John. But I wish you wouldn't say you're in love with me. I thought we agreed that we were just friends."

"Are you still in love with Henry?"

"Yes." It seemed the easiest way to explain things to John. "Or, at least, I'm in love with him when I'm writing to him or reading his letters. The truth is that I don't have the energy to think about romance. I'm a struggling young actress, remember?"

John took her hand and said, "If I get a chance to help you, Roxanne, I will. I hope your mother understands that."

"I hope she understands how angry she

made Bertram today. One more scene like that and I'm on the bus for home."

"You wouldn't do that." John's voice sounded really anxious.

"What else could I do? Go back and ask Rudy for a job in his restaurant?"

"You could marry me," John said.

"I could not marry you," Roxanne said gently. "For a lot of good reasons. One, I'm not in love with you. Two, we're both too young. Three, your father would have a fit and disown you."

"I wouldn't care," John said.

"Yes, you would care," Roxanne said. She waved her hand around her living room and said, "See this room? Well, you think it's kind of cute, but to me, it's a mansion. I've been dirt-poor in my life, poorer than you can ever imagine. Believe me, it would be hard to get used to canned beans instead of steak béarnaise. You spend more money when you take me out on Sundays than most people make in two weeks. And you don't even know that the way you live is unusual. You wouldn't like being poor, John."

"I wouldn't mind, if you loved me," John said. "Anyway, my father wouldn't disown us for long. He really loves me."

Roxanne almost laughed at the uncertainty in his voice. She wasn't sure whether it was doubt that he could learn to enjoy life as a poor boy or that he could count on his father's love. Gently she said, "That's really not the point, is it?"

"Because you don't love me?"

"John, I just want to be a star. It's all I want." In her heart Roxanne knew that wasn't completely true. If it were Gary sitting beside her and offering her love, she had an idea that her response would be very different. But Gary would never offer her anything but heartbreak, and John was too good a friend to be anything but honest with.

John kissed her on the cheek and said, "Good luck tomorrow, Roxanne. I've got to get home."

"And I've got to get to bed so I can be a beautiful bathing beauty," Roxanne said.

Chapter Eighteen

SHE made the bathing beauty short in three days. All she really had to do was stand around in a tight-fitting bathing suit and look helpful. The only other person in it with a speaking part was Harry Burns, who looked ten years older than when he'd played opposite Roxanne during her screen test.

"He didn't even remember me," Roxanne told John the evening the feature was finished. They were sitting on the front steps of her pink bungalow, enjoying the warmth of the early June evening.

"His contract's being dropped because of his drinking," John said. "I heard my dad and Bertram talking about it last night after supper."

"Poor man," Roxanne said. Though she didn't really like Burns, she felt sorry for any actor who was having trouble with his career. "I can guess how he feels."

"They're going to drop you, too," John said quietly.

Roxanne was shocked at the news. She had hoped that her professional behavior and willingness to do the short feature would help her career, not hurt it. Her face drained of color and she felt faint, but she managed to sound calm as she asked, "How do you know? I'm not important enough to talk about at dinner, am I?"

"Dad's having trouble with the stockholders again," John explained. "He told Bertram to cut out the fat."

"And Bertram offered me up for slaughter?"

"You and about ten other girls. He said that he had more starlets than he needed. I'm afraid he did mention you by name—or rather he mentioned your mother."

"It was the fight she had with him, wasn't it?" Instead of feeling defeated Roxanne was surprised at how angry she felt. The funny thing was that she was angry at both Bertram and her mother. For that matter she was angry at Cyril Randolph as well. She asked, "How does your father manage to sleep at night? The way he builds people's hopes up and then just drops them for no reason?"

"It's not a very secure business, Roxanne. You knew that."

"I thought I'd get a fair chance, though." Roxanne was crying in the darkness. "But they let me stand around for four months, then they cut out my part. Now the only thing I have to show for my six months in Hollywood is that stupid short feature. Do you know what I say in that thing? Exactly seven words. I say, 'Oh, Mr. Burns, I think that's wonderful.' Isn't that a fine way to end a brilliant career?"

"You're not finished yet," John said. He put his arm around her and held her quietly as she sobbed out her disappointment.

Finally she stood up and said, "Let's take a drive, John. I don't want to go in until Ma is asleep. I'd like to wait till I get official notice before I tell her."

"Don't tell her yet," John agreed. "You never know if they'll change their minds. In fact, I have one idea that may work. It depends on my grades."

"You still don't know if you passed?"

"I'm sure I did, but I'm hoping if my grades are high enough, Dad will let me make a movie for my birthday present. I've been working on him to give me one chance to show what I can do. He's still sure law school is a better idea, but I may be wearing him down a bit. At least I hope so. And it *is* my birthday."

Roxanne laughed. "That would be quite a present."

"If I do get to make a movie, I can pick the stars."

"John, don't spoil your chances just for me," Roxanne spoke seriously. "I'd hate to think I'd ruined your career, too."

"Your career's not ruined yet," John said. Then he laughed and added, "If I ever get a chance to direct, maybe I'll be the one to do that for you."

When she went in that night, Laureen was asleep. Roxanne went to her mother's small desk in the living room and rummaged through the papers until she found the bankbook. She knew her mother would be angry with her for meddling, but she felt that she needed to know exactly how much money they'd been able to save in the last six months.

From time to time she had tried to talk to Laureen about money, but her mother always answered her as though there was plenty. Roxanne worried all the time about the expensive suppers and clothes they bought, but until now she'd been content to let her mother manage things. Now she was dismayed to find that the bank balance showed $289. That was actually less than they'd had when they started out from Oklahoma. She bit her lip to keep from crying out in dismay. Wouldn't they have anything to show for her hard work except some fancy clothes?

Roxanne didn't hear from John again that week, and she was mentally packing her bags for the trip back to Oklahoma. Though she tried to tell herself how happy she would be to see Henry, she knew in her heart that she would be much sorrier to leave John and Gary behind. The fact that Gary was on location in northern California, making another big costume picture, didn't make her any happier. It seemed terrible to think of leaving town without even saying good-bye.

Chiding herself for her foolishness didn't really help, but worry about her work did erase most thoughts of Gary from her mind. On Friday afternoon she went to pick up her paycheck with trembling hands. She opened the envelope quickly, searching for the pink slip that would announce the death of her career. There was nothing there.

She was almost happy as she walked home with Laureen that night. Another week of work at Randolph meant another hundred dollars. She told herself that if they were able to hold onto most of this week's and next week's pay, it would stretch a long way in Oklahoma. They would be able to count this California adventure as profitable.

John's little yellow car was sitting out in front of her house when they turned the corner. He was standing beside it, holding a bouquet of flowers that were exactly like the ones he'd brought that first night. "Good news," he said as soon as they were in hearing distance. "I've got my chance to direct."

"Oh, John! You're going to do a movie?"

"And you'll be the star," John said. "I've got it all worked out. Come on and I'll take you both to dinner. Tell you all about it then."

That night they went to a small Italian restaurant with checkered tablecloths and opera music playing on a phonograph in the background. Over a soprano's aria John explained his bargain with his father. "It's a low-budget picture. Really low budget. I don't mean a B picture. I mean C minus. Ten thousand dollars total."

"*Gone with the Wind* will cost over a million," Laureen said.

"I have to use the old western set on the back lot, but that's all right. This is a real strong drama, but it's set in the West. Based on a true story that happened early in the Depression. This poor farm family got kicked off their land and started walking to California. They died of thirst in the desert. The dramatic part is that the woman—that's you, Roxanne—died just fifteen feet from a cistern full of water."

John looked proudly from one to the other, waiting for their reaction. When neither of them said anything, he added, "I've always wanted to do realistic movies. This is strong stuff."

"Yes," Roxanne said. "And I'm sure you'll do well with it. But are you sure I can handle the part? I don't know much about dying of thirst, John."

"I hope she gets to wear pretty clothes in this one," Laureen said. "I'm sure she would never have been cut if they'd listened to me in *Starlight Majesty* and let her wear the ball dress to the guillotine."

"This is a realistic movie," John replied.

Laureen looked as though she would like to argue the point, but Roxanne leaned over and put her hand on John's arm. "Thank you, John. I'll do the best I can."

"I can see you as the young mother," John said. "I really can. You'll look so beautiful as you lie there dying, only fifteen feet from water. I'll use a lot of back lighting to soften your face and hair. You'll look like an angel. It will make your career, you'll see."

"John, don't you think the picture sounds a little depressing?" Roxanne ventured. "Wouldn't it be safer to do a light comedy? I'd love to do a comedy, and they're very popular now."

"Comedies may be popular, but they're not art," John said. His eyes were burning with enthusiasm for the project, so Roxanne offered no more objections. The director made all the decisions in Hollywood, not the actor, and John was going to be the director, not her. The fact that he was young and seemed to believe that there was something romantic about death, poverty, and despair wasn't anything she could control, Roxanne told herself.

Laureen also had the good sense to remain quiet, but later that night she asked, "Do you really have to do this movie with him? I think the story sounds grim."

"He's a good director," Roxanne said. "Maybe he can pull it off."

"People like cheerful movies," Laureen said doubtfully. "It would be different if it were a love story. People don't mind star-crossed lovers dying at the end like Romeo and Juliet, but having a young mother and her baby die of thirst when there's water just around the mountain is going to drive the audience out in droves."

"Ma, John's been good to me. Besides, I don't really have any choice. He saved my contract."

Roxanne didn't have time to learn all her lines before they started filming because she was in nearly every scene, and John's bargain with his father was that the movie had to be shot in three weeks. When she got the script and read her lines, she was really worried, but there was nothing to do but go on with the project.

They shot several scenes each day, hardly pausing for retakes of anything except the most dramatic scenes. John seemed supremely confident that he could pull it off, but Roxanne was more and more concerned about the movie. She not only hated the lines she was supposed to deliver, but she was convinced that the story was too depressing to appeal to anyone.

Laureen grumbled constantly, complaining because Roxanne's costume was just one old plaid cotton dress, complaining because her makeup was too light, and nagging the cameramen to be sure to photograph her best side. At every possible moment she tried to convince John that he had to do something to lighten the mood of the movie.

Two weeks into the shooting Laureen came

up behind John while he was setting up the shot for the final scene when the young mother died. She tugged on his arm and said, "I have an idea. Let's change the ending. Let her find the water and live happily ever after."

John whirled around and roared, "Mrs. Wilson, get off this set!"

Several people laughed loudly, and Roxanne heard one cameraman whisper to another, "Sounds just like his old man."

"He should have ordered her off the first day," the other one responded.

Roxanne was humiliated by the scene and surprised that John hadn't handled her mother with his usual sweet manners. On the other hand, she recognized that the time had come to put a stop to Laureen's interfering once and for all. Even if she never had a real career of her own, it wasn't fair to John.

Laureen didn't leave the set, but she did return to her canvas chair on the sidelines. That evening she refused John's ride home from work, saying, "I prefer to walk. Come along, Roxanne."

"I'll go with John, Ma."

Laureen looked as though she would like to say a great deal about her daughter's revolt, but Roxanne interrupted, "Don't start shouting at me here, Ma. We'll talk when we get home." Then she took John's arm and turned her back on her mother.

John and she drove down to the ocean and watched the sunset before he drove her home.

They talked of many things, but neither of them mentioned the movie or her mother until they drove home and parked in front of Roxanne's house. Then she sighed and said, "Poor Ma. I guess she'll be mad at me for a month now."

"I'm sorry I lost my temper," John said. "I wanted your mother to like me."

"She'll get over it eventually."

"I wish I could be as understanding of my father as you are of your mother."

"I saw today that I have to stop her from ruining things," Roxanne said. "I hate to do it, but there's no other way."

"Can you really stand up to her?"

"Yes," Roxanne said. "I'll have to. It's just that I love her. She had a lot of dreams, John, and reality is hard for her."

"Too bad she doesn't have something of her own," John said. "She acts like it's her acting career, not yours."

"She wanted an acting career," Roxanne admitted, "but she had me instead."

"And you've been trying to make it up to her ever since?"

"Not anymore," Roxanne said. "She won't be there tomorrow, I promise you that."

Chapter Nineteen

"I wouldn't go back there if you paid me," Laureen said when Roxanne announced that she couldn't come to the studio with her the next morning.

Roxanne was too relieved to get out of the house without a fight to worry about how angry her mother was. In fact, she was determined never to let Laureen's moods run her life again. She was going to be a professional actress and not let her personal life interfere with her work, she promised herself.

The last week of the picture, she worked furiously to give John the best performance she was capable of. His father came by the set one day for about fifteen minutes and watched her work. It made her nervous to have the older Mr. Randolph watching, but she did her best to follow John's directions closely. If Cyril Randolph was impressed by her performance, he didn't show it.

The night they finished the picture, John invited her to go to the Coconut Grove to celebrate. He included Laureen in the invitation, adding, "I hope she's not still mad at me."

"She's mad at us both. It's been a week since she's said anything to me except 'Pass the mustard.'"

"I'll call her on the telephone and invite her specially," John said.

The next morning a dozen roses arrived for Laureen, and John followed his flowers up with a telephone call. Laureen agreed to go out to dinner with them and was actually cheerful as she came into the living room in a brand-new silk dress. It was a dark silk with bright red roses on it. Draped over one shoulder and the hip, it looked very expensive and elegant. Roxanne immediately began to worry about money and then told herself not to spoil the party mood. She could talk with her mother about money soon, but tonight they would celebrate John's movie.

It was another three weeks before the movie was cut and edited into final form. Then John invited Roxanne, his father, and Bertram for a preview at the studio. Roxanne was very nervous about the event, not only because she'd never actually talked with Mr. Randolph, but also because she knew a great deal was hinging on their reception of John's film.

She dressed carefully in her best white suit and a bright blue silk blouse that opened at the neckline. She chose a bright red lipstick that was exactly the color of her shoes and bag. If nothing else, Roxanne decided, her appearance was the very best she could do.

She was on time, but when she got there, the small studio theater was already dark and the credits were playing. She sat down, and John whispered, "Dad has another appointment. Sorry."

Roxanne squeezed his hand to show it was all right and then sat back to watch the movie. It was a shock, seeing herself on the screen, and she was amazed at how plain she looked. She'd known that John wanted a new kind of realism, but she wasn't prepared for the dismal grays and sad music, nor was she prepared for the long string of woebegone words and expressions that she delivered.

Even her face looked different from the other times she'd seen herself on the screen. Her hair was parted in the middle and dragged down on each side, then pinned back in a loose bun. With no makeup and those sad expressions her face looked long and tired. After she sat through the first half hour of the movie she realized that she hadn't smiled once. And the most depressing parts were yet to come.

Suddenly Cyril Randolph stood up, calling, "Lights."

The lights went on, and he turned to his son, saying, "It's terrible. We won't release it."

"But, Dad —" John began.

"There's nothing to discuss," Cyril Randolph said. "It's a flop."

"Won't you at least look at the ending?" John's voice cracked, and Roxanne hoped he wouldn't cry. She knew how much he had counted on this movie to prove he had talent but also to get his father's love and approval.

Roxanne felt furious, and she lost her control. She said, "You might at least be courteous enough to look at the whole movie. After all, it's your son's first film."

"It stinks," Randolph said. Then he asked Bertram, "Who's she?"

"Roxanne Wilson, the girl on the screen."

Randolph shook his head and said, "Never would have recognized you. Face photographs too long."

He turned, glancing at his gold watch and saying, "Got an appointment."

"You're not even going to give your son a chance, are you?" Roxanne was so furious she didn't care what happened next.

"I gave him his chance," Cyril Randolph answered, then he left without another word.

John watched his retreating back with a crestfallen expression.

"Your father's a bully," Roxanne said. "You've got to learn to stand up to him."

"I don't want to stand up to him," John said sadly. "I want to stand beside him. As long as I can remember I've been trying to get my father to recognize me, and I thought if I could make a really good movie —" His voice broke and he said, "I'm going home now. Want a ride?"

"I can't," Roxanne reminded him. "My contract calls for my presence on the set from eight till five. I've got a job, remember."

John left without saying good-bye, and Roxanne spent the rest of the day planning what she would do when she was dismissed from Randolph Studios. She actually took out a piece of paper and made a list of possibilities. The first word on her list was *Oklahoma*. After staring at it quite awhile she drew a line through it and wrote "Rudy's." Soon she crossed that one out, too. One by one she eliminated choices until she knew exactly what she was going to do and how she was going to do it.

The pink slip was in her pay envelope the next Friday, and when she went home, she put her plan into immediate action. "I'm finished at Randolph Studios," she announced to her mother. "They let me go, and a lot of the reason was because you were too bossy on the set."

"That's not true," Laureen said, defending herself.

"Yes, it is," Roxanne said. "And you know it. Now it's time to decide whether to go back to Oklahoma or change the way we're doing things right here in Hollywood. Which do you want?"

"Hollywood."

"I'd rather go back to Oklahoma," Roxanne lied, "but I'll keep on trying, on the condition that you agree to following my plans."

"What plans?" Laureen seemed really frightened by the news of Roxanne's dismissal and the possibility of having to go back to Oklahoma.

"It's simple," she told Laureen. "We'll both start working as extras. We can earn ten dollars a day when there's work. On the other days I can make the rounds of the studios and try to get parts while you do the housework. We'll have to let Lupita go, or would you rather move back to the Clintlocks'?"

Presented with two unhappy choices Laureen agreed to let Lupita go.

"Good," Roxanne said. "I'm sure we can get a lot of extra work now that we have all these clothes and some experience. Charlotte will probably give us all the work she can, because we took her out to dinner a couple of times to celebrate my success. Between the two of us we may be able to earn quite a bit."

"You'll never get to be a star working as an extra," Laureen protested. Roxanne noticed that Laureen didn't complain about the possibility of working in the movies herself. She was relieved about that.

"I've thought about that, too," Roxanne said. "What I need is another break, only this time I'll handle everything differently."

"You mean, you won't let me on the set."

"Yes," Roxanne said simply.

"I don't think you're being fair," Laureen complained. "It's certainly not my fault that John's movie was so depressing. I tried to help him with it."

"Ma, do you want to go back to Oklahoma?"

"It might be as much fun as sitting in this house alone all day long. I don't have anything to do but listen to soap operas. I'm tired of Ma Perkins."

"But I just told you that I expect you to work. When you can't get extra work, you can catch up on the housework." Then Roxanne decided that she might as well get all the bad news out at once. "I'm taking over the money management."

"You're a minor. . . ." Laureen began.

"But I'm better with money than you are. To put it bluntly, I don't want to end up with nothing to show for all my hard work. Clothes go out of style fast, Ma. Look at Mrs. Clintlock. Don't you think she'd rather have the cash than those fancy dresses Gus bought her twenty years ago?"

"Your father would be shocked at the way you talk to me." Laureen was crying now.

"Yes," Roxanne agreed. "I know he would. But, Ma, someone's got to have good sense in this family. Otherwise we'll both end up on the garbage heap."

"What about John?" Laureen asked, suddenly switching the subject. "Can't he make his father change his mind? Get John to make his father give you another contract?"

"John can't," Roxanne said. "His father still thinks John is a little boy, and he doesn't listen to a word he says. Anyway, after the movie preview he sent John to New York for a couple of months. It was a second birthday present, to make up for the disappointment of the first."

"I thought John was in love with you. He should have refused to go."

"Haven't you figured out by now that John does exactly what his father tells him?"

"It doesn't seem fair." Laureen pouted. "Cyril Randolph fired you because John's movie was a flop, but he gave his son an expensive trip. Does that seem fair to you?"

"No," Roxanne answered bluntly. "But you know what? I'd rather be me with all my problems than trade places with John and take on his father."

"You mean someone else has a parent who's worse than I am?" Laureen's voice was as sarcastic as she could make it, but Roxanne sensed that she was pleased by the backhanded compliment.

"Yes," Roxanne answered. "I never doubted for a minute that you love me very much. I'm not sure John ever believes it for a minute that his father loves him. That's sad, Ma. That's really sad."

"Still, I'd rather be rich," Laureen said.

Roxanne hugged her mother and laughed. "Wait and see. We will be."

Chapter Twenty

WHEN she went to Star Casting on Monday morning, Charlotte said, "Hi, Roxanne. I saw you in the movies last night."

"You did?" They hadn't wasted any time releasing the short feature.

"You looked cute in that bathing suit. Is Harry Burns fun to work with?"

"About the same as most leading men," Roxanne said. "I don't suppose you've heard, but I've left Randolph Studios. I'm looking for extra work again. But now I have a whole wardrobe of beautiful clothes and quite a bit of experience. Think you can help me?"

"Sure," Charlotte said. "In fact, I think I have a call you can answer tomorrow. MGM needs some high-class background for a shipboard romance. Calls for slinky evening gowns and jewelry. Ten dollars a day."

"Great," Roxanne said. "My mother wants

work, too. She's also got a good wardrobe."

"They don't like old people usually."

"My mother's not really old," Roxanne said. "A little plump but pretty. Thirty years old," she lied. Laureen was really thirty-five.

"How can she be thirty and be your mother?" Charlotte laughed, and then said, "Bring her tomorrow and I'll see what I can do. Dress up."

They were at Star Casting at seven in the morning, and by eight they were at the gates of MGM, waiting to be admitted to the set. The job lasted a week, and Roxanne was elated. "We earned as much together as I did at Randolph Studios."

"Can we hire Lupita back?" Laureen asked. She seemed to have accepted Roxanne's new role as money manager completely.

"No, but we can go to the movies tonight," Roxanne said. "And have a nice Chinese dinner."

The next week they only got work one day, and Roxanne was glad she hadn't let her mother talk her into spending money too quickly. She was pleased that once she started being a little thrifty, the money didn't seem to disappear overnight. On Friday night the second week after she'd left Randolph Studios, she wrote a letter to Henry and then another to John. In both of them she bragged about how well she and her mother were doing, despite the layoff. "I really think Ma likes to work," she wrote.

"She seems to feel better and be happier than ever."

But if Laureen was happy with the extra work, it was pure frustration for Roxanne, who had tasted the possibility of greater success. She watched the leading actors with a real hunger as she stood in the background, adding "color" to their work. On Monday of the third week she was called to be part of a mob scene that reminded her a bit of the mob scene in *Starlight Majesty*. She shouted and raged with the other extra players, but her emotions were real as she thought of how close she had been to proving herself in that movie.

During that mob scene she devised a new plan that seemed as though it might lead to another chance for success. Gary Marlowe had been very lucky for her in the past, and she decided he might be lucky again. It wouldn't do any harm to try to contact him again. What could she lose?

She knew he was on loan to another studio, because her mother had read her a long piece in one of her movie magazines about how studios loaned their stars at exorbitant prices but kept the money for themselves. A famous actor who was stuck in a low-paying contract at Randolph might be earning five hundred dollars a week but be on loan to Warner Brothers for a thousand or more a week. Randolph pocketed the difference.

Gary was at Berkeley Studios doing two

movies for them. Roxanne didn't know anything about the movies except that the first one was a pirate movie. She hoped Berkeley Studios would need extras sometime soon and devised a plan to make sure Charlotte sent her out on any Berkeley calls. She took her a box of chocolates and told her that she would really like to get work inside Berkeley Studios.

"I'll try," Charlotte promised. "And thanks for the candy. I love chocolate-covered caramels."

"Get me a job inside Berkeley and you'll have a washtub full," Roxanne said.

Charlotte laughed and held up her hands to stop Roxanne's promises. "No bribes. Besides, I don't need that many. They'll only make me fat. What's so special about Berkeley? You're getting plenty of work at MGM."

"Can you keep a secret?"

"Sure."

"I'm in love with someone who's working there." She knew Charlotte was very romantic and hoped that the story would spur Charlotte to action.

"Who is it? Ashley Anderson?"

When Roxanne shook her head, Charlotte guessed a long line of male stars, and Roxanne laughed as each name was mentioned.

"All those men are at least a thousand years old," she protested. "This is someone my own age or close to it."

"Then it must be real love," Charlotte pronounced.

"Maybe," Roxanne answered. "But he barely remembers me. I've got to get inside Berkeley and make him notice me again." She felt funny telling Charlotte that story, not so much because it was a lie as because there might be a little truth in it. The daydreams about Gary had stopped, but she sometimes dreamed of him at night, and she often thought about him at odd moments during the day.

A few days later, when she went to Star Casting, Charlotte greeted her with a big grin and said, "I've got a call for you, and I figured out who it is. Gary Marlowe."

Roxanne blushed, wishing she hadn't made up that story about being in love.

"Unfortunately it's not the Marlowe movie, but it is inside the gates. This one is a circus movie." Charlotte handed her the call card. "I figured out it had to be Marlowe, because he's the only star out there who's young enough. Besides, you're blushing."

"Thanks, Charlotte," Roxanne said. "I'll find some way to pay you back."

"Not chocolates," Charlotte warned. "I gained three pounds on that last box."

She was delighted to find that the call would last almost a week. That meant that she would have more than one chance to persuade Gary to give her a break in his film. She was also honest enough to admit that she was looking forward to seeing him again.

Her job as a circus extra was as boring as most of them. That morning she was supposed to walk into the circus tent, holding on to the hand of a small boy. The boy was kind of cute, and she had some fun talking with him during the breaks, but by the time lunch came, she was thoroughly bored with walking back and forth under the big tent.

"Eat lunch with us," the boy's mother offered. "I brought extra sandwiches." Because extra work was so unreliable, most extras conserved money by bringing their own lunches. Now they were settling down on the benches inside the circus tent, swapping stories about the movies they'd worked on and sharing their tuna salad sandwiches and oatmeal cookies along with their dreams.

Other extras ate outside the cafeteria on wooden benches and tables. They were allowed to buy the same food as the regular employees for the same prices but kept out of the studio cafeteria on the pretense that they were only temporary workers. The real reason was that most extras were aspiring actors. Because their ambition or desperation sometimes drove them to hounding directors or stars for attention, the studios had a policy of segregating them as much as possible.

Since that was exactly what Roxanne planned to do to Gary, she thanked her lucky stars that she'd been around studios enough to know the ropes. She stopped outside of the circus tent and asked one of the crew members, "What's the guard's name in the cafeteria? He's my mother's cousin and I'm supposed to say hello, but I've forgotten his name."

"Billy," the sweeper answered promptly.

"Thanks," Roxanne said, and soon sailed past the guard, smiling as she said, "Hi, Billy."

Gary was sitting at a table with two men and three beautiful girls. The girls were dressed in rags but made up as though they were going to a ball. Gary wore a white linen shirt with oversize sleeves. He was telling a story, and everyone was laughing as he used his hands to describe whatever it was that he was saying. As he talked his sleeves rustled through the air, making Roxanne think of angel's wings.

She smiled at her own silliness, knowing that she must be very nervous to let her mind run away with her like that. Gary Marlowe was no angel, but he might turn out to be her lucky star.

She was standing beside him before she spoke, saying, "Hi, Gary," very softly.

"Roxanne!" he said, and stood up immediately. For a minute he seemed genuinely glad to see her. "What are you doing here? Are you on loan, too?"

"I'm working here," she answered. "As an extra. Randolph dropped my contract."

"I heard John's movie was a flop," Gary said. "But I didn't know that they dropped you."

Roxanne tried to smile. "It wasn't just John's film. It was getting cut out of your movie and not knowing how to get along with the bosses. I'm older and more professional now, and my mother . . ." Roxanne hesitated, torn between treating Gary like an old friend and confiding in him, and keeping their conversation strictly business. Whenever she was close to Gary, she was confused. "Mother's working as an extra now, too."

Gary threw back his head and roared with laughter. "That's wonderful. Who thought of that? John?"

"I was the one who suggested it," Roxanne said stiffly. She hated it when Gary laughed at her, and she hated having to ask him for favors. "She seems to enjoy the work."

"Your mother's probably as good an actress as mine is," Gary said. "Maybe she'll make it to the top."

Roxanne was determined to ignore his sarcasm. She plunged in, "It's hard to make it anywhere if you're stuck as an extra. That's what I wanted to talk to you about."

"I'll see what I can do," Gary promised before she actually asked him for a favor. "If I hear of anything, I'll let John know."

"John's in New York City. He won't be back until school starts."

Gary raised one eyebrow and said softly, "Poor Roxanne. John gets a trip to the big city and you get fired. Life's not fair, is it?"

"Don't make fun of me," Roxanne snapped. "You've no right to be rude."

"Is this your new professional attitude?" Gary teased. "I said I'd see what I can do."

"Thank you, Gary. I'd appreciate that."

Roxanne went back to her job as an extra with mixed feelings. It was hard to know if Gary would really try to help her or not. It was easy enough for him to say he would see what he could do, but she wasn't sure he meant it. Sometimes Hollywood people made promises but didn't keep them. It was called the soft no, and Gary might have been turning her down politely by promising so quickly. As the afternoon wore on her doubts grew. After all, Gary was a big star and he was always surrounded by beautiful starlets. What would he want to bother with her for? He had probably forgotten about her by the time he finished his dessert.

She decided she couldn't make Gary help her, but she could make sure he didn't forget about her. She was back the next day at lunchtime to ask him if he'd made any progress. This time he was sitting with only one beautiful girl, and he stood up immediately, then carefully introduced Roxanne. He invited her to join them. The starlet frowned at the thought and looked relieved when Roxanne declined, asking, "Did anything turn up?"

Gary smiled and patted her arm. "You know what I admire about you? Your determination. With determination like that you're bound to make it."

"You said once that I had talent," Roxanne reminded him.

Gary laughed. "If you don't make it in

Hollywood, you could always try selling Fuller brushes door-to-door. Put that pretty little foot inside the door and push."

"I don't mind if you insult me, if you really intend to help," Roxanne said. "Go ahead and have fun. But the question is whether you really plan to help me."

"I said I'd try. Now sit down and eat with us or leave, because I'm tired of standing up while my dinner gets cold."

Roxanne whirled around and left them, telling herself that she'd never speak to Gary Marlowe again as long as she lived. But the next day she was back at his table. This time he was sitting alone and took her by the wrist and said, "Now sit down and eat. You'll get too skinny, skipping lunches like this. What will you have? The roast duck?"

"A cheese sandwich and a cherry Coke."

"I'm buying."

"A cheese sandwich and a cherry Coke."

Gary shook his head. "You're a funny girl, Roxanne. You ask me for a favor and then you act mad when I want to buy you lunch. Does that make any kind of sense?"

"It's because you make fun of me," Roxanne said simply.

"Do I?" Gary asked. "I'm sorry. I really kind of like you and your funny mother, you know. I find you . . . refreshing."

"That's exactly what I mean. You talk as though you were on a mountaintop and I were way down at the bottom looking up."

"I'll admit there is a distance between us,

but it's not like that," Gary said. "You don't know me as well as you think."

"I know you're arrogant and rude."

"Then why did you ask me for help?"

"You were the only person I knew . . ." Roxanne began. Then she stopped because he looked hurt and it wasn't true. "I think you might be lucky for me," she said in a softer voice. "I mean, you were the first Hollywood person I met and then I was in your picture."

"You're superstitious?" Gary shook his head. "You amaze me, Roxanne. I thought you were as levelheaded as anyone I'd ever met."

"I am," she said. "Sort of."

"Well, I hope I'm lucky for you," Gary said. "And I am really trying to get you work, you know."

"Thank you," Roxanne answered.

"No thanks in order," Gary answered. "After all, John's one of my best friends. Besides, I said I was trying. That's all I can do."

"I'm on the circus set," Roxanne said. "I'll be there all day tomorrow."

"Yes, ma'am," Gary said. "I'll make a note of it. Now eat your sandwich."

The call came about three on Friday. A young man walked up to her and asked, "You Roxanne Wilson?"

"Yes."

"Follow me."

Roxanne followed him all the way across

the huge Berkeley lot to a sound set at the opposite edge of the five-acre grounds. By the time she got there she was hot and sweaty because the July sun was hot. She wished she had time to stop and comb her hair and put on fresh makeup before approaching this unknown situation, but the young man indicated that everyone was waiting.

When she went in, Gary said, "This is Roxanne Wilson. The girl I told you about."

About twenty men and women stared at Roxanne without any expression on their faces at all. Roxanne felt an almost irresistible impulse to make faces or stick her tongue out at them. Recognizing the signs of nervous strain, she worked to keep her smile easy and her posture relaxed. Finally an older man with a beard shrugged and said, "If you want her, you can have her."

"I want her, Sam." Gary's eyes were looking straight at Roxanne as he pronounced the words.

To her dismay she blushed beet-red, but no one was looking at her anymore. They had all turned back to their other concerns, and only a short, harried-looking woman in a plain brown dress was paying any attention to her. She wrote Roxanne's name on a clipboard and asked, "How much are we paying you?"

"I don't know."

The woman turned to the man with the beard and asked, "Sam, how much are we paying Wilson?"

"Hundred and fifty a week," he answered.

"Make it five," Gary interrupted.

"Five? We could get Paulette Goddard for that."

"But Roxanne Wilson is closer to my age. You said the only problem with my last movie was that the co-star looked too old."

"If she's young, she should come cheap," Sam grumbled.

"Five hundred a week is the going rate, you know that."

"Okay," Sam said. "But she'd better be good." Then he turned to Roxanne and said, "Have them give you the script tonight. I want all those lines memorized when you get here Monday morning."

"Oh, yes," Roxanne said. The words were really all she could manage. Her brain was having trouble assimilating the fact that she'd somehow been hired to be in Gary Marlowe's movie. She wanted to thank Gary, but he had already turned away and was in the middle of a conference on the other side of the lot. She waited around as long as she dared, trying to catch his eye, but he never looked in her direction again. Finally she went back to the circus set to finish out her day as an extra. Next week she would be a potential star.

Chapter Twenty-one

THIS time everything was going to be different, Roxanne promised herself. In the first place her part was too big to be cut out totally. It wasn't really a co-starring role since most of the movie took place on a pirate ship, but she was in the beginning and the last thirty minutes of the movie. That was certainly too much to cut.

One other reason why this movie would be different, Roxanne told herself, was that her mother was busy working as an extra at MGM. They had finally begun filming *Gone with the Wind*, and Laureen had a bit part as one of the wives on a neighboring plantation. With any luck she'd be busy the whole time that Roxanne was working with Gary on *Spanish Treasure*.

There were other ways that Roxanne was determined that this time would be different.

When she reported to hairdressing, she insisted on watching as they dressed her hair. The minute the stylist began to part it down the middle, Roxanne said, "I look much better with my hair parted on the side."

"You have a perfectly oval face. It should be parted in the middle," the hairdresser said. He made a straight line exactly in the center of her scalp with the tip of his rat-tail comb.

"That's what my mother always said," Roxanne said in a pleasant voice. "But if you try parting it on the side, you'll see that I photograph better."

When the hairdresser hesitated for a second, Roxanne added, "I'm sure that's what Sam Barlow wants. When he hired me, my hair was parted on the side."

"Everyone knows my business," the hairdresser said, but he moved the tip of the comb to the side and began to part her hair in a diagonal line.

When he was finished, Roxanne thanked him several times, making him think it had been his idea in the first place. She was just as definite and tactful when she consulted with the costumer about her gown. The woman insisted that she wear the pale pink satin that had been prepared for the original co-star.

"I'm sure pink was perfect for her," Roxanne said. "She was a lovely brunette. But don't you think my fair skin will show up better in a darker color?"

"Don't know why they make these last-minute changes anyhow," the costumer grumbled. "We plan weeks in advance, and then they change their minds at the last minute."

"She couldn't get away from her other commitments," Roxanne said as she thumbed through the stock costumes on the rack. It was her mother who'd told her that the original co-star was replaced because of a feud between two studios. When Berkeley refused to release one of their beautiful stars for a big musical comedy that MGM was making, MGM withdrew their offer to release Gary's original co-star.

"Studio politics," the costumer grumbled. "They mess everything up."

"And sometimes they straighten things out," Roxanne said. She was hoping the latter possibility applied to her career. She stopped her looking and asked, "Is that your daughter in that photograph? She looks just like you."

"My granddaughter," the woman said. Her face was now smiling as she picked up the photograph and handed it to Roxanne.

"She smiles just like Shirley Temple, doesn't she?" Roxanne asked. "Is she in the movies?"

"She's done some extra work," the woman admitted proudly.

"That's how I got my start," Roxanne said. "My mother's an extra on the *Gone with the Wind* set right now."

"Really? Is it true they finally picked an English girl for Scarlett?"

"Vivien Leigh," Roxanne answered. "Ma says a lot of people are really angry about the choice. They made a three-year talent search in this country and then picked a foreign girl. Are there any dark-blue dresses? I know the movie's not in Technicolor, but a deep blue always photographs well."

Within a few minutes Roxanne was dressed in a beautiful dark-blue velvet gown with a low-cut neckline, puffed sleeves, and wide hoop skirt. She was very pleased with the way she looked and walked back to the hairdresser's trailer just to show him the effect of his careful work in combination with the costume. By the time she walked onto the set, she'd made friends with both the hairdresser and the costumer, and she felt that she'd never looked better in her life.

No one seemed to notice her when she got on the set, because they were all so busy setting up for the next scene. But when Sam Barlowe did acknowledge her, he smiled briefly, and that smile told Roxanne that he was pleased by her appearance. She could only hope that her acting pleased him as well.

The first scene was fairly simple because all she had to do was stand beside her uncle, the Spanish governor, and look interested as he and Gary talked about politics. During that scene she had to manage to smile and look interested in Gary, too, but keep her eyes downcast like a good Spanish *señorita*. They wrote in a new line for her to explain her light-colored skin and hair. When Gary was introduced to her, he said, "You don't look Spanish, *señorita*."

"My mother was English," she replied. Then she waved a beautiful lace fan and covered the lower half of her face. She lifted her eyes and looked seductively at him for one second, then lowered them. She thought the whole scene was kind of silly, but she did her best to play it seriously. Either the director thought she did it well or he didn't think it was important enough to bother with because he gave her no instructions at all. The first time she got a chance, she tried to thank Gary for getting her this part. While the director was giving directions to the cameraman she whispered to Gary, "I tried to call your house to thank you, but the butler said you were gone for the weekend."

"Palm Springs," Gary said. "I go there whenever I can."

"I was in the desert once," Roxanne said wistfully. "It was beautiful."

"So are you," Gary whispered back.

His compliment made her glow and made up for the fact that he ignored her the rest of the morning. They filmed her one scene in about an hour and a half, and she had the rest of the day free. She spent her free time carefully watching the other actors and learning as much as she could. She also spent some time getting to know each of the crew members and learning to call them by name.

When Gary didn't invite her to lunch, Roxanne told herself not to be disappointed, that he'd done what she'd asked of him. But she had to admit that she felt left out and lonely when he went off with two pretty starlets and the assistant director, who was also very young. Roxanne ate with the crew, partly because she was too shy to go to the commissary alone and partly because she wanted to learn as much about moviemaking as possible.

The head cameraman was happy to show her all his equipment and explain some of the basics of his art to her. "It's all in the use of lights," he said. "Got to keep those lights tilted at just the right angle to catch the best aspects of the faces. Close-ups are crucial. Take your face, for instance. You're young and your face needs definition. I use low lighting to bring out the cheekbones. When you get older, you'll need that less but you may need other special touches."

She learned a lot while she was working on *Spanish Treasure*, and she had a very good time. Everyone was nice to her, and without her mother on the set, she felt much freer to make friends. Her only disappointment was how little attention Gary paid to her.

But as she watched him work she understood that most of the time he was too involved in making the movie to worry about anything else. Even though he was usually surrounded by beautiful girls, his attention seemed to be totally on his work. He gave every scene his all and obeyed directions instantly. He also watched every detail, pointing out very politely those things that might make a difference in the final result.

The crew seemed to like him and admire the way he worked. More than once Roxanne heard someone say he was a lot like his parents. By the time she'd worked on the set a week, she understood that in the Marlowe family were some of the best-liked actors in Hollywood, and she came to believe that Gary was doing everything he could to follow in their footsteps.

She admired his professionalism and tried to imitate it. It was the days when he went to lunch with friends and never even thought to include her that really hurt. She wished it didn't bother her but it did. Once in a while he asked her if John was back yet, and except for that, they exchanged no personal words.

They worked well together, though. On the set Gary Marlowe was all business and so was Roxanne. She was pleased when the costumer told her she was developing a reputation as being an excellent actress. "They're saying you're a real winner," the costumer confided. "I heard the rushes are terrific."

"Thanks, Annie, it's nice to hear."

"You mark my words, you'll be a big star."

"I hope you're right," Roxanne said, and she dared to believe that it might be true. She'd noticed a difference in the way Sam Barlow and the others were treating her after the first week. Now she could assume it was because they liked what they saw on the screen.

In the last scene of the movie Gary was supposed to rescue her from his own pirates and carry her back to her uncle's ship. It called for some strenuous athletics on Gary's part, since he had to swing her into his arms and walk across a narrow plank with her kicking and screaming in his arms.

She reported to work very early the morning they were to film that scene, just because she was so nervous. To her surprise she found Gary already there. "Hi," she said. "You worried about that plank, too?"

"I always worry," Gary admitted.

That was one of the most confusing things about him. Most of the time he was distant and formal with her, and then suddenly he would let his guard down and she'd feel as though she were talking to an old friend. "By the time you carry me across that thing a few times, you'll wish you'd never bought me lunch," she said. "Maybe you should have picked a smaller girl."

"You're the right size," he said. Then he smiled and said, "Have they shown you the rushes?"

"No."

"Then you've got a treat in store for you. You look great."

"I'm glad. You risked a lot by getting me this part. And I *am* grateful."

"Just tell John he owes me one," Gary said lightly. Then he stepped onto the plank and jumped up and down, testing its strength. "I always get to the set early and check everything out," he said. "Don't like any surprises when I'm working."

"You're the most professional actor I've ever seen," Roxanne said. "You work harder than anyone else."

She meant it as a compliment, but Gary obviously heard it as criticism. "If you were a Marlowe, you'd understand why I have to," Gary said. "What if I were the first Marlowe to be a bad actor?"

"I suppose it does add an extra risk," Roxanne said.

"But you're also thinking that it gave me a great start," Gary said. "That's what everyone thinks, but I'm not so sure it isn't doing it the hard way. There are a million fans out there just waiting for me to fall on my face." He raised his voice to a mocking high pitch. "There's the little Marlowe boy."

Roxanne laughed and shook her head. "You sound so sorry for yourself. How much fun do you think it is to break in the hard way? Instead of being angry about being the son of a famous acting family, you ought to be grateful."

"Let's not fight again, Roxanne." Gary's voice told her he was very angry. "Let's just get this scene done and wrap up the movie like professionals. Shall we?"

"And then we never have to work together again, right?" Why did she always lose her control when she tried to talk to him?

The others were coming in now, so even if he'd wanted to answer her, he would have restrained himself. Roxanne went to get into her costume without another word. If Gary wanted a professional relationship, that was what they would have. She was back on the set and ready to go in thirty minutes.

Most of the morning was spent just standing around waiting for them to adjust the cameras and lighting. They started filming at about eleven, and Roxanne was really nervous about having Gary lift her and carry her in his arms. The first time he almost stumbled, and the second time, Sam Barlowe yelled, "You both look as stiff as boards. You're supposed to be in love, remember. Make it a love spat, not an armed truce. Roxanne, show your legs when you kick."

By the time the noon break came, Gary had carried her across the plank eleven times, and Barlowe still wasn't satisfied. "You two loosen up a little bit," he growled. "You still look scared to death of each other. I want excitement between you, and I know you can give it to me. Now go eat and be back here in forty minutes."

"Eat lightly," Gary warned, and then he winked at her.

Roxanne giggled at his joke. Even though she was still mad at him for the way he'd dismissed her attempts at friendship this morning, his joke cheered her up. She was still smiling as she ordered a cup of tea and half of a cheese sandwich for lunch. What she ate wouldn't really make that much difference to Gary, but it would be easier for her to kick and scream on an empty stomach.

They reported back to the set on time, and Sam Barlow's only instructions were, "Electricity. That's what I want."

This time Roxanne slipped her arm a little tighter around Gary's neck and snuggled in closer to his broad, muscular chest. She could feel his heart beating beneath the soft linen shirt, and she could feel her body grow warm from the heat of his exertions. "Action," Sam called through his megaphone.

Roxanne kicked higher and held on tighter than before. Gary held her closer and marched swiftly across the plank. Two overhead cameras followed their movements, and Sam Barlow seemed a lot more pleased with their efforts. "Fine," he said. "Now we'll do it a couple of more times just like that for close-ups."

They went through the whole thing several more times, "Just for insurance," Barlow said. By the end of the day Roxanne felt as though she must be as heavy as a ton of bricks for Gary.

"One more time," Barlow said, and Gary groaned.

"Professional," Roxanne whispered in his ear.

She saw his jaw muscle tighten and then release, and she felt him sweep her into his arms once again.

"This time I want you to kiss her," Barlow commanded.

"That's not in the script," Gary objected.

"It is now," Barlow said.

"But I thought this was a kid's movie. Heroes never kiss the girl in kids' movies."

"Kiss her!" Barlow roared. "Action."

Roxanne was so angry at Gary's refusal to kiss her that she kicked and screamed for real. But when he let her slide to the ground and kept his arms around her, drawing her close for the kiss, she felt her anger dissolve into a stronger emotion. Once again she responded fiercely to Gary's kiss. This time she felt as though she might melt into his arms, she wanted to kiss him so much.

"Cut," Barlow called, and they broke apart as though they were in a daze.

Gary stared at her and then turned abruptly and walked away. Roxanne looked after him with tears in her eyes. Why did every encounter with Gary seem to end in disaster?

Chapter
Twenty-two

THREE days after *Spanish Treasure* was
finished Roxanne got a call from Bertram at
Randolph Studios asking her to come in for
a conference. She wore her new aquamarine
dress with polka-dot gloves and a deeper
turquoise straw hat with a matching polka-
dot bow. Being dressed so stylishly gave her
the confidence she needed to face Bertram
once again.

Since her shoes were very high-heeled and
it was a hot day, she took a taxi to the studio.
She felt foolish stepping out of the taxi after
only a five-block drive and tipped the driver
extravagantly. As she gave him the money,
he asked, "Are you famous?"

"Not yet," Roxanne said, "but I'm hoping
for the best."

She was still smiling as she walked into
the reception room and asked for Bertram.

The beautiful young woman at the desk said, "Oh, yes, Miss Wilson. He'll be right here."

Thirty-five minutes later Bertram came over to her and said, "Roxanne, I'm glad to see you again. Hope I didn't keep you waiting."

Roxanne couldn't figure out what an appropriate answer might be, so she kept silent. She was nervous and off-guard and knew that the long wait was intended to accomplish exactly that feeling. Though she'd sailed through the door with polka-dot confidence, she felt like the timid little girl who'd started at Randolph Studios six months ago, after her long, anxious wait.

She followed Bertram down the long hall and into his office. He sat behind a huge mahogany desk and smiled at her, as though he were waiting for her to begin. His leather-bound books and two golden Academy Awards on the wall behind him made her extremely nervous. Sometimes, when she was in an impressive environment like this office, she had the strangest feeling that she might wake up and find she was back in high school in Oklahoma.

"What did you want to see me about?" she asked. She tried to control the level of her voice and the dryness in her throat.

"We're thinking of giving you another chance," Bertram said. He smiled pleasantly and said, "I've persuaded Mr. Randolph that you didn't really get a fair shake here at the studio, and we are thinking of offering you another contract with a few conditions."

"Conditions?"

"Now that you're older, there's no real need for your mother to be on the set, is there?"

"My mother is working herself." Roxanne breathed a sigh of relief. If Laureen was the only problem, then there was no problem.

"The other condition is really a standard aspect of an actress's contract. You understand that the studio has a real interest in the personal life of an employee and that no hint of scandal can reach the press."

"There's no scandal in my life." Roxanne was genuinely puzzled by what he was saying.

"As your employer," Bertram said, riding right over her objection, "we have a real interest in who you see, who you date. Mr. Randolph is very concerned about your friendship with his son. Mr. Randolph is prepared to offer you a contract with all the original terms. He'll even throw in the limousine your mother wanted if you'll agree to stop seeing his son."

"Why doesn't he just tell *John* to stop seeing *me*?" Roxanne was pressing her fingertips together to relieve the tension she was feeling. The gesture would be invisible to Bertram and help her control her emotions. She'd learned that trick from an older actress on the set of *Spanish Treasure*, and she was grateful for the many acting skills she'd picked up in the last six months. She didn't want to lose any small advantage she might have in the negotiation.

"Mr. Randolph felt it would be better to speak to you about the matter than approaching John. He wants to make sure that you understand that you must break off the relationship without letting John know that his father had anything to do with it."

"Why doesn't he want me to be friends with John?" Roxanne asked. "What if I promised Mr. Randolph that I wasn't seriously interested in him. That it really is a friendship, not love."

"The point is that he wants the friendship broken off," Bertram said. "I don't think it's personal, Roxanne. I think it's that he fears any influence that may dissuade John from his chosen career as a lawyer."

"John hasn't chosen to be a lawyer," Roxanne snapped. "His father chose it for him."

"Mr. Randolph is prepared to offer you the same terms as you had before. In addition, he will offer you a limousine and promise you at least two movies this year. Mr. Randolph wants an immediate answer."

Roxanne sighed and stood up. "There's only one answer to give."

"Then you'll accept the terms?" Bertram stood up and held his hand out to her.

"Of course not!" Roxanne answered. "Did you really think I'd trade John's friendship for a contract?"

Bertram seemed stunned by her answer. He sat back down and then said in a different, softer voice, "Roxanne, John will have to solve his own problems with his father eventually. Do you know what you're throwing away?"

"I know what I'm not throwing away," she answered. "John is the only person in this town who's treated me decently. I'm not throwing away his friendship."

"I must warn you that marrying John won't solve anything. Mr. Randolph will disinherit him and see that you never work in Hollywood again."

"You sound like one of your corny movies," Roxanne answered. She knew she'd totally lost control of herself again, but at the moment, she just didn't care. "I don't want to marry John, and I don't think Ruthless Randolph can stop me from working. I just wonder why a talented director like you would do his dirty work. Why don't you take a good look at yourself, Bertram?"

She stamped out of his office before she had a chance to change her mind. Turning her back on another chance at success hurt a lot, and by the time she was out the door and walking toward her little pink bungalow, she was wondering if she'd made a mistake. Had there been some other way to handle things so she wouldn't lose as much?

Her mother thought so. She listened to Roxanne's recounting of her interview with Bertram and shook her head sorrowfully. "I should have gone with you. An older person could have handled him better."

"Ma, you have a worse temper than I do. The first time he hinted that there was anything wrong with my reputation, you would have hit him over the head with one of his little golden Academy Awards."

"Maybe you could pretend to accept the offer and let me explain things to John. He'll understand that your career comes first."

"He'd pick a fight with his father and I'd lose, anyway."

"You could just drop John, and when things settle down, you could be friends again."

"Ma, John has been the best friend we've had in this town. You don't really want me to do that, do you?"

"You say yourself that you're not in love with him."

"But I like him," Roxanne said. Then she said, "Know what? I'm really thinking about packing up and going back to Oklahoma."

She went over to her mother and knelt beside her, putting her head on her mother's lap. Then she lifted her head and said, "How about it, Ma? We could go home tomorrow as winners. I've been in the movies, and we have almost two thousand dollars in the bank. We could buy a little restaurant in Norman."

"Over my dead body."

"I'm tired, Ma. It seems like everything I do goes wrong. It's a tough town, just like everyone says."

"I'm not going back to Oklahoma," Laureen said. "I don't even like to think about it.

That boy's voice gave me the shivers, when I heard that twang, I just felt —"

"What boy, Ma? Did Henry call?"

"Yes."

"When? Is he all right? Why did he call long distance? Is something wrong?"

"It wasn't long distance," Laureen admitted. "He's right here in Hollywood."

"When, Ma? How long has he been here?" Roxanne was as angry with her mother as she'd ever been. How could her mother keep such important news from her?

"Two days," Laureen admitted. "I told him you couldn't be disturbed because you had a big appointment. I told him you were dating John Randolph, too."

"Ma!" She was standing over her mother now, and she said in a quiet, serious voice, "Don't you see what you've done? You're just as bad as Cyril Randolph. I have a right to decide whether or not I want to see Henry. Where is he?"

"I don't want you to see that boy, Roxanne. I forbid it."

"Ma, if you don't tell me where he is, I'll never speak to you again, and I mean it."

Laureen answered quickly, "Normont Hotel. He's only going to be here another two days. His uncle Henry is here on business."

"And you thought you would stall him so long that I couldn't see him." Roxanne went to the telephone, pausing before she dialed to say, "Ma, I'm really angry about this."

Laureen was crying as she said, "I was going to tell you eventually." Roxanne ignored her and dialed quickly. When she got Henry on the telephone and began to make arrangements to meet him, her mother got up and went to her room.

They agreed that Henry would pick her up in half an hour, and Roxanne raced into the bathroom to take a bath, fix her hair and makeup, and get dressed. In exactly twenty-seven minutes she was sitting quietly in the living room with her hands folded on her lap. She was wearing a soft blue crepe dress cut in a princess style. There were tiny covered buttons all the way down the front, and the sleeves were short and slightly puffed. The collar was made of the finest Belgian lace, which had been dyed to the exact shade of the dress.

Roxanne knew she looked her very best, and she was pleased with every detail of her costume. Her shoes were soft, gray suede pumps and her small purse matched exactly. She didn't need a coat, but California evenings were sometimes cool even in August, so she had a soft gray cashmere cardigan draped across the back of the couch. She would carry it just in case.

Henry pressed the bell with three short, nervous rings, and Roxanne almost ran to the door. She threw her arms around him and hugged him, saying, "Henry, I missed you so much."

His arms circled her shoulders, and he held

her tightly for a moment, burying his face in her soft blonde hair. Then he whispered, "I missed you, too, Roxanne. That's why I made Uncle Henry let me come with him. Come with me, Roxanne. Marry me."

She laughed and took his hand, saying, "Not so fast. I want to hear all the news and show you my little house. Do you think pink is a pretty color for a bungalow?"

"Houses shouldn't be pink," Henry said. "We can get married on the train trip home. I checked it out and we can get off overnight in Nevada or Arizona. There's no wait in those states."

"Come look around. Let me show you our kitchen. It has Mexican tile. We had a Mexican maid for a while, but we don't right now. But I have money in the bank, Henry. Over two thousand dollars. That's about what it would cost to buy this house."

"I saw you in the movies," Henry said. "In the Bijou. Some of the kids told me you were there and I went to see you. I was ashamed, Roxanne. You took your clothes off in front of all those people."

Roxanne laughed. "Henry, you sound like an old fuddy-duddy. I had to wear that bathing suit or get fired. It doesn't matter, anyway. Everyone wears bathing suits in California."

"Not in Oklahoma," Henry said. "I was afraid Uncle Henry would find out about it. He wouldn't give you a job if he knew you appeared in public like that."

"I don't need your Uncle Henry's job," Roxanne answered. "I could *buy* a restaurant if I wanted to."

Henry stopped and looked at her in dismay. He said, "You've changed a lot, Roxanne. Your hair is different."

"It's parted on the side, that's all."

"I liked it with the little bows."

"Little bows are old-fashioned," Roxanne said. "Anyway, I thought you loved me, not my hair bows."

"You've changed in other ways. You never used to talk so sharp. And who's this John your mother told me about?"

"He's a friend. You mustn't pay any attention to Ma."

"I don't. She's the one who talked you into this foolishness in the first place. But you know something, Roxanne? Your letters are beginning to sound as foolish as she does."

Roxanne took his hand again and leaned her head on his shoulder. "Let's not quarrel, Henry. I'm so glad to see you. Tell me about school. Did Alice get to be prom queen?"

"I wrote you that in my letters."

"Yes, of course, you did. Now, where are you taking me to supper?"

"I thought some place close. But you're all dressed up." Henry sounded as though he were accusing her of some wrong.

"I got dressed up so you'd tell me I was pretty," Roxanne teased. "Not so you'd tell me I had a sharp tongue."

"You are pretty. Marry me, Roxanne, and come home."

"There's a good Chinese restaurant about six blocks from here. I'll bet you've never had Chinese food. Ma and I love it. We could walk down Hollywood Boulevard. Maybe we could go see Graumann's Chinese Theater after that. Wouldn't that be fun?" Roxanne realized that she was "managing" Henry the way she sometimes had to manage her mother. It made her feel sad and also showed her that she was a whole lot older and wiser than she'd been when she last saw Henry. She smiled at him and took his arm. "Come on, Henry. We'll have some fun and talk seriously later."

Henry allowed himself to be led to the Chinese restaurant and tried a little bit of each of the dishes that Roxanne ordered. He liked the cooked vegetable dishes fairly well but turned down more than one bite of the sweet and sour pork and fried shrimp. "These are the best things," Roxanne chided him as she helped herself to his share.

"Meat shouldn't be cooked in sweet stuff, and I don't like fish."

"Shrimp isn't fish," Roxanne argued. "But I'll bet you'd like the fish here in California. They take it right off the boats and deliver it to the restaurants. Best fish in the world."

"Sounds like you spend a lot of money on restaurants these days."

"Some," Roxanne admitted. Why did every question Henry ask her make her feel so guilty? It occurred to her that Laureen probably felt that way lots of times when she had chided her about money. Mentally Roxanne made herself a promise to worry less about money and start enjoying life more. Her mother would be pleasantly surprised at the outcome of this evening with Henry.

"What are you laughing at?" Henry asked.

"I was just enjoying myself," Roxanne said. "I am so glad to see you, Henry, I really am. Is the corn real tall on your place now?"

"Drought's still there," Henry admitted. "Corn isn't as tall as it should be this time of year. But things are pretty, just the same."

"Have you decided where you're going to college?"

"I thought we'd get married," Henry said. "I thought I'd come get you and bring you home. I guess I was crazy, but when I saw you standing there on that big screen in that bathing suit, I just knew this wasn't any place for you."

"I felt silly in that feature," Roxanne admitted. "Not because of the bathing suit so much as they made me look so foolish. And I didn't get a chance to act. But I've got a real picture coming out, and you'll be proud of me in that one. You'll see."

When Henry looked unconvinced, Roxanne stood up, saying, "Let's go to the movies now. There's a good show at Graumann's Chinese, and I want to show you the stars' footprints in the cement."

They walked to the theater, holding hands

but not talking much. Henry was obviously not impressed by the fancy Oriental architecture of the theater. Instead of praising the red tile roofs and golden trim, he said, "Big waste of money here. People hungry and they spend money on this foolishness."

"It was built in the twenties." Roxanne didn't know why she was so defensive about everything he criticized. Only a few hours ago she'd been talking about what a terrible town it was and how she wanted to move back to Oklahoma. But now that she was actually beside Henry, she knew that was not what she wanted at all.

"Come over here and let me show you the footprints," she said. She led Henry to the famous sidewalk and pointed out some of the stars' prints. "That's Norma Shearer's there. And the little ones belong to Shirley Temple."

"Looking for a soft spot in the cement?" a deep, rich baritone asked.

"Gary?" Roxanne couldn't see him, but she would know his voice anywhere.

Gary stepped out from behind the freestanding wall that held the coming attractions posters. He was wearing a dark felt hat that was pulled down over his eyes and a funny tweed coat that turned up around his neck. He also had on little round glasses and a fake mustache.

Roxanne began to laugh and asked, "Are you going to a costume party?"

"Just to the movies," Gary admitted. "My

folks are already inside. It's funny to run into you. I was going to call you tomorrow. Maybe we are linked together by fate."

"This is my friend, Henry, from Oklahoma."

Gary shook Henry's hand and was charming, but his expression was one of amusement. "Forgive the disguise," he explained, "but I wanted to avoid being mobbed by fans."

"It must be terrible to be so famous," Roxanne said, not letting the sarcasm show in her voice. "I don't see any mobs around."

"You'll see what it's like pretty soon," Gary predicted. "Have you heard from John recently?"

Why did everything Gary say make her so uncomfortable? Now he was insinuating that she should feel guilty about going out with Henry while John was away. She was also uncomfortably aware of the fact that Henry's sleeves were a little too short and that his hair was parted in the middle. Middle parts were definitely out of style for men. Then she reminded herself that she didn't care what Gary thought about her friends or anything else. Their last words together had been a quarrel and soon they would be in another one. "We've got to go in," she said.

"Enjoy the movie," Gary said. Then he asked, "Isn't John coming home this week?"

"Next week."

"I hope he's been having a good time in New York," Gary said.

"So do I," Roxanne said sweetly. She

wasn't going to fall into Gary's trap tonight. She knew he was deliberately trying to bait her.

The movie was wonderful, and Roxanne watched in absolute fascination as she saw Gary's mother and father play against each other with perfect timing and tone. She loved the plot of the light, sophisticated work, and she loved watching the couple on the screen.

On the way out of the theater Gary introduced her to his folks, and she conquered her shyness enough to tell them what she thought. She ended with, "I would love to do that sort of thing. Sophisticated comedy, I mean."

Ruth Marlowe raised one eyebrow in the same quizzical expression that Gary used so often. She said, "You're a little young at the moment, but you'll get older." Then she made a small face and added, "Unfortunately."

"You look wonderful," Roxanne said sincerely. "It's hard to believe you're Gary's mother."

Ruth Marlowe beamed and she said to Gary, "You told me she was a good actress, but she's also a lovely girl."

"Or a *very* good actress," Gary said, but when he saw Roxanne's hurt expression, he added, "I told them how great you look in *Spanish Treasure*. In fact, Mother was going to call you in the next day or two with an invitation. How would you and John like to come to our Santa Barbara house for the weekend?"

248

"What?"

"Come alone if John can't manage it," Ruth Marlowe added. "We like to have Gary's friends visit."

"Next weekend?" Gary repeated. "Will you come?"

"Yes." Roxanne was so stunned by the invitation that she left almost immediately after that. On the walk home her mind raced over all the possible reasons why the Marlowes would invite her to their fabulous Santa Barbara house, but she couldn't come up with any good ones. The puzzle was simply too much for her.

"So you're not coming back to Oklahoma?" Henry asked.

"What?" she had almost forgotten that Henry was walking beside her.

"You're not coming back to Oklahoma?" he repeated.

"No. I'm staying in Hollywood as long as there's any chance I can make it. I'm sorry, Henry. Really."

"Don't you love me at all?"

"I do love you, Henry. At least I think I do, but I want this so much. You'll just have to forget about me and find some nice girl. What about Alice? She was always crazy about you."

"What if I can't forget about you?" Henry asked.

"You will," Roxanne promised. "You'll see."

"I'll wait," Henry said. "Another six

months and maybe you'll change your mind."

"Don't wait for me," Roxanne warned. She felt it was only fair to tell him that there was no real chance that she would leave Hollywood anytime soon. She could tell by her excitement about the Marlowes' invitation that she hadn't given up hoping for the very best. "I've got time to work on my career," Roxanne said. "I'm young. Most girls don't even start till they're seventeen or eighteen and I'm just sixteen. I've still got a head start."

"Head start on foolishness," Henry said.

Roxanne leaned her head on his shoulder and said, "Henry, don't be mad at me. I can't helping wanting what I want."

"I'm not really mad." Henry suddenly softened and pulled her close to him. He kissed her cheek, then whispered, "I missed you so much. I wanted you to come with me, Roxanne, but if you won't, I'll find some other way."

He kissed her then, pressing his lips on hers, demanding that she return his love. Roxanne tried to respond, but her head was swimming with other feelings, and she knew that she was thinking more about Gary than Henry, even at this tender moment.

Chapter
Twenty-three

JOHN came home in time to accept the Marlowes' invitation, and they drove up the coast together in his little yellow car. As they left Ventura and headed into the last leg of the journey toward Santa Barbara, he said, "Gary said your Oklahoma boyfriend was visiting while I was gone."

"Yes, I'm sorry you missed him."

"I am, too. I'd like to size up the competition."

"John, the real competition is my career."

"I can wait," John said. "I've still got another year of college and then I'll have to get a job."

"What about law school?"

"Out of the question," John answered. "I gave the whole thing some serious thought while I was in New York. Talked to some friends of my dad's. Talked to a couple of people who weren't really his friends. I can get a job in the theater, Roxanne. Then, when I make a name for myself, I can come back to the movies."

"Your father really hates the idea of your being in the movies," Roxanne said. She considered telling him about her offer from Bertram but decided it would just make more trouble.

"Yes," John said. "But he can't stop me. I'm a lot like my father in some ways. At least I think I could be if I ever got over being scared of him."

"I'm a lot like my mother, too," Roxanne said. "After Henry came to visit I did some serious thinking. I've been blaming her for our being here, and every time something went wrong, I said I wanted to go back to Oklahoma. But it isn't true. I love Hollywood but I get scared. I'm scared today."

"Scared? What of?"

"Of this invitation. Of meeting the Marlowes socially. Or feeling like a little girl from the sticks in their fancy house. Just scared. You'd never understand."

"You still think I'm a spoiled little rich kid who's incapable of understanding anyone who wasn't born with a silver spoon in his mouth?"

Roxanne laughed. "Sort of," she admitted. "I don't think you're spoiled exactly, I just think it's hard to understand some things if you've grown up the way you and Gary have."

"What things?"

"The Depression. Drought, for instance. I don't think you have any idea how not having any water changed the lives of people in the Midwest."

"What about my movie?" John demanded.

"That's my point," Roxanne said. "I think the movie made it seem like it was noble to die that close to water. But that's not the truth, John. It's silly to die when you can live. It's wrong to be unhappy when you can be happy."

"Think you could be happy here?" John asked. He turned the corner and started down a long driveway. About two hundred feet in, a guard tipped his hat and swung open a heavy wrought-iron gate. They went a little farther along the tree-lined road and then turned sharply. Ahead of them was the biggest house that Roxanne had ever seen. "It's a castle," she exclaimed.

"Actually it was built by a German baron for his American wife," John said. "The Marlowes picked it up at the beginning of the Depression for a song."

Those were exactly the same words Ruth Marlowe used as she showed Roxanne the house and led her to her room on the second floor. As Roxanne admired the lovely pink-marble staircase and ran her hand along the smooth banister, Ruth Marlowe said, "We picked it up for a song, my dear. No one else wanted it because it was so far from Hollywood. But we like to invest in real estate, and we thought this would be a good retirement home."

Then she laughed again and said, "Not to retire in, of course. But real estate is going to be a very good investment in California. More and more people will want to live here, and everything will go up in price. You must invest in real estate, my dear, as we do. One of the days we'll sell for a profit and we'll have enough money to buy something simple in Mexico or the Caribbean."

Roxanne was overwhelmed by the splendor of the house. Everywhere she looked there was another marble fireplace, French tapestry, or Oriental vase to catch her eye. She had never seen so many beautiful things collected together under one roof, not even in the museum. Her room was on the second floor and had French doors that opened out onto the balcony. "You can see the ocean from your room, Roxanne. That's why we put you here. After all, you're the guest of honor."

"Guest of honor?"

"Yes," Ruth Marlowe said. "We've invited several other people, but most of them are quite a bit older than you. I'm afraid that you three will have to entertain yourselves most of the weekend. Of course, this is a business weekend, but we do hope you'll enjoy yourself as well."

"What business do we have with each

other?" Roxanne hoped she didn't sound too rude, but she couldn't wait another minute to ask her hostess.

"Not really with me," Ruth Marlowe said. "That is, I'm always an interested party in anything my son does, and I won't say I didn't put a word or two in his ear. But the decision was really his."

"What decision?"

"I can't spoil my only son's little surprise, now can I? All I'll say is that you'd do well to look your prettiest this evening. We're having an early supper and showing a movie. Guess what one?"

"*Spanish Treasure*," Roxanne answered promptly.

Ruth Marlowe looked at her approvingly. "You're not only exceptionally pretty, my dear. You're very clever. Now get yourself all gussied up. We'll see you at five-thirty for drinks. On the terrace."

Roxanne tried on all four dresses she'd brought and finally decided on the pale ivory jersey that she'd never worn. It was slinkier than anything she'd ever owned, and her reflection almost scared her when she looked in the mirror, she looked so grown-up. The dress had long sleeves and a heart-shaped neckline. Since the fabric clung to her body, it showed off her figure more than most of the clothes she wore, and she almost traded it again for the pink chiffon evening dress with the full skirt. But after some hesitation she gathered her courage together and walked down the marble staircase to join the others on the terrace.

There were several older people, and as Ruth introduced her to them, she recognized some famous Hollywood names. Most were writers or in the production end of the business. Roxanne was surprised that there were only three other performers, and they were all older character actors.

Ruth Marlowe was a relaxed and charming hostess, and Gary seemed quite comfortable as he helped his mother serve drinks and make the guests comfortable. Roxanne noticed that even though there had to be a lot of servants in a house like this, there was no butler or maid in view during the time on the terrace. It was just one of many ways that the Marlowes managed to make the huge house seem cozy.

Roxanne sat as close to John as she could, smiling at the appropriate times and being extremely grateful that he was such a good talker. No one seemed to expect her to say much, and she found much of the talk about the old days in the movie business quite interesting. Ruth Marlowe and an older actress were laughing about how hard it was to make movies before the studios developed sophisticated equipment and safety devices.

"I remember one time I was supposed to fall off a raft into icy water," Ruth Marlowe reminisced. "That was before there were stuntwomen or stand-ins. I fell into that water fifteen times before they figured out how to get a shot of me without having water splash on the camera lens. I was in bed sick for one whole week."

"How did they get the shot?" Roxanne asked.

"Actually, they let the water splash and the director was praised for his originality and dramatic effects. What made me maddest was that I'd suggested that the first time we tried the scene. But they never listen to women."

"They listen to you now," the other actress said.

"Somewhat," Ruth Marlowe said. "But I'll never get a chance to direct just because I'm a woman. That is, unless I buy my own studio. If we sold this place . . ."

"Not that again," Evan Marlowe's voice rang out over the heads of two other conversation groups. "Whenever Ruth gets started on wanting to direct, I feel the roof over my head crumbling away."

Roxanne was fascinated by Gary's parents. His voice was a lot like his father's, and many of his mannerisms were like his mother's, but he didn't really look much like either of them. "Penny for your thoughts?" John asked, and Roxanne blushed. She was thinking about Gary once again.

Gary seemed to be studiously avoiding her, and it made Roxanne even more curious about what sort of business they might have together. She knew it had to be connected to the movies in some way, and she was beginning to hope, against her better judgment, that it would mean a new part. Everyone was being so nice to her that she was certain that whatever was coming next would be good news.

Dinner was short, and though Roxanne had never eaten in a room like this one before, she guessed it was informal. The table was long enough for at least thirty people, and there were three maids who served the roast beef, baked squash, and fresh broccoli. For dessert there was a fresh fruit cup and small coffees.

"Cake and ice cream after the movie," Ruth Marlowe announced, "but first, the main feature." She led the group out of the dining room and through the huge living room, down a long hallway, through an immense library that was lined with books, and into a private theater. Roxanne looked around carefully, trying to memorize the exact shade of the wallpaper, the exact color of the carpet, and every detail of this room.

"Planning for the day when you have a theater of your own?" Gary's breath touched her shoulder and neck as he whispered behind her. She shivered and didn't answer him. Why was it that Gary seemed to know what she was thinking so much of the time?

The lights went down and the sound went on. Roxanne held her breath as she saw the credits flash on the screen. When her name appeared, she let out a little sigh and behind her, she heard Gary say in a low voice, "Looks good, doesn't it?"

She was surprised at how pretty she looked in the first scene and then waited impatiently till she would appear again. She wasn't surprised that Gary looked so great on the screen, knowing by now that he was a fine actor, but the closer they got to the part where she would appear, the more nervous she got. By the time her face reappeared, she was feeling almost sick at her stomach, she was so scared. She kept telling herself over and over again that there was nothing to be frightened about, that she had enough hints from other people to be fairly sure she looked good.

In fact, she looked very good. And what was even more apparent was how good she looked next to Gary. His dark, handsome hair and eyes flashed next to her blonde beauty. She was amazed at how loving she looked as she turned toward him, and the scene on the plank was a mixture of fun and romance. Several people in the room laughed as she kicked her skirts high. The movie ended with the kiss, and Roxanne turned red just remembering that day.

When the lights went on, she was still blushing. John said, "You looked great, Roxanne. But I still see you as a great dramatic actress."

Roxanne had to resist laughing. Comparing her pitiful performance in John's tragedy with the delightful look of this movie was very funny to her, but she surely didn't want to hurt John's feelings. He was still very sensitive about his one attempt at movie-making.

"Like yourself?" Gary asked.

"Yes," Roxanne answered. "If I liked you, too."

"Everyone thinks this will be a big hit," Gary said. "And I have another one to do for Berkeley Studios. It was supposed to be a Civil War drama."

"Will there be a part for me?"

"No. Not in that one." Then Gary whispered, "Now, don't have a temper tantrum, Rosie. Just hang on a few more minutes and everything will turn out fine."

"I'm not going to have a temper tantrum," she said. As usual he'd managed to make her furious. "But you have no right to tease me like this. Are you going to offer me a part or not?"

"I'm not, my mother is."

"Oh." Somehow, though she knew she should be thrilled at the idea of working with Ruth Marlowe, she was disappointed. She'd hated to admit it, even to herself, but she'd hoped that she would be working with Gary again.

Chapter
Twenty-four

"WASN'T Gary's movie wonderful?" Ruth Marlowe asked her guests. After they agreed she added, "And wasn't Roxanne the best young talent you've seen in years?"

They clapped then, and Roxanne was so pleased that she could hardly believe it was happening to her. Ruth nodded her head and said, "Roxanne, why don't you tell us what it feels like to be Hollywood's next overnight success?"

"It feels fine," she confessed. After everyone laughed she added, "But it's not exactly overnight. My mother and I came out here almost a year ago. Well, almost nine months ago."

That brought more laughter, and Ruth said, "My dear, some of us wait years and have much less success than you've achieved in nine months."

"I'd like to thank John and Gary," Roxanne stammered. She was uncomfortable making speeches and afraid that she might say the wrong thing. "They both helped me so much."

"Hollywood brats have to stick together," Gary said. He was smiling and looked very happy for her. For once Roxanne didn't have to be confused about his motives.

"I asked you all here tonight because I have a plan for Gary's next movie that requires your help, as you know, because some of you are involved in it already, Gary is supposed to do a Civil War drama for his second Berkeley movie. We weren't happy with the script to begin with, but now that the pirate film is such an obvious success, we want to scrap it totally. We'd like to use this little weekend party to polish up a second pirate movie package. If you're all agreeable, I'm going to take the proposal to Berkeley on Monday morning. If we have everything ready to go, I'm sure they'll agree."

She turned to Roxanne and said, "Will you be the leading lady in a sequel? At the same terms but a bigger part?"

"Yes."

Then she turned to the older character actors and asked, "Would you play pirates instead of Civil War characters?"

"Of course."

"Good, now all that we need is a plot and a script, and we're in business." She turned to three guests who were writers and asked,

"You can whip up a sequel to this in two days, can't you? Tom? Mary?"

When they began to protest, Ruth Marlowe smiled and said, "I'm willing to pay you a month's salary for one good weekend's work. I need something solid to present to Sam Barlowe on Monday morning."

One of the writers stood up and said, "I guess I'll get to work. We'll want more of that comedy conflict between the two of them. That was where the electricity came from."

The other two writers stood up, and one asked, "Ruth, will you have the maid send up some coffee before she turns in?"

"All-night coffee," Ruth Marlowe promised. Then she laughed and said, "This is the best party I've had in a long time."

Roxanne had a lot of trouble going to sleep that night and made up for it in the morning. When she finally came downstairs, it was close to eleven in the morning. Evan Marlowe was in the dining room, drinking coffee and reading the newspaper. He looked up and said, "Hello, Roseann. The others are all either working or went to the beach."

"Roxanne," she corrected. But he was already reading again. Roxanne poured herself some coffee and ate a piece of toast. Then she asked, "Mr. Marlowe, do you mind if I call home?"

"Home? Of course not."

Ordinarily Roxanne would not have dared to call long distance from someone else's home, but the Marlowes seemed to have so much money, it couldn't possibly matter. Her mother answered on the third ring.

"You can hire Lupita back," Roxanne said. "And you can buy yourself that new fur jacket that you were talking about yesterday."

"Good news?"

"I'm doing another Marlowe movie," Roxanne said. "Same terms. Now aren't you glad I didn't take the Randolph offer? Five hundred a week is a lot better than one."

"I'll buy the jacket this afternoon," her mother said. "I saw a little red fox that I'll get for you."

"A fur jacket? I'd feel like a silly squirrel or something."

"It's fox, not squirrel. You'll need it for the premiere of *Spanish Treasure*, and it will soon be winter."

"Ma, we both lived in Oklahoma for a long time without fur coats. And it snows more in Oklahoma than it does in California." Then she laughed and said, "Okay. Buy me one, too. They say I'm going to be a star and I just hope they're right."

"I'll start house-hunting tomorrow," Laureen said.

"I like my pink house," Roxanne objected.

"A limousine will look silly parked out in front of that little house."

"No one promised me a limousine."

"Ask them," Laureen commanded, but then she softened her tone and said, "You need a big car if you're a star, Roxanne. And I'd like to ride to work in it, too. Remember, we're both working girls."

When she met Ruth Marlowe walking through her lovely rose gardens later in the afternoon, Roxanne asked, "Mrs. Marlowe...."

"Please call me Ruth. I know I'm old enough to be your mother. After all, I am Gary's mother, but it makes me so unhappy to have you call me Mrs. Marlowe."

"Ruth, I have a favor to ask. I don't want you to think I'm not grateful, because I am. I really am very grateful to you and to Gary and to John and to everyone who's helped me. I'm most grateful to my mother because she's the one who got me started in the whole idea. What I'm trying to say . . . I'm trying to ask . . . I wouldn't want you to pay for it, of course. But when you talk to Sam Barlowe, do you think they'd give me a limousine?"

"Don't you have one?"

"No."

"How did you get to work?"

Roxanne began to laugh because Ruth seemed to be another one of those rich people who had no idea how the poor lived. But she didn't want to offend her hostess, so she quickly stopped herself. "I took a bus to Berkeley Productions, and I walked to Randolph Studios."

"You must have a very long, very beautiful limousine from now on. I'll see that the studio puts one at your disposal." Then she added, "You should also get an agent. Not for this picture, please, because I need you to work for the price we agreed on, but for your next pictures. You need someone to represent you."

"Do you know any good agents?" Roxanne asked.

Before she could answer, one of the writers called to her out of the window of his room and Ruth hurried away. Roxanne walked in the garden for a while, dreaming of all the things she would do with the money she would earn as a star. She decided that as quickly as she could she would invest in real estate as Ruth Marlowe suggested. She wondered what sort of place she could afford on five hundred dollars a week. Nothing this fancy, of course, but something nice. As she walked alone she kept hoping that Gary and John would come back from the beach. It would be fun to talk about her success with them, but they didn't show up. About four, she went back to her room to dress for the evening gathering.

The group was quite a bit smaller at dinner that night, because two of the three writers were in their rooms working. The third one seemed too preoccupied to know what he was eating. When Roxanne, who was sitting beside him, asked how the script was coming, he nodded his head and said, "Good soup."

Most of the other guests had gone home early that afternoon, either to prepare for the new movie or because the gala party they'd expected had turned into a rather dull work party. Only two of the older actors and John remained. That evening they watched a first release of a movie that starred Gary's uncle, and there was a sad silence following the ending credits.

Ruth sighed and said, "Poor Herbert. He does pick some soggy stories."

"I liked it," John said on the way out of the theater. "At least I liked the part where he went bankrupt and died."

"No one ever died from bankruptcy," Roxanne protested. "Ruth was right, it was a soggy story."

"You only believe in happy endings," John protested. "Don't you know that films can be great art?"

"I know that. But because something's sad doesn't make it great art."

John turned to Gary and said, "Roxanne thinks we're supposed to keep them laughing out there in Kansas. She says we don't know anything about reality, anyway."

"Maybe she's right," Gary said.

"That's easy for you to say," John pouted. "You enjoy playing with swords and walking gangplanks, but I want to be an artist."

"I want to be the best craftsman in the business," Gary said. "And I'll be happy to leave the dramatics to Uncle Herbert. Besides, I like happy endings."

"See, the great Gary Marlowe agrees with me," Roxanne said. She was delighted to find that she and Gary were on the same side for once. "Movies should be entertaining; that's what people want. Isn't that right?"

"Whatever the great Roxanne Wilson says," Gary said, and bowed from the waist. "She's the expert." Then he yawned and said, "See you at the studio on Monday afternoon. I'll be going home early tomorrow morning."

"Ride with us," John offered.

"No. You two love birds will have a better time alone."

Gary left them then, and Roxanne wasn't sure whether she'd made him mad again or not. It seemed as though everything she said and did was wrong in real life, though Gary had certainly been complimentary about her work. She told herself that was all that mattered. After all, Gary was nothing to her except a comrade at work.

Chapter
Twenty-five

BERKELEY Productions not only bought the idea of a second pirate movie, but they started Roxanne's salary that Monday. She rode home from work in a white limousine that had the longest, sleekest lines of any car she'd ever seen. What's more, the driver was Mike, the man who'd picked her up for her first screen test at Randolph Studios. He remembered her and seemed genuinely delighted by her success.

"I drove the big boss one time too often over at Randolph, so I just up and quit," he confided. "Plenty of jobs for good drivers in Hollywood. Now I've got my personal movie star to take around. You just let me know where you want to go. I'm on call twenty-four hours a day."

"Will you wait here? I think I'll take my mother to the Coconut Grove to celebrate."

"Why not try a better restaurant?" Mike suggested. "Mr. Gable always preferred the PickWick when I was his chauffeur."

"Some other night," Roxanne said. "Ma thinks the Coconut Grove is the fanciest place in the world. Can you give me a few minutes to change?"

"You got it all wrong, Miss Wilson. You don't ask, you tell. You're the star now."

"Wait till you meet my mother," Roxanne promised. "She'll give you lots of orders."

But even Laureen was impressed by the white limousine that waited for them when they walked out of the little pink bungalow. She drew her new fur jacket closer around her and said in an awed voice, "It is a very long car."

"Mrs. Marlowe asked for the longest one in the studio. It's older than some, but it's elegant. Do you like it, Ma?"

"I love it."

"Do you think they'll be impressed when you arrive at Star Casting in this? Or do you want to quit work now? We'll have enough money."

"No." Laureen shook her head quickly. "I may never be a big name, but I like working in the movies."

Mike held the door open for them, and they got into the lush backseat. Roxanne ran her hand along the upholstery and said, "It's real leather. And Ma, there's a telephone so you can give orders."

Laureen's face lit up, and she lifted the

telephone off the hook and said, "1236 Mirador Road, please. That's right off Sunset, in the hills. Next door to Cyril Randolph's brother's house."

She turned to Roxanne and said, "The house is for sale, but the real estate woman said we could probably rent it for a song. It's a real mansion with a swimming pool and a tennis court. It has a little house for Lupita and seven bedrooms."

"Sounds very big," Roxanne said doubtfully.

"She says we can probably just move in for almost nothing if we fix it up. Says we might just have to pay the utilities and taxes. She's checking on it and will let me know tomorrow."

"Ma, I like my pink bungalow," Roxanne said. "It means a lot to me."

"Just wait and see," Laureen said. "If you don't like it, we'll look for something else."

They were turning off Sunset now, and the limousine slowed down as they came to the end of the little road. The car stopped and Roxanne said, "It's pink!"

"Looks like a giant model of the one we're living in," Laureen said. "That's why I said we'd take it."

They got out and walked around in the twilight, carefully stepping over the broken tree branches that littered the walkway to the house. As she walked Roxanne fell in love with the place. "It's kind of shabby," she said.

"Built in 1918 by a silent screen director.

He moved back to Germany seven years ago. It's been on the market for a while."

There were brilliant bougainvillaea vines everywhere. The scarlet flowers climbed over the pink stucco walls and onto the tile roof. Though the grass was dry and brown, Roxanne could see that the place could be beautiful with a little work. "It needs an awful lot of fixing up, Ma. We don't have time."

"I talked to Lupita. She has a cousin who is a good carpenter. We'd be putting some poor people to work if we rented this, Roxanne. Of course, I can't tell you what to do. You're the one who's earning all the money."

"How much is he selling it for?" Roxanne asked.

"I didn't ask," Laureen admitted.

"When she calls tomorrow morning, find out," Roxanne said.

"Then you do like it?" Laureen asked. "It was the only one I saw that was really suitable for a big star like you. And think how wonderful the limousine will look parked out in front."

"I haven't promised anything," Roxanne warned. "Let's go eat. I'm starved."

It took them two weeks and several overseas telegrams, but they bought the pink mansion for five thousand dollars. Using all her savings as a down payment made her very nervous, but Roxanne reasoned that if she put the money in real estate, she would have something to show for it even if things didn't work out well in the movie business.

After Casa Feliz, which meant "Happy House" in Spanish, was fixed up, it would be worth more than she'd originally paid for it.

"You'll never regret this," the real estate woman assured her as they signed the papers for the final closing.

"No, I don't think we will," Roxanne said as she looked around the large living room. Lupita had already managed to clear out a lot of the debris and shine up the few pieces of furniture that came with the house. Roxanne looked down at the beautiful wooden parquet floors and smiled. She said, "I'd like to find some Oriental rugs like the ones the Marlowes have. Do you have any idea where I might start looking?"

"Some of those Orientals cost as much as this house," the woman warned. "But if you ask around, you can probably pick up bargains. There's always someone on the way up or down in Hollywood."

"My daughter's on her way up," Laureen bragged.

"So is my mother," Roxanne teased. Laureen had spoken several lines in *Gone with the Wind*, and the director told her she did a good job. She'd already had a nibble on a small role in an Andy Hardy movie with Mickey Rooney.

When they moved in on Sunday, it took several trips in the limousine to collect all their clothes. John came to take them out to supper that afternoon, and Roxanne asked, "Remember when you moved us from the

Clintlocks' to the pink bungalow? We got it all in your little car."

"You've come up in the world," John said. "And I heard today that your new film is wonderful."

"Did Gary tell you that?" She hoped he would say yes. Though she'd worked with Gary almost a month and they seemed to be getting along well together, she still didn't know what he thought about her. Or, she admitted to herself, she kept hoping he thought about her more than he seemed to. Gary was always cool and polite on the set, but he never had more than two or three friendly words for her. Working with him every day was painful in some ways, because she found herself wanting to please him too much. And it hurt that he always seemed to have a different girl on his arm. Where did he find them all? Central Casting?

"I haven't talked to Gary," John answered. "I heard it from someone who was talking to my dad. He had a chance to see the rushes, and he was raving about you."

"That's really nice." Roxanne had heard a lot of good things about her work recently, but she still experienced a real thrill every time someone praised her.

"Why didn't you tell me about the contract Bertram offered you?"

"You were the one who told me, remember? You brought roses, and I thought it was bad news."

"No. I mean the second contract."

"I didn't see any sense in it, John."

"I heard them talking about it by mistake. They thought I'd gone to my room to study, but I came down for a Coke. You gave up your chance, for our love. Roxanne, I wish you'd told me."

He took her hands in his and leaned toward her, as though he intended to kiss her. She pulled away and shook her head. "John, I'm not in love with you. I've tried to be honest about that."

"You can't still be in love with Henry. Gary said he looked like a country boy and parted his hair in the middle."

"That's just like a couple of Hollywood brats. If all you can find to say wrong about him is how he parts his hair, then he must be all right." But Roxanne was laughing a little bit under her stern answer.

"You don't talk about him at all anymore."

"There's not much to say," Roxanne said. "He's working in the bank in Norman. He was lucky to get the job, but he says that things are finally picking up there. But it's not just Henry. . . ." She took a deep breath and told him the truth. "I don't love you, and I don't think I ever will."

"Why don't you love me?"

How could she explain to John that he wasn't the kind of man she could take seriously? Even his question seemed childlike and petulant to her. If she ever did fall in love, it would be with a man who took himself and his work seriously. A little voice within asked her if she wasn't already in love with just such a man. Gary might be a sensible person when it came to work, but he was just another playboy the rest of the time. Actually, of the three men who were in her life, Henry was the only one who had the qualities she wanted in a man. She sighed, knowing that she didn't love Henry, either.

Roxanne took his hand in hers and stroked it gently. "John, you can't always choose who you love. If I could choose, it would be you. I like you so much, but it's just not the same as love."

"You could learn to love me," John said. "I don't finish college until next June. Then we can get married and you'll learn to love me. You can star in my Broadway plays."

"No, John."

"You will, Roxanne. You'll see. You'll learn to love me when you get a little older."

Roxanne was dismayed by John's need to believe that. Why couldn't she make him see that she was serious? It hurt her that he seemed to want her so much, and yet his very eagerness warned her that he was not the man for her. She could never be happy with a man who clung to her the way John wanted to cling. The whole thing seemed very sad, somehow.

Her mood of sadness carried over to the next day on the set, and try as she would, she couldn't shake the feeling that she had been unfair to John. Yet she had never lied to him about her lack of feelings. His hurt expression haunted her all day, and around two in the afternoon Gary asked, "What's the matter? Your puppy dog die?"

"I don't have a puppy dog." Why did Gary always sense her mood and then find exactly the thing to say to make her feel terrible?

"You look so sad. Is something wrong with your mother?"

"No. I'm worried about John," she confessed. After all, Gary was supposed to be John's best friend. Maybe he could advise her.

"So am I," Gary said.

"Has he talked to you about me?"

"No, but I can see he's crazy about you and that the feelings are not mutual. You used him to get this far and now you want to dump him."

She drew back her hand to slap him and then dropped it. It wasn't Gary's fault that John was unhappy. It was hers. She said, "That's not what happened."

"But it is true that he helped you and now you're not interested in him, isn't it?"

"Yes and no."

"Ambitious women," Gary taunted. "Deliver me from them."

"You're always making cracks about my ambition. What about yours? Isn't it ambition that drives you to work a half an hour before everyone else in the morning? But you act like I'm a criminal to want to be a star."

Roxanne waited for Gary to reply, but he

only smiled and raised one eyebrow in that infuriatingly superior manner of his. His lack of response made her more furious, and she went on, "You've been laughing at me and my mother ever since you met us. Is she really so awful because she wants me to succeed? What about your mother?" Roxanne was close to tears now. "She arranged this whole movie just so her little boy would be happy and successful. She's every bit as bossy and ambitious as my mother."

Gary laughed at that and said, "I don't know how our mothers got into this. We were talking about John." Then he shook his head and said in a teasing manner, "And my mother thinks you're such a nice girl."

"I am," Roxanne replied, "and I didn't say I didn't like your mother. I liked her a lot. I like my mother, too. And I liked John. You're the only one I don't like."

Gary's eyes widened and then shut, as though she had actually slapped him. She saw, for one split instant, that she had hurt him terribly, and she was immediately sorry. Then Gary's face took on a perfectly calm expression, and he said in a detached voice, "If you don't want John, you're going to have to tell him the truth. Poor guy."

"I have told him," Roxanne said. She was near tears now, and she wasn't sure whether it was over hurting John or Gary. She was never quite sure what she was feeling when she was around Gary.

278

"So now you'd like me to convince him?"

"Would you?"

"No. Do your own dirty work." Gary picked up the script and swiftly changed to his most professional tone. "Did you get what they're doing here? When they changed the lines? Want to run through it again?"

"All right." It was hopeless to expect any real help from Gary Marlowe. For the hundredth time she'd promised herself that she'd never try to have a personal conversation with him again. She always seemed to get driven into some extreme position and come out looking like a fool.

But the look in his eyes when she said she didn't like him haunted her the rest of the day, along with her guilt about John. She didn't really want to hurt Gary, and though her feelings for him were very confused, she knew she was closer to loving Gary than either Henry or John. While she had no intention of ever telling him that, she didn't want him to hate her, either. Later in the day she tried to tell him, "I do like you, Gary. I admire your work very much. And I'm grateful for what you've done for me."

"Anything I did for you was for John or because I think you're a very talented actress," Gary said curtly. But his voice sounded very different from usual, and she understood that he was hurt, very hurt.

"Thanks, anyway," Roxanne said. She was determined to remain humble and not lose her temper again. She'd seen the look on Gary's face that said he was vulnerable despite his handsome facade of detachment. She was beginning to understand that in some ways Gary was still the same little boy that John remembered.

Chapter
Twenty-six

THE closer they got to the end of the movie, the clearer the signs of success became. First there was an extra courtesy on the part of all the staff at Berkeley Productions. Then, about halfway into the second picture, the director, Sam Barlow, suddenly started referring to her as Miss Wilson when he spoke about her to the others on the set. He still called her Roxanne, but all the others except Gary switched from her first name to the more formal title.

By that time the first pirate movie, *Spanish Treasure*, was about to open, and she noticed that much of the publicity included her name. One morning at breakfast her mother jumped up and shouted, "It's here!"

She pointed to a line of newspaper print and said, "Your name is here in Hedda Hopper's column. Roxanne, you've made the big time."

Roxanne was pleased and amused by her mother's reaction. "What does it say?"

"What unknown Hollywood starlet is about to become the hottest leading lady of 1939? R. W. is a real buried treasure. Her golden hair and winning smile will be big box-office news for Berkeley Productions."

"My name's not there," she teased her mother.

"It's better than a name," Laureen said. "Keep them guessing."

"They won't be guessing much longer," Roxanne said. "I've seen the coming attraction billboards, and my picture is plastered on all of them. And my name is almost as big as Gary's."

"One of these days it will be bigger," her mother predicted.

"Ma, you'd better start enjoying these days," Roxanne warned. "We don't know what the future holds."

"Good times," her mother insisted.

"I think so," Roxanne agreed. "But we've already accomplished so much. This wonderful house is half paid for. We've got pretty clothes and a fancy limousine. At least we'll have the fancy limousine for another three weeks while I'm under contract with Berkeley Productions."

"They haven't offered you another picture?"

"Not yet, but everyone is sure they will. I need an agent, Ma."

"And your own publicity man and a personal hairdresser. They say Shirley Thompson never goes anywhere without her butler and five other servants."

Roxanne laughed and shook her head. "You're incorrigible. But I've got an appointment with Benny Foyle on Saturday morning. He's coming here."

"Is he the best agent in town?"

"I checked around, and he has a reputation for being tough. I need someone who can really get me the best contract possible. We want to get as much as we can out of these first years. Buy some more real estate and invest in stocks. Henry says he's learning a lot about money management. He can help us with that."

Laureen shook her head. "There's no sense hanging on to Henry. He's not in your league."

"My league? What am I supposed to be, a baseball player?"

"A winner like Babe Ruth," Laureen teased. "Hitting home runs, not just walking from base to base. Henry was a nice little boy back in Norman, but he's not in your league."

"Henry has a very important position in the bank," Roxanne answered. Then she stood up, stretched, and kissed her mother on the cheek. "But let's not argue about Henry this morning. Let's go to work and have a great day. How's *Gone with the Wind* coming?"

"My part is finished. But I'm testing for the mother in the Hardy movie."

"You'll get it," Roxanne said.

"How do you know?"

"Because I inherited my acting ability from you," Roxanne said. "So you've got the original source all tucked away inside you somewhere. Now go out there and hit a home run."

"What's your day?"

"Watching Gary Marlowe's swordplay, I suppose."

"Boring."

"Not really," Roxanne said. "He's awfully good at it. But it's not as much fun to watch now that they make them wear masks.

"Masks?"

"Just for the practice. Word came down from on high that all actors had to keep their faces covered except for the actual filming. Gary had a fit."

"I should think he'd be glad not to have that pretty face in danger."

Roxanne shook her head. "Gary's a funny guy. He works hard and worries more about his career than anyone I know, except maybe me. But he's not vain."

"You two have a lot in common," Laureen said. Then she stood up and said, "I wonder if I should call Hedda Hopper and give her an interview."

"Ma, you promised."

"It might help."

"Ma."

"All right." Laureen frowned and then smiled. "I have to worry about my own career, anyway. Can Mike drop me off first this morning?"

As Roxanne watched Gary fencing that morning she reviewed the way things were going in her life. The best thing was the way she and her mother seemed to be getting along so well these days. In so many ways her mother was still a little girl, but Roxanne had grown up enough to manage her better. Laureen seemed quite happy in the new house, spending her own salary on clothes and other luxury items. She was having the time of her life.

Now, if Roxanne could just get her own career on a steady course, she would be a very happy young woman, she decided. Then she smiled and shook her head, chiding herself because she was not following the advice she'd given her mother this morning. She was going to learn to enjoy each day and not live so much in the future. It was silly to let your life slip by in dreams and plans, when there was so much really happening.

She forced her attention back to Gary's swordplay and soon lost herself in the enjoyment of watching real professionals work. When Sam called the lunch break, Gary came over to her, lifted his mask, and asked, "How did I do?"

"You're great," she answered. "How did you ever learn fencing so well?"

"If I tell you, you'll think I'm a spoiled brat," Gary said. But today his voice was light, almost flirtatious.

"You started fencing lessons before you could walk," Roxanne guessed.

"On my seventh birthday," Gary admitted.

"I started ballet when I was ten," Roxanne said. "But my folks couldn't keep paying for the lessons, so I had to drop out." She wondered if that simple recounting of the truth was going to offend him.

He kept right on smiling and asked, "Are you still a good dancer?"

"Not professional quality," she admitted. "But I can tap and do some simple ballet."

"We danced together once," he reminded her. "I thought you were very graceful."

Roxanne wished his compliments didn't mean so much to her. Why was it that any small praise from Gary felt so important? It frightened her that she wanted to please him so much. "Thank you," she said.

"Like to have lunch?" Gary asked.

Roxanne was astounded at the invitation. In the year she'd known Gary, he'd never actually asked her to do anything with him. Once or twice he'd invited her to join his table when not doing so would have been rude. Even the invitation to his Santa Barbara estate had really come from his mother. She rose from her chair, trying not to let him know how surprised and pleased she was with the invitation.

At lunch they chatted about moviemaking and the very good chance that their pirate movies would be a big success. "I'll be glad to get back to Randolph Studios, though," Gary admitted. "I hated being on loan."

"You don't mean you actually like working for Ruthless Randolph?" Roxanne asked. She was having a very good time and used John's father's nickname half in jest.

"He's always been nice to me," Gary said.

"I should think he would be," Roxanne said. "The Marlowe family has practically made his studio."

"I also think he likes me because John and I are friends," Gary said. "How are things going between you two?"

"Better. That is, I think I've finally convinced John that my career comes first."

"And I think I've finally convinced him that movies should have happy endings," Gary said. "John's a good guy, but he's got some growing up to do. You and I have already done a lot of that."

"You know, you do seem years older than John. How do you account for that?"

Gary shrugged. "My folks drilled it into me that I would have to work for a living. They were a little tougher on me than John's were on him."

Roxanne laughed. "Your parents are crazy about you. John's father picks on him. I think you've got it all backward."

"My parents would do anything they could for me, as long as they were sure it was good for me," Gary agreed. "John's folks were different in a lot of ways. His mother spoiled him a lot when he was a baby, and then, when she was killed, there were a lot of servants and governesses."

"John told me he had governesses until he went to college."

"I went to military school and was treated like the other kids," Gary said. "Maybe that helped me grow up faster."

Roxanne nodded. "I know what made me grow up fast. It was having to take care of my father when he was sick and then . . . my mother isn't very grown-up herself."

"So you were a parent to your parents. Well, it didn't hurt you, did it?"

"Except one of these days I'd like to have more fun," Roxanne confessed. "I'm earning all this money now, but I never seem to do anything with it that's fun. Most of the people I know are a lot older than I am, and I'm making all these important decisions by myself. Riding around in a fancy car and wearing pretty clothes is nice, but it's not —"

"Not like real teenage fun," Gary finished for her. "You're young and you want to forget you're in the toughest business in the world once in a while. Most kid stars go through something like that. They find a way to be like regular kids at least part of the time."

"What do *you* do for fun?" Then she laughed and said, "Besides date pretty starlets."

"The starlets are for my image," Gary

confessed. "The studio was worried about starting me in romantic parts when I was so young. They wanted me to develop the reputation for being a very romantic fellow."

"And you love it," Roxanne teased. Then she shook her head and said, "I would never let them tell me who to date."

"You don't know what you'd do," Gary said.

"Yes, I do," Roxanne said. "I'd never sign a contract that gave them that kind of control over my personal life."

"We were talking about fun," Gary reminded her. "How would you like to go to the Santa Monica pier with me Saturday? I'll show you how to have fun. I go there all the time. Well, I've been there a few times. Come on."

"What would we do?" Roxanne could hardly believe that Gary was asking her out.

"Swim in the ocean. Ride bicycles. Shoot wooden ducks in the shooting gallery. Maybe ride the merry-go-round."

Roxanne laughed and said, "It sounds like fun. But won't anyone recognize you? You have to sneak into the movies in a mustache."

"I wear funny clothes and a wig," Gary admitted. "Pick you up at ten?"

"Would noon be all right?" Roxanne asked. "I have an appointment at ten."

"On Saturday? Another real estate deal?" Gary teased.

"No, but I decided I need an agent."

"Who did you hire?"

"I'm thinking about hiring Benny Foyle. Know him?"

"I've heard good things," Gary said. "Now finish your sandwich. I'm due back on the set."

On Saturday, the first thing she said to Benny Foyle when he sat down in her living room was, "I hear good things about you, Mr. Foyle."

He nodded and said, "I hear you're doing fine, too. Knew you were a winner first time I saw you. They cut you out of that movie, though. I went to see it. So what happened after that?"

Roxanne gave a brief accounting of her days as an extra and getting the part in the first Gary Marlowe movie. She finished with, "So now I'd like to find another good studio to take me on. I'll go anywhere except Randolph Studios."

"Wrong thinking," Benny Foyle said. "You'll go anywhere if they pay you enough. You said yourself that you wanted to be a rich woman."

"I guess you think that's awful," Roxanne said, "but I've been very poor and I know the value of money."

"You got a good head on your shoulders for a pretty little girl," Benny Foyle said. "But pretty little girls have a way of letting their emotions rule their lives. That's why they need ugly old men for agents. No emotional decisions. We'll go for the cash."

Roxanne laughed and said, "Randolph Studios would have to offer me twice as much before I'd go back there. I hate Cyril Randolph."

"But if Cyril Randolph decides he loves you, we'll have to consider his highest and best offer." Benny stood up and said, "I'll call you later this week. I'll be testing the water till then."

As she led Benny to the door she decided that he was right about one thing. She was a lot more emotional than she wanted people to believe. Right now she was much more excited about her date with Gary Marlowe than any deal Benny Foyle might put together.

Gary was wearing a funny yellow wig and a straw hat when he picked her up. On top of that, he had on overalls and a checked shirt. "You're kidding?" she said. "You're not really going out looking like that?"

"I like to look like this," Gary said. "It's my favorite disguise."

"Do you have many of them?"

"Sure. You'll need them, too, as soon as the public gets to know your face."

"If the public gets to know it. There's always the chance that I'll be just another pretty blonde."

"No," Gary said. "No chance."

"You don't think I'm pretty?" Roxanne asked.

"I don't think you'll miss. You're a good

actress, Roxanne, and you'll get better. But I can't go out with you looking like that."

Roxanne looked down at her new white sharkskin slacks and her brilliant red-and-yellow Hawaiian silk shirt. She said, "I spent a fortune on these clothes. The woman in the store said they were the top of her 'cruise line.'"

"You're not going on a cruise. Don't you have any overalls?"

"Of course not." Roxanne laughed at the idea.

"I thought all girls from Oklahoma had overalls."

"If you start that, we'll have a fight before we get off the front porch," Roxanne warned. Then she offered, "I do have some navy slacks and a checked cotton shirt."

"Red?"

"Red," she admitted.

"Put it on," Gary ordered. "With the same red-checked shirts and my blond wig, people will think we're twins."

"You're silly." Roxanne said.

"That's the point," Gary said. "I'm supposed to be showing you how to have fun. To have fun you have to learn to be silly."

They parked his red Cadillac convertible with the matching red-leather unholstery half a mile from the pier and walked along the wooden boardwalk to the pier. "First thing to do is to eat so many hot dogs that you get sick," Gary advised.

"And cotton candy," Roxanne said. "I always wanted to taste pink cotton candy."

"Never ate that fuzzy spun sugar?" Gary raised one eyebrow in mock dismay. "You really did have a deprived childhood."

They ate hot dogs and cotton candy, then shot wooden ducks and rode the merry-go-round. They swam and walked on the sand, picking up shells, and then went back to the shooting gallery for another round. As they walked together on the sand Roxanne asked, "Mind if I ask a serious question?"

"As long as it's not too serious."

"Why didn't you speak to me that day in the restaurant? When you saw me at Rudy's?"

"I'd been dreaming about you for weeks. When I saw you in person, I got scared and ran away."

Roxanne laughed.

"I went back the next day, but you were gone. And the only name I could remember was Rosie."

For a minute Roxanne almost believed him, then she remembered the time he'd given her mother the same fast answer when she insisted that Roxanne enter the talent contest. Gary was a joker, and she dismissed his words as exactly that, a joke.

Roxanne was having so much fun, she could hardly believe it when Gary said, "Sun's going down. We'll have to get back to the car before we turn into pumpkins."

"I want to have my fortune told," Roxanne said. They were staring at a large tin hand that had Madame Geneva written in bold purple letters across the bright pink skin tones.

"We'll both have our fortunes told," Gary agreed.

"Not with you." Roxanne laughed. "If she sees that wig, she'll think you're a spy or something. I want a serious fortune."

"No serious fortunes today," Gary reminded her. "Besides, you know your fortune is all good. Aren't you the girl who makes her own luck?"

"Did John tell you about that?" It bothered her to think that Gary and John must be talking about her behind her back. The idea erased much of the pleasure of the afternoon. She shivered and said, "It is cold. We'd better be going."

"John didn't tell me anything," Gary said. He took her hand and said, "I just know you believe in making your own luck because I know you."

"Why?"

"Why what?"

"Why do you know me so well?" Roxanne had forgotten the funny disguise now, and was looking directly into Gary's dark, beautiful eyes for an answer.

His eyes seemed to hold answers to many things as she allowed her gaze to probe deeper and deeper into their shiny depths. He neither blinked nor answered, and for a moment she thought he was drawing closer to her. Her breathing stopped, and she leaned toward him, as though pulled by a magnet.

He broke the mood abruptly, pulling his head away and taking her hand as he said, "You're freezing, Roxanne. I'll race you to the car."

The mood was broken, and they ran back to the car together. As she raced along the wooden boardwalk, Roxanne was aware of the music of the waves in her ears and the beautiful colors of the red-and-gold sunset over the ocean. She reached the car a long time after Gary did, and when she got there, she was gasping. "I had fun," she said.

"So did I," Gary said, "but we've got to get home."

He didn't explain why he was suddenly in such a hurry, so Roxanne assumed that he had a real date with one of his large collection of starlets. But she was determined not to break the mood of this beautiful day again with any serious questions or worries. As they drew up to the front of her door she said, "I think blond hair is definitely your style. You ought to talk to the studio about changing it permanently."

Then she slipped out of the car, pausing just long enough to say, "See you at the salt mine."

Chapter
Twenty-seven

THE next morning Sam Barlow asked if she would have coffee with him. The director almost never left his set, and Roxanne was amazed that he considered talking with her important enough to turn the last few feet of the fencing scene over to his assistant. She never believed for a moment that he just wanted a cup of coffee.

"Would you rather have it in my office or the commissary?" Barlow asked.

"The commissary," Roxanne said promptly. Though Barlowe's office didn't have the same terrifying Academy Awards sitting on the shelf that Bertram's office did, it still made her nervous.

He disclosed the real reason for the meeting even before the coffee was served, and Roxanne was grateful for that. "We think you look very good in this one. With a little help we believe you can be a star. How would you like a contract?"

"Yes," Roxanne answered. "I'd prefer a long-term contract to moving from studio to studio." She tried to keep her voice free of excitement. Her instructions from Benny Foyle were to look unimpressed by any of the offers that might be coming her way and let him handle the negotiations.

"We'd like to start you in another adventure film right away. I'll be directing it, and Harry Burns will be your leading man."

She didn't blink an eye as she said, "I've hired Benny Foyle to represent me, so you'd better call him."

Barlow looked disappointed as he said, "I'd hoped we could make a deal without involving anyone else. We're prepared to offer you a three-year contract at five hundred a week. That's a lot of money, Roxanne."

"Yes it is," she replied. "Talk to Benny and get his reaction."

"Foyle's a difficult man to deal with," Barlowe growled. "I thought we were all friends on this set."

"We are. I love working with you, Mr. Barlow, and I hope you and Benny can come to an agreement." Roxanne had to remind herself not to skip back to work. If the three-year contract didn't have too many loopholes and she could really stay on that long, she'd be earning $15,000 a year for three years. That was a total of $45,000. More money than her father had earned in a lifetime.

Benny Foyle was not impressed with Berkeley's offer. "They know they've got a hot property, kid. They'll farm you out and make double that."

"You didn't say *no*?" Roxanne was really alarmed as she gripped the telephone in her hands.

"Never empty out dirty water till you're sure you've got clean to put in the bucket," Benny said. "I said we'd think about it. But I know Randolph will top that. They're losing Betty Nelson, and they need another blonde bombshell."

"I don't want to work for Cyril Randolph."

"Emotional decisions don't put money in the bank," he reminded her. "What if I got you seven-fifty for five years with a clause to negotiate upward if your pictures gross over a hundred million?"

"Do you think they might?" Roxanne was beginning to understand that her career looked more than promising to these men. They all seemed certain that she was destined for real stardom.

She wrote to Henry that evening, telling him about her new agent and ending her letter with, "I can hardly believe that things will be as good as everyone says, but maybe they're right. Maybe my name will really be as famous as they say. They keep comparing me to Jean Harlow and Carole Lombard. They say the only real competition is a new girl called Lana Turner. Funny thing about that is that she wears sweaters a lot of the time, just like I do, and she was discovered in a drugstore. Louella Parsons, she's the new gossip columnist who's competing with Hedda Hopper, called last night, and she's doing a story about both of us. She's calling it 'The Sweater Girls.' "

Benny called again the next evening, saying, "Randolph's got you. Seven-fifty for five years with a renegotiating clause. You can't beat that, kid. We've got to take it."

"Does it say in there that they're going to tell everyone I'm an English orphan?" Roxanne said.

"I'll check on it," Benny promised.

"I want to be myself in all their publicity stories," Roxanne said. "And, Benny, I want it written right in the contract that I can date anyone I please."

"Roxanne, you know they won't do that. They've had so much trouble with the Hays Office."

"Then have them write in that I can date anyone my mother says is all right. They know what a fight my mother put up over that short feature when I had to wear the bathing suit. Besides, they're not really worried about my morals, believe me."

"Studios always like to have a say in a girl's public and private life, Roxanne."

"I won't sign with Randolph unless that's in there, Benny. I have my reasons, believe me." As far as John knew his father was unaware that their friendship continued despite his long New York vacation. In fact, he seemed to think his father was too busy at the studio to worry much about him these days.

Benny was back in three days with a contract that included her right to date anyone she wanted and all the other conditions they'd promised. Roxanne signed, though she still wasn't sure that going back to Randolph Studios was a good idea. "They didn't treat me very well before," she said.

"Forget the past," Benny advised. "This time you'll have your own dressing room and the real star treatment. Brand-new limousine as long as a trailer, and a gold uniform for your driver. You're a hot property, Roxanne."

"Did you ask them about picking my own chauffeur?" she asked.

He hit his forehead and said, "I forgot. Took so long to iron out the dating thing that I forgot. But I'm sure they'll hire whoever you want."

"I want Mike," Roxanne said. "He wants to work for me, too."

"Then there won't be any problem," Benny assured her. "Believe me, baby, they'll treat you like a queen this time. They even offered to have your mother's name printed on a brand-new canvas chair. Gold letters."

"She'll love it," Roxanne said. "But she won't have much time, I'm afraid. She's working nearly every day now."

"Maybe I should be representing her, too," Benny offered.

"Why not?" Roxanne said. "I'll ask her if she wants to sign a contract with you. But she's not earning as much as most of your clients."

"Salt the cow to catch the calf," Benny said. "I'll represent her as a favor to you. You're going to be my top money earner in a year or two, Roxanne. And with this new contract we got from Randolph, I'll be very busy negotiating raises."

"I hope you're right," Roxanne said.

"I know I'm right," he answered. "The studio will send a limousine for you tomorrow morning at eight. They want to give you the full treatment in the publicity department. You've got an interview with *Photoplay* in the morning and a full afternoon of publicity posing. They want you to start autographing photos in your spare time for your fans."

"My pictures aren't even released yet," Roxanne said. "How do they know I'll have fans?"

"The premiere of *Spanish Treasure* is set for a week from Wednesday. They want wardrobe to choose your costume."

"Why does Randolph Studios have anything to say about it?" Roxanne asked. "It was a Berkeley picture."

"But you're a Randolph property, so they care. And they want to know who your date will be."

"I'm not sure," Roxanne answered.

"The studio can fix you up with some budding young star," Benny said.

"Not on your life," Roxanne said. "I'm going to hold them to that no meddling in my personal life clause all the way. I don't care if I have to go alone."

"You can't go alone," Benny said. "It would kill your image with the fans."

"I'll think of somebody," she promised.

That evening she related her whole conversation to John and her mother. She asked, "Who do I ask? John's the only boy I know in Hollywood, and his father will have a fit if I ask him. The only reason he let me agree to choose my own dates is that he thinks John has forgotten all about me."

"Ask Gary Marlowe," her mother said.

"Ma!"

"Why not? He asked you out last week."

"But that wasn't a real date," she said. "We just went to the beach together. He'll have some beauty draped on his arm. Maybe two."

"It would be nice for the fans to see you together."

Roxanne put the problem to John later that evening, and he promptly offered to escort her.

"No. I'm not going to ruin your chances with your father. You graduate very soon, and he may still give you a job at the studio."

"I don't care," John said. "I've got a job in New York. Montesque says I can work for him. He's a very famous Broadway director, you know."

"I know. But your first love is movies. I'm not going to let your father dictate my private life or stop our friendship, but I don't want to begin by infuriating him and ruining your future."

"I'd love to be your escort," John said wistfully, but Roxanne noticed that he didn't pursue the matter. She didn't really blame John, but she did wish he could work out some way to stand up to his father.

"And I'd love to see you working at your chosen career," Roxanne answered. "I'll find someone who won't mind being seen with me."

"Any man in his right mind," John said gallantly. Then he stood up, saying, "I've got to get home and hit the books. But I'll be glad to do it for you, Roxanne."

"Thanks, John, but somebody will turn up."

Chapter
Twenty-eight

HER first day back at Randolph Studios was so different from the old days that Roxanne felt as though she were in a dream. In the first place, she rode to work in the longest, sleekest, most beautiful limousine she'd ever seen. The guard at the gate not only tipped his hat, but also he called her by name, saying, "Good morning, Miss Wilson."

Everywhere she went on the set people spoke to her respectfully, nodding and smiling and saying, "Morning, Miss Wilson, glad to have you back."

She was amazed at how many of the ones who ignored her when she was there before suddenly seemed to be her very best friends. One writer who had consistently snubbed her while she was on the set of *Starlight Majesty* threw his arms around her neck and kissed her on the mouth. By the time she got to her appointment with the *Photoplay* writer, she wished she had one of those silly wigs or phony mustaches that Gary enjoyed so much.

It was the *Photoplay* magazine writer who told her that she was set to begin work on another costume adventure with Gary Marlowe. "They say it will be very romantic and exciting," the writer gushed. "And, of course, the Technicolor will be a first for you, won't it, Miss Wilson? May I call you Roxanne?"

"Please do."

"Your official biography here at Randolph Studios says you were born in England, Roxanne. What part?"

"I was born in Norman, Oklahoma."

"But I found your old publicity sheets in my files."

Marsha Walters, the publicity director, was sitting in on the interview and was obviously very nervous about what Roxanne would say next. She stubbed out her cigarette and said, "We had a young writer with us at the time. She was given to flights of fancy, and I'm afraid she got carried away. I understand she's doing very well writing romances these days."

Roxanne resisted the temptation to say that Marsha had written that biography herself.

"Well, tell me about yourself," the writer said. "Is Roxanne Wilson your real name?"

"Certainly," Marsha interjected, and glared at Roxanne, daring her to deny it.

"And your family?" the writer prompted.

"My father is dead. My mother works as an extra in the movies."

"Isn't that wonderful?" the writer gushed. "So everyone you're close to is in the movie business. Your boyfriend and your mother."

"What boyfriend?" Roxanne asked.

"Gary Marlowe." The writer was beaming now.

"Gary's not my boyfriend," Roxanne said.

"Come now, everyone knows —"

"Then everyone knows wrong," Roxanne snapped. Then she added, "I do have a boyfriend, though. He's a boy from high school in Norman."

"His name is Norman?" The writer was scribbling fast now.

"His name is Henry Scott, and he works in a bank."

"Does he own the bank?"

"No." Roxanne laughed. "He's a clerk there. Last I heard, he was making fifteen dollars a week."

"Roxanne isn't really serious about this Scott boy," Marsha said. "Please don't print that."

"News is news. Sorry," the writer said. Then she turned to Roxanne and asked, "You live in a very large mansion, just off Sunset Boulevard," the writer said.

When Roxanne looked surprised, the writer said, "I happened to attend a party on your block, and your name was mentioned. In fact, that was why I called and asked to do your story. I wonder how your young man feels about the difference in your incomes? I'm not sure exactly how much you're making, but it must be quite a bit more than fifteen dollars a week. It's a very large house."

"I got it for a song," Roxanne said.

"What Roxanne means," Marsha interrupted, "is that the house makes her feel as though she wants to sing. It is a beautiful Spanish home with marble interior and gorgeous grounds. It once belonged to a very famous director."

When Roxanne looked at her quizzically, Marsha smiled and said, "I was scouting locations for your photographic sessions. We'll do several in your charming mansion."

The interview was eventually over, and Roxanne sighed with relief. After Marsha walked the writer to the door she came back and said, "Roxanne, I want you to make every effort to be gracious to the press and tell them what they want to hear."

"What do they want to hear?" Roxanne had a feeling she wasn't going to like the answer.

"That you live in a big, expensive house, that you're deliriously happy with your career, and that you're crazy about Gary Marlowe."

"But none of that is true," Roxanne protested. Then she said, "If you check my contract, you'll find that I have complete control over my personal life and publicity releases. So no more nonsense about Gary Marlowe, please. And I did get my house for a song."

Despite her quarrel with Marsha, she enjoyed her first week at the studio. Most of it was taken up with posing for publicity shots, trying on new clothes, and lounging in her own private dressing room. She loved the small, efficient trailer with her name on the brass star that hung on the front door.

There was a small couch to lie on, a chair, and a makeup table of her own, as well as her own private toilet and running water. She knew that some of the older, more established stars had bigger and better dressing rooms, but she loved this one. She even liked the lavender- and pink-flowered wallpaper that clung to the walls. By the end of the week she'd hung photographs of her mother and father on the walls and had African violets growing on the dressing table under the bright makeup lights. She felt as though she were at home.

She was in her dressing room at about five o'clock on Thursday when Gary knocked on her door. He had to duck to get in the door, and he looked around critically, saying, "I like everything but the wallpaper."

"I like that."

"Probably reminds you of your grandmother's parlor or something," Gary said.

"I suppose your dressing room is fancier?"

"Yes, but it was a hand-me-down from Uncle Herbert, so it really doesn't count. They only had to change half the name on the brass star."

She laughed in spite of herself. She hadn't

seen Gary all week and realized she'd missed him. "I'm glad to see you," she said. "Want some coffee or tea?"

"Coke?"

Roxanne went to the tiny little cooler under her sink and took out one of the Cokes. As she opened it she said, "The ice melts too fast, but the Cokes are still cool."

"That's fine, and I don't need a glass." He took the Coke and then said, "I was wondering if you'd like to go to the premiere with me?"

"The two of us in one car?"

"Yes."

"Did the studio put you up to this?"

"No. John told me you needed an escort, and I didn't have a date. I thought it might be fun."

"Yes, I'd like that," Roxanne said. She had told Benny that someone would turn up, but it never occurred to her that it might be Gary.

"Good. I'll pick you up around seven at your house."

"Do you mind picking me up here? The studio is dressing me."

"Sure," Gary said. "Seven-fifteen, then?"

Roxanne laughed and asked, "Why did you shave fifteen minutes off the time?"

"I thought I should spend that much time talking with your mother," Gary admitted. And then he asked, "How is she?"

"More ambitious every day," Roxanne answered. She wasn't sure why she didn't feel like quarreling with Gary today, but maybe it was because she was so very pleased by his invitation.

But Gary only smiled wider and said, "Good for her." Then he opened the trailer door and ducked under the door.

She reported to the studio at five that afternoon and stood patiently while they twisted her long blonde hair into a million curls. Once it was finished, Roxanne reported to wardrobe where the costumer said, "I have a dress fit for a princess for you, sweetie. You'll look gorgeous."

The dress was beautiful, and Roxanne sighed with pleasure as she stepped into it and Annie zipped her up. The skirt of the dress was an off-white jersey with a little fullness, but it clung seductively as she walked. The top was sleeveless with tiny spaghetti straps, and the whole bodice was sewn with tiny sequined beads.

The sequins sparkled and looked iridescent under the lights, and the wardrobe woman assured her, "Wait till you get all those spotlights on you. You'll look like walking moonlight."

"You should have been a poet," Roxanne teased. But she agreed that the dress was spectacular-looking.

When she brought out a long, soft feather boa, Roxanne laughed and said, "I hope I don't trip on that."

"You won't," she assured her. "Just hold

your head up high and look as though you were born in a feather boa."

"I'll try," Roxanne said. She twirled the boa around her shoulders and threw back her head, then strutted across the wardrobe room, waving her arm to her fans in a disdainful manner.

The wardrobe woman laughed and clapped her hands. "You'll do fine," she promised.

Gary was right on time, and he looked very handsome in his white dinner jacket and dark tuxedo pants. He was wearing a red carnation in his buttonhole and offered Roxanne a bouquet of white roses.

"They're lovely," Roxanne said, and bent to smell the flowers. Then she said, "But I'm not sure I can manage them and the feather boa at the same time, Gary. I'm nervous."

"We'll leave the flowers in the car. You can take them home to your mother."

"I'll take them home and enjoy them myself," Roxanne said.

Most of their conversation on the way to the premiere was small talk about their next movie, which they would be starting in a week. Gary said he was very pleased to be working with her again, and Roxanne said she was pleased that he was pleased. Then they were turning the corner, drawing close to the theater where the premiere was being held. "You've never been to one of these before," Gary warned. "The important thing is to keep smiling and walking. Don't stop no matter what you do."

"You make it sound dangerous," Roxanne said.

"Just keep walking," Gary answered. "It's not really dangerous, but it can be frightening."

The limousine drew up to the curb, and several people crowded around the car. Roxanne saw their faces peering in at her, and she wondered how they would ever get out of the car. The driver got out first and came around to the street side, pushing aside the crowd as though he were going to open the the door. Gary took Roxanne's hand and said, "Now we go the other way. It's an old trick, but it works."

She slid across the wide seat and let Gary help her out of the car. Then he took her firmly by the arm and said, "Remember to smile. They're the ones who make you rich and famous."

Roxanne smiled and waved, but she was very glad that Gary was holding on to her firmly. The number of people and the noises they were making were very confusing and almost frightening. They stepped onto the sidewalk that was roped off, and Roxanne breathed a sigh of relief. At least now there was no real chance of being mobbed. Still, the voices she heard around her were so excited, it was easy to believe that they were angry instead of enthusiastic.

They called Gary's name over and over, and once in a while she heard her own name being called. That told her that all the publicity Marsha was working so hard to get was paying off. Still, she was surprised that anyone knew who she was in such a short time. She was even more surprised when the radio announcer who was covering the premiere called them over and said, "Here's Gary Marlowe and his beautiful leading lady, Roxanne Wilson. Roxanne, you look absolutely smashing. Will you tell the folks listening to us at home what the dress you're wearing is like?" He pushed the microphone in front of her face, and Roxanne almost panicked. She'd never talked over one before.

"It's white with sequins on top and a jersey skirt," Roxanne managed to say.

"White sequins, folks," the announcer said. "I didn't know what you called these little things, but I did know they showed off Roxanne's lovely shoulders. Of course, she left out the most interesting part of the dress design. What do you call that no-shoulder look, Roxanne?"

"I'm not sure," she stammered.

"We call it beautiful at Randolph Studios," Gary rescued her. "In fact, Roxanne is known as the most beautiful blonde in the whole industry. I'm very fortunate to have her as my leading lady in *Spanish Treasure*. I'm sure everyone will love her as much as I did. In fact, I loved her so much, and so did my boss, Cyril Randolph, that she's got a much bigger part in the sequel."

Roxanne didn't know whether she liked everything that Gary was saying, but she was very grateful for the fact that he was talking. The bright lights shining in her face, the screaming crowds, and all the confusion and excitement were almost too much for her. She hated to think that she was in danger of fainting on her first opening night. It seemed a sad way to celebrate the beginning of her stardom.

Clark Gable came up behind them, and the announcer let them go so he could interview the most romantic man in Hollywood. Roxanne let Gary lead her into the theater lobby, and she clung to his arm as he moved easily from one group of industry people to another, being charming to them all. When the dimming lights finally signaled that it was time to go inside, Roxanne whispered, "I don't know how you do that. You acted like you love these things, and I happen to know you hate them."

"Lower your voice," he whispered. "You never know who's listening."

"Why would anyone want to listen to me?" Roxanne said.

"Because you're a star, and that means you have power. It also means that you're good newspaper copy. Anything you say in public can be twisted and turned into excitement or scandal, Roxanne. You'll have to watch that charming honesty."

"You're the one with the charm," she whispered. "But I'm glad to hear you think I'm honest."

"I always have," Gary whispered back.

"You were the one who thought I thought you were dishonest. I just called you ambitious, that's all. And you were offended when it might have even been a compliment."

She laughed and shook her head. Then she whispered, "Don't try to charm me, Gary Marlowe. The things you said to me were no compliment."

"A man can change his mind," Gary said. Each time they talked he had to lean his head down closer to hers so that they could hear each other. Sometimes his lips almost brushed the top of her hair. Once, his breath brushed against her ear, and she felt a thrill run all the way down to her toes.

During the movie she wondered if it was possible that Gary could be interested in her romantically. She knew it was foolish to hope such a thing, but she also acknowledged that she did hope it. But after the movie was over and they'd accepted everyone's applause and compliments and they climbed back into the limousine to go home, Gary seemed more interested in getting her deposited on her doorstep than anything else.

He did walk her to the door and ask to be remembered to her mother, but when she invited him in, he shook his head quickly and said, "No, thanks. I'm going to stop at Charlie's for a hot dog and Coke, and I have to get up early tomorrow. So do you."

As Roxanne let herself into her fancy mansion she told herself to enjoy the wonderful things she did have and to forget about Gary.

He was more interested in a hot dog and Coke than her. What's more, he hadn't even thought to ask if she was hungry. Gary might have changed his mind about her, but he hadn't changed his heart.

Chapter Twenty-nine

THE newspaper printed a picture of Gary and her as they stepped out of the limousine, and both Hedda Hopper and Louella Parsons mentioned in their columns how madly in love they were. Roxanne was so furious that she marched straight into Marsha's trailer and complained.

"I didn't have anything to do with it," Marsha said. "Do you think I stay up all night phoning columnists with romantic stories just to aggravate you?"

"Yes."

"Well, think again. Something you said or did must have given them that impression. Anyway, you're going to read a lot of things about yourself in the newspaper you may not like. You'd better learn to handle it if you're going to survive in this business."

Roxanne knew that what Marsha was saying was true, and she apologized before she left her office. "I guess I'll just stop reading the gossip columns and concentrate on my work," she said.

"Good thinking," Marsha said. "Besides, it doesn't do any harm for the fans to think you two are in love. You're doing another picture together, aren't you?"

"Yes."

"Good for box office."

That was a term she had grown to hate, but when the first box-office figures came in for *Spanish Treasure,* she had to admit that she loved the idea that they might bring greater success to her. "Keep this up and we'll renegotiate right after this picture," Benny promised her.

The third picture that she was working on with Gary was more fun in a lot of ways than the first two. For one thing she was getting along with him a lot better. He was always polite, sometimes he made little jokes that made her laugh, and there weren't any starlets around the set. But Gary didn't ever step over the magic line of friendship into romance, and Roxanne had made up her mind that he never would.

Sometimes, as she watched him work, she dreamed that things might have been different between them, but she never mentioned her thoughts to anyone. She concentrated just as hard as she could on her work and tried not to worry about her lack of a personal life.

She might have been very lonely during those first weeks of stardom, except Cyril Randolph did an abrupt about-face and gave his son a job in the studio. As Bertram's assistant, John was assigned to a different movie, but he dropped around once in a while to chat. They had lunch together every few days, sometimes with Gary, and sometimes alone, but he didn't come around in the evening much. Roxanne was pleased that he was finally doing what he wanted and just a bit hurt that he seemed to be losing interest in her.

John explained his father's decision to let him work at the studio by saying, "I think my dad was worried I might turn out to have some talent. Then Montesque would get the credit for discovering me. So he offered me a job if I promised to do exactly what Bertram said. No soggy stories. And this musical I'm working on is really quite a fine artistic achievement."

John was as enthusiastic about musicals now as he once had been about realistic dramas. Roxanne just hoped that his judgment was better. But she suspected that it would be, because now that John was an accepted member of Randolph Studios, he had become a carbon copy of his father. He wore the same tweed jackets with patches on the sleeves and the same English caps. He even wore the same dark-red and blue neckties. But John was tall and slim and his father was short and fat, so people on the set sometimes laughed behind their backs.

Cyril Randolph had apparently given up any objection to her dating John, now that she was one of his stars. It seemed like an ironic twist of fate that his son was losing interest in her just when he was beginning to notice her. Cyril Randolph spoke to her whenever he saw her and sometimes pinched her cheeks, telling her how pretty she looked. She endured Cyril Randolph's friendliness, just as she endured the hot lights and standing around for hours at a time. It was part of the job.

Her social life was surprisingly dull. Since she was working and had to be up so early, she spent most evenings at home. John took her and her mother out some Sunday afternoons, but he no longer spent all his time professing his love to her. In fact, she had an idea that John might be just a little bit interested in one of the chorus girls who was working in his musical.

She saw Gary on the set every day and grew closer and closer to him professionally, but that was all. He took her to the premiere of their second movie, and the stories that they were madly in love with each other continued to pop up in the newspapers. It added an extra sadness to the reality of their relationship. Then, as they were finishing their third movie together, word came from Cyril Randolph's office that he'd lined up three more stories for them as a team.

"Do you mind?" Gary asked her the day they'd heard the news.

"No," Roxanne said. "Do you?"

"No," Gary said. "Romantic teams are big news this year. There's always that extra interest in a movie that has two well-known stars. Look at Myrna Loy and William Powell. Or my mom and dad. Of course, they're older."

"Look at Judy Garland and Mickey Rooney," Roxanne said. "They're younger. I guess we're supposed to be the team somewhere in the middle."

"Anyway, we work well together, and you're a good actress," Gary said.

"Thanks." She wished her heart didn't thump every time he paid her a compliment. She wished she didn't care so much what he thought.

"I thought you might like to come up to Santa Barbara next weekend," Gary said casually. "In fact, my mother thought you might like to bring your mother along."

"I'm sure she'd love it." Roxanne was very surprised by the invitation and said to her mother, "There's probably some ulterior motive. We'll find out when we get there."

But there was no ulterior motive at all, and they had a perfectly lovely weekend. The only unpleasant moments were when Gary forgot that he had a photographer's appointment and asked Roxanne if she'd mind waiting a few minutes before they went to the beach.

It took closer to an hour than thirty minutes, and Roxanne got tired of waiting, but she didn't complain. Later, Gary apologized three times, and she decided he must care a little bit about what she thought.

"I had a wonderful time," Laureen admitted when they drove home on Sunday afternoon. "And I thought Ruth Marlowe was charming."

"You two seemed to hit it off very well." Roxanne said. Then she yawned and said, "I think I'll try to sleep a little bit."

"You won't be able to sleep on this curving road," Laureen predicted.

"Then I'll just rest my eyes." She was really dreaming of being married in the lovely Santa Barbara estate and didn't want her fantasies interrupted by any conversation at all. She was ashamed of the fact that she was daydreaming about Gary again.

Gary invited her out the next Saturday night. They went to the Coconut Grove and were almost mobbed by photographers. As he took her home she said, "Why don't we try going somewhere in disguise again?"

He laughed and said, "I told you that you'd get around to wearing wigs and mustaches."

She did find that it was easier to go for walks with her blonde hair wrapped in a silk scarf and wearing dark glasses. Then her lovely Casa Feliz was put on the movie star maps that they hawked to tourists on every Hollywood corner. She never knew when she would be accosted by gawking strangers who not only wanted autographs, but also wanted to talk for a long time.

Much as she hated to, she had a high stucco wall built to keep out the tourists, and then she hired a guard to stand at the gate. Laureen complained that she was getting parts just because she was Roxanne's mother, and threatened to change her name. But no matter how much she hated the loss of privacy, she loved the work she was doing.

In the fourth picture she felt she really had learned enough to hold her own with Gary. There were scenes between them that the critics called "pure magic."

She tried not to read the silly publicity stories about how she and Gary were in love because it made the reality so much sadder. Gary continued to invite her out nearly every week, but he never even tried to kiss her.

She sometimes wanted to tell Gary how she felt about him, but it seemed as though it was never exactly the right time or place to do it. They usually went out to public places, and even when they tried to find secluded spots, the photographers seemed to be able to find them. Besides, Roxanne was too shy to broach her feelings to Gary, partly because she feared a confession of love might endanger anything that was growing between them.

One night they went to the Hollywood Bowl to hear a concert, and photographers interrupted the performance by taking flash shots of the two of them. They held hands as they ran toward Gary's car, and once inside,

Roxanne said, "That does it. I won't go out with you again unless I can wear a mustache."

When he laughed, she said, "I mean it, Gary. It's just not a lot of fun being followed by photographers everywhere we go. I don't think we really even get to enjoy each other's company."

"But it's good for box office," Gary said. He laughed, and then he stopped his laughter as he saw the look of understanding in Roxanne's eyes.

"That's why you've been asking me out, isn't it?"

"I don't know what you mean."

"Yes, you do, Gary." She couldn't decide whether she wanted to scream or cry. "You've been taking me out as a publicity stunt, and I was dumb enough to fall for it."

"Not dumb, Roxanne," Gary began to explain.

She shook her head. "And the reason all those photographers always found us is that you told them where we'd be. Even those awful pictures of me in my bathing suit that they took in Santa Barbara. You set that up, too. Didn't you?"

"Let me explain, Roxanne. You're young, you don't understand this business as well as I do."

"I understand one thing, Gary Marlowe. I'll never speak to you again as long as I live." She was out of the car and walking down the steep mountain road that led from Hollywood Boulevard to the Bowl. But before she got thirty feet, there were a pack of photographers hounding her.

"Get in," Gary ordered, opening the door for her. Then he said, "And for Pete's sake, smile. You want those tears on the front page of tomorrow's paper?"

She allowed Gary to drive her home because she had no real choice, but she refused to speak to him. When he called the next day, she had her mother tell him she wasn't home. On Monday she called in sick to the studio, and on Tuesday, Benny Foyle was on the telephone. "You have to go in tomorrow, Roxanne, or they'll suspend you."

"Let them," she said. The tears were gone, but her face was still puffed and red from crying. "I can't come in, anyway. My face looks awful."

"Your mother says you've been crying for three days," Benny said.

When Roxanne didn't answer, he said, "No guy is worth that, sweetie. And if you hold up production, the studio can fine you a bundle. We all lose money if you don't work, Roxanne."

"I don't care."

"Yes, you do," Benny told her. "You're a trooper, remember? And you like being rich and famous."

"I hate Randolph Studios," she said, "and I hate Gary Marlowe."

"Finish this picture," Benny cajoled. "And I'll see what I can do about getting you out of the others."

Chapter Thirty

WHEN Roxanne went to work on Wednesday, the first person she saw said, "You look terrible."

"Thanks, Annie. You look great." But the criticism worried her a lot. A star's fortune depended on her appearance, and she knew her eyes were still red and puffy.

Gary said the same thing when she went onto the set. "You look terrible."

"I had the flu," she answered briefly.

"Roxanne, I want to explain to you —"

"There's nothing to explain. Shall we get to work?"

"How can we work together if you won't listen to my side of the story?"

"I can't," Roxanne said, and she felt the tears crowding into her eyes again.

He nodded, apparently understanding that

she meant exactly what she said, and then he said, "Okay. We'll work."

They worked together all of that day without talking. The next day, Gary tried once again to talk to her. "I don't think there's any point in going over it," Roxanne said. "You took me out because the studio wanted it."

"But I didn't know you really cared about me," Gary said. "I'm sorry. . . ."

"I didn't care about you." Roxanne tossed her head. "I've tried to tell everyone from the beginning that I'm in love with Henry. Now we'd better get to work. They're ready."

"Then why did you cry over me for three days?"

Roxanne laughed, using all her acting skill to deliver the lines. "I was slightly upset to discover that you were using me, but I certainly wouldn't waste a lot of energy on that. It happens that I had a bad case of the flu. Would you like to call my doctor for verification?"

They worked together after that, and their work seemed to go as usual, but there was no kidding and no happiness on the set. Within a week the gossip columns were filled with stories of their "lovers' spat." Roxanne read Hedda Hopper's column on Saturday morning, crumpled it into a ball, and threw it on the floor. "Trash. Pure trash. They wouldn't know real love if it hit them in the face."

"Would you?" her mother asked.

She stomped out of the room and upstairs.

Donning a dark blue sweater with a hood and some baggy slacks, she put on her dark glasses and started out the door.

"Where are you going?" Laureen asked.

"For a walk."

"It's cold," Laureen warned. "Almost Christmas."

"I hate Christmas in California," Roxanne grumbled. "No snow."

"You hate everything today," Laureen said, and then she smiled at her new nail polish. "Think this pink is a nice shade?"

When Roxanne didn't answer, her mother added, "If I were in love with a handsome young leading man, I wouldn't snivel about it. I'd go after him."

Roxanne slipped out the door quietly and stuck her hands into the sweater pockets. It was cold, but she tucked her head down low and started into the wind. A little walk would do her good. She got to the corner of Sunset Boulevard and saw a tall young man with a suitcase standing there, looking at an envelope as though he were searching for directions. "Henry!" she cried, and flew into his arms.

Within seconds they were back in the house, laughing and talking. She said, "Ma, Henry's here. He's on vacation from the bank, and he's going to look for a job here. Isn't that wonderful? I said he could stay with us for a while."

Laureen managed to frown and smile at

the same time as she said, "Hello, Henry. I hear you're a banker now."

"Hello, Mrs. Wilson. I hear you're an actress."

"How's your father?"

"Fine. Your Cousin Margaret sends her love. She saw you in the previews of *Gone with the Wind*."

"Really?" Laureen was thawing now, and she asked, "Would you like a Coke or coffee or something? What did she say about my performance?"

"We all thought you were just fine," Henry assured her, putting his suitcase on the floor. "Everyone in Norman is proud of you both. You're celebrities."

By now Laureen was bustling around the kitchen looking for something to feed Henry and telling him all about the filming of *Gone with the Wind*. She finished by putting a piece of cold pie in front of him and saying, "It will be nice for Roxanne to have a friend around for a while. She's had a little disappointment in love."

"Ma, that's not true."

"I read the gossip columns all the time," Laureen snapped. "I know what I read."

"I read those stories, too," Henry said. "So I decided to come out and see what was really happening. You aren't going to marry Gary Marlowe, are you?"

"I'm not ever going to speak to him again after we finish this picture," Roxanne promised.

"Then there's still a chance for me," Henry said, and put his fork into the pie.

Since it was not a question, Roxanne didn't feel that she had to reply. During the first weekend Henry was there, they talked mostly about Henry's work and his new interest in money management. "I figured you wouldn't have left me, except that we were all so poor," he explained. "So I decided to get rich. Of course, it will take me a lot longer than you, but will you wait?"

Roxanne avoided the question by asking his advice on her investments, explaining, "I want to put as much of my money in safe investments as I can. But I'm afraid of the stock market after the big crash of 1929. What do you think about real estate? A lot of movie stars are buying ranches in a place called San Fernando Valley. It's hot and dry there, but I kind of like it."

"Blue-chip stocks." Henry advised, and he lectured her for two hours on the stock market.

As she half listened, Roxanne's thoughts drifted back over the time that had passed since she'd left Henry to come to California. A lot had happened to her, but Henry had changed as well. He seemed older, stodgier, more like his Uncle Henry in a lot of ways. She closed her eyes and tried to imagine what her children would look like if she really were to marry him. But the idea made her laugh.

"You're not listening," Henry accused.

"Let's go get some ice cream," she said. "I'll show you the sights. Would you like to go to a movie? Sunday nights are best because there aren't so many fans looking for you."

"I'd like to finish explaining this to you, Roxanne. If you don't know the difference between short- and long-term bonds, you won't ever be a good investor."

She jumped up and said, "I've got a good idea. I'll call my friend John and see if he wants to go to the movies with us."

"Is that the other boyfriend?" Henry asked. "The one you were in love with last time I was here?"

"There was never anything between John and me," Roxanne said. "We're just friends."

John agreed to come over but asked if he could bring a date of his own. Roxanne was delighted, and within the hour, the four of them were crowded into John's little yellow car. Despite the fact that John had grown so much like his father, he still was driving his beloved toy. But Roxanne had an idea he wouldn't be for much longer.

"This is ruining my hair," Doreen, his date, complained. She had long red hair that hung below her shoulders like Rita Hayworth's.

"Your hair looks beautiful," he said, and dropped his arm around her shoulder. "Doesn't she have pretty hair, Roxanne?"

"Yes," Roxanne shouted from the rumble seat.

Later, as they waited for their dates to return from the lounges, Roxanne said, "I like your new girl."

"Me, too," John said. "I've been meaning to introduce you to her. And when you called, she was having dinner with me and my father, so I just invited her along."

"Your father doesn't object to your dating starlets anymore?"

"She was sort of a consolation prize," John admitted. "When we agreed that you would start dating Gary, he said I could take Doreen out."

She turned and stared at him, her face turning beet-red with anger. "You mean you were in on it, too?"

"Sort of," John answered. "Naturally Gary didn't want to do anything to hurt me, so when the studio told him to start dating you, he came right out and asked me if I was still in love with you."

"He didn't want to do anything to hurt you, but he certainly didn't mind hurting me!"

"It wasn't really like that," John protested. "It was good for box office, and it seemed like a good plan. No one thought you'd really fall for him. You never seemed to like Gary very much, you know. I'm sorry, Roxanne, I really am."

Henry came back then, and Roxanne said, "We're taking a taxi home."

"Aren't you going to ride with your friends?" Doreen asked.

"I don't have any friends in this town," she answered, and she dragged Henry out into the night.

Chapter Thirty-one

THE next morning Laureen was waiting for her when she came downstairs. She told her a little bit about her quarrel with John and said, "John's getting to be too much like his father to suit me. He honestly didn't see a thing wrong with the way they all tricked me."

Laureen said, "Henry will have to leave today, I'm afraid. The papers have already reported that he's staying here. You know the studio will never stand for that."

"I'm not allowed to have guests in my own home?" Roxanne said.

"Not young men you've publicly declared your love for. If he stays, the studio will have a fit. And they'll blame me." Laureen added, "And they'll use it as a reason to make you stay in the next Marlowe movies. You know how they operate. Do you want to continue playing opposite that boy?"

"No."

"Then Henry will have to move out," Laureen said.

"I suppose you're right," Roxanne said. "But I'm beginning to hate being in the movies."

"Do you hate this house?" Laureen asked. When Roxanne didn't answer, she asked, "How about that satin dressing gown you're wearing? And you seem right fond of the money in the bank."

"Ma, do you think I was too emotional about the way Gary tricked me?"

Her mother patted her hand and said, "It's only natural to be emotional about the man you love."

"I don't love him."

"Yes you do, and he loves you."

"You read too many gossip columns."

"Maybe," Laureen admitted, "but if you're looking for a decent future, I'd just point out that his parents are very nice people."

"I'm going to work," Roxanne said.

She was early, but Gary was already there. He said, "You didn't lose any time, did you?"

"He's just here for a visit," Roxanne said. "He's moving out today."

Gary looked confused and then said, "I meant that I heard that you were trying to get out of our next pictures together. Do you really hate me that much? I don't care where Henry stays. I'm not jealous of Henry."

"Obviously," Roxanne answered.

"I am mad at you for picking a fight with John, though. He called last night and he was pretty upset, Roxanne. You know, John's been a good friend to you. And I'm sorry I hurt you so much, Roxanne. I really am."

"All right, you're sorry. What are we doing today?"

"The love scene."

"Oh, no!" Roxanne groaned.

"Do you want me to ask to rearrange the schedule?" Gary asked. "They'll have a fit, but if I say you have a cold and I'm afraid I'll catch it, they'll do it."

"No one would believe I had a cold. We might as well get it over with."

"Roxanne, I really want to talk to you. I want to explain."

"Here comes Marsha, and she's got fire in her eyes," Roxanne said. To the publicity director she said, "He's leaving today."

"How in the world did that hick manage to ask directions to your house of someone who would know enough to call Hedda Hopper? And why did he tell the guy his whole life story?"

"People are friendlier in Oklahoma," Roxanne explained, then she added, "Besides, he said the man was real polite and asked a lot of interested questions." As Roxanne explained, she laughed. It was the first time she'd laughed in several days, and it felt good. It felt even better when Gary joined in.

Marsha turned on them and said, "You two

and your lovers' quarrels. Now Roxanne has some stranger living with her. You both ought to be fined or suspended for this."

"For what?" Gary demanded.

"For not falling in love," Marsha snapped, and wheeled around, marching back to her office.

Roxanne shook her head, though she was still laughing. "What a crazy business. Only in Hollywood would your boss think he had a right to decide who you ought to fall in love with."

"Maybe they're right," Gary said.

But before she could find out what he meant by that, the set was filling with crew members who were busy setting up. They both went to get dressed for the day's schedule, and the moment was gone.

She was nervous as she dressed and went through makeup, because she wanted to do well in today's scenes. She knew that even if she intended never to work with Gary again, much of her acting future hinged on how well she came across in the romantic scenes. More than one young actress had her contract dropped because she didn't "sizzle" on the screen. In the other movies she'd made with Gary her main job had been to look pretty, but this film had a bigger and more demanding part for her.

In today's shooting she had to deny that she loved him, then melt in his arms as he forced her to kiss him. She was wearing her hair loose and soft around her face. A soft rose-colored satin dressing gown fit her tightly. Because it was her first Technicolor movie, she was also nervous about how well she would photograph in color. Some of the other blonde actresses hadn't fared well under the harsh lights, and their hair looked gray or yellow. This was the only scene in the movie where her hair flowed unbound, and she had to keep reminding herself that she was naturally blonde and would photograph better than the peroxided heads did.

Her nervousness increased dramatically when she went onto the set and discovered Cyril Randolph in the director's chair. He smiled at her and said, "I've decided to direct this sequence myself. Just to keep my hand in. You don't mind?"

"Of course not," Roxanne said. But she really did mind a lot. She'd never worked with the great man, but she knew his reputation for high standards of excellence. There were too many stories of his impetuous firings of stars who didn't live up to his expectations. She was trembling as she walked onto the set.

"All I want from you two is magic," Randolph said, then he smiled and rubbed his hands together. "I see you as the most famous lovers of the forties. You're young and talented, and I see you working in film after film together. Now let's get going."

Roxanne strained to hear every nuance of his commands and to obey completely. She thought she was doing fine until he frowned and shook his head, saying, "Miss Wilson, you look like a sweet little geranium up there. I want a violet — no, I want an orchid. Make me an orchid, Roxanne, dear."

Roxanne had to bite her lip to keep from laughing out loud. Now she knew where John had found his love for the dramatic. This time when she said, "I don't love you, Charles," she positively dripped sweetness.

"Wrong!" Randolph roared. "All wrong!"

They went over her lines again and again, and each time she seemed to please him less. By the time they'd done twelve takes, Roxanne wanted with all her heart to pick up her rose-colored skirts and run from the set. When Randolph turned to bawl out one of the cameramen, Gary whispered, "Steady, Rosie. This is no time to turn tail and run."

Her eyes widened and she asked, "How do you do it? How do you know what I'm thinking?"

He shrugged. "I'd like to run, too."

She smiled, grateful for his encouragement and forgetting for the moment that she hated him. Compared to Cyril Randolph, she thought Gary Marlowe was absolutely marvelous.

"Let's play this for real, Rosie," Gary said. "I know you really love me, and I've been trying to get you to talk to me about it. So let's talk right now."

"Don't be ridiculous," she snapped. "We've got work to do."

"Is that all you think about? Isn't your

love life more important to you than your work?" he teased.

Randolph called, "Places. Lights, camera, action."

"I know you love me," Gary said, delivering his line with more conviction than he'd managed before.

"I don't love you," Roxanne snapped back, forgetting everything she'd been instructed about sweetness and orchids.

"You do," Gary insisted. The extra insistence was not in the script.

"I do not love you," Roxanne said. This time there was almost a break in her voice, and she knew she was fighting tears.

Gary took her arms then and tried to kiss her. Roxanne was taken by surprise and pulled away, and beating her hands on his chest, she said, "I do not love you. I do not."

This time Gary's grip was firmer and he managed to whisper, "You're doing fine, now kiss me."

Roxanne understood that the cameras were still running and that they were actually filming. She turned her face toward Gary's and lifted her lips for a kiss. He circled her waist and drew her closer to him, kissing her softly and then more passionately.

Behind them, Roxanne could hear Randolph calling, "That's fine. Now let's do it again and get the close-ups. Tim, I want softer lighting on her hair. And Gary, look stronger when you pull her close. A few more times and you've got it."

Gary still had his face close to hers, and he whispered, "Think you can stand it?"

"Yes," Roxanne answered. She hoped he couldn't see the way she was having trouble catching her breath. It was humiliating to be so attracted to someone who thought of her as just another actor.

"I hope I can," Gary said. "Kissing you is always a shock."

"A shock?"

"Yes, at first I thought it was just because you were such a good actress. You almost took my breath away during that first love scene in *Spanish Treasure*. Remember?"

"I remember you walked away from the set very quickly."

"I was trying to keep my wits about me," Gary admitted. "I thought you were just showing off that day."

"Showing off?"

"Pretending to react that way to show me what a fine actress you were."

"All right, one more take," Randolph called through the megaphone. "Places at the beginning."

This time they had no trouble with the beginning lines. He seemed pleased enough with their delivery, but he made them do the kiss over and over again, never seeming quite satisfied with the result. Finally he said, "I think we got it. I think we've got the magic. You're a great team."

Roxanne managed a small thank you and tried desperately to control her racing pulse and whizzing mind as she turned away from Gary. She noticed that his thank you was as thin as hers had been. She also noticed that he was still holding her hand, as though unwilling to break the contact between them.

Cyril Randolph opened his arms wide to paint a picture in the air. He said, "I see a great future for you two together. Mark my words, you'll be Hollywood's favorite couple. We'll star you in movie after movie, and the fans will stand in line for hours to see the latest Marlowe-Wilson picture. Raises for both of you, of course. You'll be as famous as your mother and father, Gary, now that you've found the perfect girl."

Roxanne's emotions were still too clouded to think clearly, so she didn't know whether to be pleased or frightened by Randolph's predictions. Could she stand to do another movie with Gary? Their love scenes were breaking her heart, but after that last scene together she knew she was too much in love with Gary to resist the temptation. But wouldn't it be tragic to play love scene after love scene with someone who never really cared about anything but his career? And yet his kisses. . . .

She was glad when Cyril Randolph announced, "Lunch," and turned his back on them. At least she would have a few minutes to think before she had to respond to any questions. Randolph turned as he reached the edge of the set, and rubbed his hands together, smiling broadly as he repeated,

"Hollywood's most romantic couple."

Gary squeezed her hand and asked, "Have a date for lunch?"

"Gary, I don't know. I'd like to be friends but . . . it never seems to work out."

"It's the cheese sandwiches," Gary said gravely. "Order something a little fancier and you'll enjoy it more. Come on."

Since he was still holding her hand, she allowed him to lead her to the commissary before she knew exactly what had happened. She was still stunned by their love scene and sat quietly until the waitress left. Gradually, she was able to remind herself that Gary was just being professionally charming. By the time her steak arrived, she was clear-headed again and telling herself that no matter how great things were on film, he still spelled trouble for her off the set.

As she cut into the steak, he said, "I can see your mind clicking and I know what you're thinking, but you're wrong. I'm not nearly as bad a guy as you think I am."

"I just think you're interested in your own career. I can't blame you for that. But I still think it was wrong to trick me." She put down her knife and fork and stared directly into Gary's eyes.

He covered her hand with his and said, "It was wrong. But I had no idea you were in love with me. I thought you were just being stubborn and that you really wouldn't care once you found out how good it was for your career."

"I'm not in love with you," Roxanne said. She withdrew her hand and picked up her knife and fork, sawing viciously at the steak in front of her.

"Yes you are, Rosie. And I was a fool not to figure it out sooner. But I thought you thought I was just a spoiled brat who'd had his career handed to him on a silver platter. I believed you when you said you didn't even like me. You never even hinted that you loved me, Rosie. In fact, you acted like you wanted to chop me up, the way you're chopping up that steak."

She put the silverware down again and turned, with blazing eyes, to face him. His face wore that arrogant smile with the raised eyebrow that always infuriated her. "I don't love you," she said in such a loud voice that other people stared. Then she added in a lower voice, "And nobody calls me Rosie anymore — not even Henry."

"Good. It can be my pet name for you." Gary was still smiling as Roxanne rose from the table and marched from the room.

She was in her own dressing room before he caught up with her. At first, she refused to answer his knock, but he called out to her in a voice that she knew could be heard all over the set.

"You don't want that silly lover's quarrel publicity all over again, do you? So I've decided on a new publicity stunt. If you don't let me in, Rosie, I'm going to call Hedda

Hopper and Luella Parsons and announce our engagement."

She opened the door. "You wouldn't."

He was laughing as he stepped inside and took her in his arms. "I wouldn't," he admitted. "But it was the best thing I thought of to get you to let me in."

"You tricked me again."

He ignored her complaint and pulled her closer to him, bending his head to say softly, "I love you, Rosie." Then he kissed her gently, holding her as though she were the most precious person in the world.

When she finally pulled away from him, she asked in a husky voice, "This isn't another trick?"

"No. I've loved you for a long time. Since Kansas City, I think. But there were a lot of reasons to stay apart. There was John. . . ."

"And all those starlets." She could tease him now about other girls. Gary loved her, really loved her, and her heart was humming with happiness.

"The girls were never important." His lips brushed her cheek and he was stroking her hair. "But I thought you didn't like me. You said you didn't like me, Rosie."

"You said I was ambitious. You said. . . ." She stopped talking. It didn't really matter what had been said in the past. What mattered was the wonderful, warm feeling she had now. She smiled and lifted her arms to circle Gary's neck, drawing his lips closer to hers.

The kiss seemed exactly like all their other kisses, whether on or off camera. Roxanne felt as though she would like to stay in his arms forever.

A knock on her door broke the spell of the kiss, and a voice called out, "You're wanted on the set, Miss Wilson."

They held hands as they walked to the set and Roxanne asked, "When did you decide that I loved you?"

"When you came to work with your eyes all puffy and swollen. I knew you were too professional to cry that much over anything except love."

Roxanne laughed in delight. "You mean, all I ever had to do was look ugly to make you notice me?"

"You'll always be beautiful to me," he said. "Now let's go to work."

"More Ruthless Randolph, ugh!" Roxanne pretended to be upset at the prospect. In truth, she was too happy to dislike anyone, even him.

"He's a brilliant man," Gary whispered in her ear. "Didn't he just say we'd be the most romantic couple in the world? And aren't we?"